PRAISE FOR

THE STOLEN

'Gripping, heartfelt and intelligent, *The Stolen* is an emotionally rich thriller that crackles with tension'

Christian White, author of *The Ledge*

'*The Stolen* is compelling, down-to-earth Australian crime fiction that delivers on absolutely every page. Vikki Petraitis is the real deal!'

Hayley Scrivenor, author of *Dirt Town* and *Girl Falling*

'To read a Vikki Petraitis crime novel is to be let in on the secret of how things really work, both at a procedural level, and in terms of the best and worst ways humans behave. It was a treat to revisit Senior Detective Antigone Pollard as she unravelled another twisty and topical mystery with the help of her authentic and (mostly) faithful support crew. Like *The Unbelieved*, *The Stolen* is a clear-eyed, fast-paced take on the reverberating effects of a crime on survivors and their community, making it a must-read for anyone who likes to go beyond the headlines, to where the true story waits'

Jacqueline Bublitz, author of *Before You Knew My Name* and *Leave the Girls Behind*

'Vikki Petraitis knows how to draw us into a story and hold us there. She has the gift of making us become emotionally invested in her characters. If you begin *The Stolen*, you *will* finish it, and you will have experienced a richly satisfying range of emotions along the way'

Robert Gott, author of *The Port Fairy Murders* and *Naked Ambition*

'I couldn't put *The Stolen* down. Vikki Petraitis has a way of getting under your skin, not just with her tight plotting, but with the emotional weight behind every chapter. Antigone Pollard is such a refreshingly real character: no clichés, no tropes, just a smart, tough, deeply caring cop doing the work. This isn't just crime fiction, it's fiction that makes you feel'

Anonymous *Casefile* host

PRAISE FOR

THE UNBELIEVED

'A beating heart of a novel, *The Unbelieved* sweeps you up in its rhythms from the very first pages. Petraitis handles this exploration of the corrosive consequences of not believing women with such assurance, it really does seem impossible this is her crime fiction debut. Compelling, clever and utterly convincing, readers are going to love Senior Detective Antigone Pollard – and her dog!'

Jacqueline Bublitz, author of *Before You Knew My Name*

'*The Unbelieved* is a triumphant debut, ushering in Petraitis as a formidable new voice in Australian crime fiction. If you read any crime novel this year, make it this one'

Better Reading

'A true-crime expert wielding skilful prose, Petraitis's *The Unbelieved* is tight, tense and unrelenting'

Candice Fox, author of *The Chase*

'A rally cry of a crime book jam-packed with great characters. Don't pick it up unless you're prepared to be held hostage. Antigone Pollard explodes off the page, she's such a fearless, memorable character'

Sarah Bailey, author of *Body of Lies*

'Fast-paced and gripping, *The Unbelieved* follows a strong, determined female detective in her search for the truth. The climax will have you questioning concepts of justice and fairness, and how we can all do better. A riveting novel tackling today's issues'

Petronella McGovern, author of *The Last Trace*

'A fast, hard ride through the zeitgeist. Gripping, important, funny – and with a great swerve in the tail'

Matthew Spencer, author of *Black River*

'A gleaming puzzle box of plot twists, conspiracy and comeuppance, *The Unbelieved* is a pacy thriller . . . Fearless, exacting, honourable and smart, Antigone Pollard is a mighty protagonist . . . A standout success'

Books+Publishing

'A rattling good crime story . . . Petraitis has used her knowledge, experience and passion to deliver a page-turning crime novel that also has something to say'

Newtown Review of Books

'*The Unbelieved* proves to be a very hard-hitting and timely read . . . a standout crime fiction text. Interwoven in this engrossing crime story is a hard-line focus on justice, the law, gender bias and reporting practices of sexual assaults'.

Mrs B's Book Reviews

'Gripping . . . Petraitis has created a wonderful character in Antigone Pollard: a kick-arse copper determined to help the terrified women of a small town kick down the walls of deceit, male privilege and patriarchy. *The Unbelieved* is a must read: gripping to the last page'

Sisters in Crime

Also by Vikki Petraitis

The Unbelieved

THE STOLEN

VIKKI PETRAITIS

SIMON &
SCHUSTER

London · New York · Amsterdam/Antwerp · Sydney/Melbourne · Toronto · New Delhi

First published in Australia by Allen & Unwin, 2025

First published in Great Britain by Simon & Schuster UK Ltd, 2025
This paperback edition first published in Great Britain by Simon & Schuster UK Ltd, 2026

1 3 5 7 9 10 8 6 4 2

Simon & Schuster UK Ltd, 7th Floor, 199 Bishopsgate, London EC2M 3TY

Simon & Schuster Australia, Sydney
Simon & Schuster India, New Delhi

www.simonandschuster.co.uk
www.simonandschuster.com.au
www.simonandschuster.co.in

The authorised representative in the EEA is Simon & Schuster Netherlands BV, Herculesplein 96, 3584 AA Utrecht, Netherlands. info@simonandschuster.nl

A CIP catalogue record for this book is available from the British Library

Paperback ISBN: 978-1-3985-5723-9
eBook ISBN: 978-1-3985-5724-6
Audio ISBN: 978-1-3985-5725-3

Typeset in 13/18 pt Granjon by Bookhouse, Sydney
Printed and Bound in the UK using 100% Renewable Electricity
at CPI Group (UK) Ltd

FSC
www.fsc.org
MIX
Paper | Supporting responsible forestry
FSC® C013604

This book is dedicated to my dad, John Burke,
taken from us on 25 February 2025.

Dad, you made me a storyteller. I have loved you
my whole life and will miss you forever.

'I have love in me the likes of which you can scarcely imagine and rage the likes of which you would not believe. If I cannot satisfy the one, I will indulge the other.'

MARY SHELLEY, *FRANKENSTEIN*

PROLOGUE

39 YEARS AGO

The young woman was delirious. It seemed like one minute she'd been at a party surrounded by friends; the next, separated from the herd, held down on a bed. The pain came in waves, dulled by a cocktail of drugs. She grabbed handfuls of the sheet beneath her to try to anchor herself to what was happening. Sweat trickled down her forehead.

She screamed.

Someone pushed her, roughly, further down the bed. Hands pulled her legs wider apart. Bursts of pain radiated through her. Every part of her ached, exhausted from fighting. She could see the masked man bending over her.

'Please make it stop,' she whimpered, but they all ignored her. She had ceased to be a person to them.

One of them stuck a needle in her arm.

'No!' she screamed. The world turned hazier. 'No . . .' Her voice grew fainter. She was aware of a sensation of pain, but a wall had sprung up in her brain that disconnected the pain from her. It was the oddest feeling. She was still there but whatever was in that needle had separated her mind from her body. The relief calmed her.

Nothing mattered now. Another wave, strong enough to break through the wall. She gasped. Tried to sit up.

'Hold her down,' said the man.

Strong hands held her shoulders.

She cried out.

A low voice in her ear: 'It's nearly over. One more push.'

With all her strength, she let out a primal scream and pushed. The man with the mask bent forward over her swollen belly. There was a tugging and a pushing that felt like it was tearing her apart. Finally, something slithered from her.

When she had imagined this moment, the doctor had held up the baby and said, 'It's a boy!' or, 'It's a girl!'

What she never imagined was silence.

In the dim room, she was aware of people closing around the doctor like a shield.

'Where's my baby?' Her voice was hoarse.

A nurse appeared by her side. 'I'm sorry to inform you that your baby has died.' She didn't look sorry.

How could the kicking, rolling, wriggling being she'd carried be dead?

She wanted this baby. She loved this baby. Despite the odds. Despite the stern nurses and the doctor who looked down on her. The ones who used terms like *illegitimate* and *unfit mother* and *too young*. The ones who had told her to give her baby up and *get on with life*. But she was stubborn. She'd vowed to do this on her own. Now it seemed she wouldn't get the chance.

'I want to see my baby!' Desperation. A tugging at her wrist. What the hell? Were they strapping her to the bed? Another needle.

Then nothing.

CHAPTER 1

A CHANGE IN COFFEE

It was a La Niña kind of summer, where the sun never really reached full strength. Two weeks into January and the milder temperatures were kind to the crime rates in Deception Bay. Crowds still flocked to the beach at the bottom of the cliffs of the Devil's Corner, but this year there had been a drop in thefts and assaults. Less heat outdoors reduced the heat indoors. Fewer calls about family violence. Fewer fights outside any of the half-dozen town pubs.

Nothing much had changed over the summer inside the CIB office except that my partner, Senior Detective Warren Harvey—Wozza to all who knew him—had switched from flat whites to iced coffee to mark the season. He was sipping one as he walked into our office with my latte. I was happy to brave the mild summer weather and drink hot coffee. He put my coffee on my desk, then settled at his. Leaned back on his office chair.

'Anything?' he asked.

'Nope.'

Our phones had been eerily silent for a Monday. I had used the time to catch up on paperwork and keep an eye on the weather app on my phone, which warned of a severe weather event coming our way. The summer storm jiggled colourfully over the map of Victoria, heading east, heading towards Deception Bay. There were too many magenta pixels for my liking. They meant the storm would bring heavy rain. While I'd fixated on the map, Wozza had played more than his fair share of Tetris. He reckoned it was a better challenge than Candy Crush. And he'd completely failed at Wordle.

'Banana cake?' he asked, reaching for a cling-wrapped plate on the shelf behind his desk.

'Do you even need to ask?'

The banana cake had become a ritual since Norma O'Mealley, the head of the Deception Bay Country Women's Association, had made a habit of dropping one off each week. She had won awards with her banana cake recipe. In honour of the work Wozza and I had done solving a decade-long murder case, we now got cake. And we weren't complaining. Well, Wozza complained that the cake could be bigger, or sometimes chocolate, but aside from that, no complaining at all. As kickbacks went, it was unlikely to be the subject of a Royal Commission, although Wozza thought *Banana-cake-gate* did have a headline-worthy ring to it.

He cut me a slice and handed it over. 'Do you reckon this is the calm before the literal storm?'

I considered that for a moment. Before returning to Deception Bay, where I had spent a good part of my childhood with my nan, I had been a city detective, stationed in Brunswick with access to some of the best coffee in Melbourne, and never a lull in crime. After a contemplative sip of the equally fine coffee that Wozza had bought from my friend Angie's cafe in the main street of town, I said, 'No idea. In Brunswick, we never had a quiet day.'

Wozza settled back in his chair with a generous slice of cake. 'So, Pollard, what's the weirdest thing you ever saw in Brunswick?'

I smiled. 'Once I was on patrol and we drove past the train station. It was late and the platform was deserted'—I paused for dramatic effect—'aside from a rather amorous young couple.'

Wozza leaned forward and slurped on the straw of his iced coffee. Then pressed a hand against his forehead like a fortune teller. 'Don't tell me,' he said. 'I'm getting a vision. They were doing the horizontal limbo.'

I laughed. 'Yep, just not the horizontal part. They were more . . . vertical. Funny thing was that once they finished, they spotted the police car and, first, they looked horrified, then he bowed, and she curtseyed.'

'Did you clap?' Wozza asked.

I shook my head. 'The performance wasn't that good.'.

'Bit different here in the country,' said Wozza. 'Jeez, if I had a dollar for every guy I've caught getting amorous with his scarecrow.'

He caught me mid-sip and it took all my power not to send a spray of coffee in his direction. 'His *what*?'

Wozza shrugged. 'It's a thing.'

'If you had a dollar for every time you've caught a guy with his scarecrow, just how many dollars *would* you have?'

Wozza blushed. 'Well, only about three dollars, but still, it's something a cop never forgets.'

At that moment the phone rang. Our eyes locked. I had the advantage because Wozza was still holding what was left of his piece of cake in one hand and his iced coffee in the other.

'Deception Bay CIB, Senior Detective Antigone Pollard speaking.'

There was a breathless voice on the other end of the line. 'Oh god! Oh god! He's gone! Help me!'

A crack of lightning nearly drowned out the woman's voice. It was followed by a blinding flash through the office window and an angry rumble of thunder.

'Ma'am, who's gone?' I kept my voice calm. On the other side of his desk, Wozza watched me.

'My boy!' Her voice cracked into hysteria. 'My baby boy!'

CHAPTER 2

THE STOLEN CHILD

The sky above Deception Bay was a deep and ominous grey and it looked cataclysmic to me. Flashes of lightning and deep grumbles of thunder provided a fitting backdrop to the drama unfolding in town. No rain yet, though the sky was tuning her strings. It took eleven minutes for the street outside Maddy Muir's house to fill with cop cars, lights flashing red and blue. The crackle of police radios, uniforms with clipboards, and Wozza and me in our unmarked CIB car. Maddy was at the front gate when we pulled up. She was a young woman, around twenty-five, I guessed. Long cardigan over a white T-shirt that had *#march4justice* printed in purple across the front. Thongs. We moved her back inside as the neighbours in her quiet little street came out to see what was wrong.

'He's gone, he's gone,' Maddy kept saying, as frantic as anybody I'd ever seen.

Wozza's calm was the perfect antidote to her panic. 'Take us through what happened,' he said in a gentle voice.

Maddy hurried into a bedroom to the right of the hallway. It was a bright baby's room with a cot in the middle and colourful giraffes and monkeys on the wallpaper. I looked around for entry and exit points. There was one window with its blind pulled down. Moving around the cot, I got a pen out of my pocket and used it to lift the side of the blind. The window was shut and locked. Dust around the catch suggested it hadn't been opened for a while. Behind me, Wozza prompted the young mother. 'So, the last time you saw him?'

'I put Ethan down for his nap about an hour ago and when I came in to check on him'—her voice cracked and wavered—'he was gone.' She put her hands over her mouth, maybe to keep a scream in. A choked wail escaped.

'You didn't hear anyone come in?' Wozza moved his weight from foot to foot and the floorboards of the old place creaked.

'No! I didn't hear anything.' Maddy's voice rose.

'Were you up the back of the house?' I asked.

She shook her head. 'I took a shower. I always take a shower when he goes down for his morning nap. It's too hard other-wise. Then I brought the washing in. Did some folding.'

'Did you leave the side down like this?' Wozza was pointing at, but not touching, the side of the cot.

Maddy's brow furrowed. 'No . . . I always put the side up.' She looked at us hopefully, like the revelation might be a clue.

'They're a bugger to figure out how to work the catch,' said Wozza, leaning over to take a closer look. Wozza had three girls and, I suspected, a lot of experience with cots. 'So someone who knew which lever to push . . .' He trailed off, lost in thought.

'How old is Ethan?' I asked. My knowledge of babies was limited. I looked around the room. 'Could he have gotten out of the cot somehow?'

Maddy shook her head. 'He's seven months old.'

Wozza looked concerned. 'They can't do much at that age,' he said to me in a low voice. 'No way he could get out by himself.'

'He is just learning how to roll.' Maddy's bottom lip trembled.

'Who else is here?' I asked. So far it was just Maddy and her panic filling the room. No sign of the baby's father.

'I—I . . .' Maddy choked on her words. 'I'm on my own. Ethy's dad . . . he didn't stick around.'

Wozza took out his notebook. 'Is there a custody dispute?'

Maddy put a hand to her forehead and rubbed. Closed her eyes for a moment. Opened them and looked straight at Wozza. 'It's complicated. He just . . .'

'Is he on the scene at all?' I asked, my voice gentle. It was important to keep things calm; we needed to get as much information as we could.

'He comes around when he feels like it. He tries to get in and see Ethan and if he's polite about it, I let him. But . . .'

'He's not always polite?'

Maddy's answer was quiet. 'No.'

'Does he threaten you?' asked Wozza.

She looked uncertain, then shrugged. Sometimes, threats were subtle.

'Do you think he's done this?' I asked, nodding towards the empty cot.

Maddy looked worried at the thought, but I could see her processing it. Seemed like every fibre of her being wanted to say no, but logic was forcing her to think otherwise.

Wozza turned a page in his notebook and took down the father's details. Josh McCreedy, aged twenty-five, lived off Main Street with his parents.

As Wozza was writing, I noticed some sort of monitor on the side of the cot. 'What's that?' I pointed.

An intake of breath. 'The baby monitor!' Maddy hurried from the room. We followed her down the hall to a big open room out the back. She picked up her phone from the bench, tapped it a couple of times to open an app. A picture of the empty cot emerged. She hit rewind. Wozza and I flanked her, fascinated. Fuzzy lines on the screen showing an empty cot, empty cot, empty cot . . . then shadows moving, legs, hands, a sleeping baby, the side of the cot pulled up, shadow legs retreating, baby sleeping. Baby safe.

A kidnapping in reverse.

My heart pounded as Maddy switched to play and we all watched, mesmerised, as golden-haired Ethan lay asleep, a curl at the top of his head swept up in a comical wave. Little fists clenched, one on each side of his face. Long pale lashes. A bright orange dummy. Rosebud cheeks. The camera pointed downwards, onto the baby. I guessed the whole point of a baby monitor was to watch the baby, not to spot kidnappers. So when the shadow legs appeared beyond the cot, it was impossible to see who it was. A hand appeared at the side of the cot rails, then the side of the cot slid down easily. Two hands reached for the baby. Picking him up. Baby disappearing from view. Legs turning. Walking away. Cot empty.

Maddy began sobbing. 'It's him. It's Josh.'

Wozza looked worried. 'How can you tell?'

Maddy wiped her nose with a tissue and rewound the video footage. 'See that?' Her voice was unsteady. She hit pause. There was a shadow of a tattoo on the hand reaching for the baby. On the side, close to the wrist.

Wozza squinted at it. 'Some kind of bird?'

'An eagle,' she said in a quiet voice. 'That's because birds travel between the land and the sky, between Earth and Heaven. That's what he always says. He got it when his brother died last year.'

'Try to ring him,' said Wozza. 'Maybe he just . . .' Then he stopped.

I watched his face. He didn't want to say it, didn't want to suggest an innocent explanation for the missing baby. Cops knew better.

Maddy tapped the contacts on her phone and called Josh McCreedy. She hit the speaker button so the sound of ringing filled the room. It went to voicemail. A deep voice said, 'It's Josh. Leave a message.' Then a beep.

'Where's Ethan?' Maddy screamed into the phone. 'Bring him back!'

I put my hands over hers and clicked the end-call button. Gave her a moment to take a deep breath.

'While you've got your phone there, can you find a couple of photos of Ethan and Josh and message them to me?' I pulled a card out of my pocket so she had my number. It was heartbreaking to watch her scrolling through what must be hundreds of photos, all featuring the same blond-haired, blue-eyed baby. She finally scrolled back far enough to find one which featured Josh holding Ethan. The baby looked newborn and I guessed that was the last time Josh had featured in Maddy's photos. She added the most recent photo she had of Ethan, taken that morning. He was dressed in the same outfit he was wearing in the baby-monitor video.

As soon as the photos pinged on my phone, I sent them to the police communication centre at D24, then followed up with a phone call to put a KALOF—a keep-a-look-out-for—alert for Josh McCreedy. I turned to Maddy. 'What sort of car does he have?' She described his car and I repeated it for the operator. 'He's driving a Holden Gemini. 1977. Lime green in colour. Personalised number plate. JOSHMC.'

I stepped away from Wozza and Maddy and moved into the hallway. 'We're going to need roadblocks set up, and uniforms at his house.' I checked my watch. How far could Josh McCreedy have driven? Fifteen, twenty ks? That's if he was heading out of town.

I finished the call and walked outside the house. Instructed the uniforms to begin canvassing the neighbours. Shouldn't be hard. By now most of them had come out to see what was happening. Police cars in a quiet street will do that. A quick scan of the scene told me all the houses on the same side as Maddy's place backed onto bushland. I called our senior sergeant. Told her we needed Crime Scene at the house, and the SES to do a search around the property and the adjoining national park just in case Josh McCreedy had dumped the baby nearby.

I finished the call and slipped back into the house.

'Keen on the old cars, is he?' Wozza was saying. Sounded conversational, but I knew he was fishing for information. If Josh McCreedy had taken his baby son, then we needed to know as much about him as we could.

'Yes,' Maddy murmured, distracted.

'Do you mind if I . . . ?' I nodded towards the kettle.

'A cup of tea sounds good,' she said.

I moved around to the other side of the bench and put the kettle on. The cups were on a shelf above the sink. I took three down and set them on the bench. The teapot and tea cannister were next to the kettle.

Wozza gestured for Maddy to take a seat at the kitchen table. Half of its surface was covered in laundry, neatly folded with lots of jumpsuits, some plain white and others featuring cartoon animals. Next to the neat piles of clothes was a tub of dummies and little plastic spoons and small bumpy rubber toys. For teething? Around the room were nappies and wipes and creams and lotions. A nice pram was parked near the sliding-glass back door. It never occurred to me that babies needed so much stuff.

'Why do you think Josh would have taken Ethan?' Wozza asked as soon as they were seated.

'I don't know. I have no idea why he would do this.' Maddy reached for the pile of baby clothes and rested a hand protectively on top of them.

'Would he have known about your shower routine?' I asked.

'He always criticised me about it. He told me I shouldn't wait till the baby was asleep before I took a shower. He said to just let Ethan cry.'

Sounds like a tosser, I thought.

'Did he have a key?' Wozza asked.

'I made him give it back when he moved out.' Maddy suddenly gasped. 'The spare key!' She got up and hurried down the hallway. We followed her outside and watched her squat next to a pot plant on the verandah and reach behind it. She pulled out a small rock. It was one of those fake rocks you hide keys in. She clicked it open. Empty.

'Did he know it was there?' Wozza asked.

She nodded miserably and we all went back inside and resumed our positions.

'What can you tell us about Josh?' I poured water into the teapot and brought it and the cups to the table.

Maddy began her story. Nothing out of the ordinary. Accidental pregnancy after dating Josh for six months. Maddy was living in her parents' Deception Bay holiday home and working as a teacher at the local Catholic school. Josh moved in and immediately expected her to take care of him. He was lazy and petulant. And soon, gone.

'At first, I figured he'd just lost his brother, so I cut him some slack, but the shine wore off pretty quickly. He'd play video games all day on the couch and he'd shout for a beer.' Maddy rolled her eyes. Small smile. 'Instead of a beer, I offered him a time machine so he could go back to the 1950s.' She shook her head. 'As if!'

'You asked him to leave?' I poured tea.

'Sure did. I was committed to the baby, but I did not want to have to deal with him as well. He didn't value-add.'

'Huh?' said Wozza.

'You know, add value to what I had here. He didn't bring anything to the table. So, what was the point?'

I admired her directness.

'And I didn't think he was that interested in Ethan. That's why this doesn't make sense.' Maddy sipped from her mug of tea.

Wozza and I looked at each other. This wasn't about the baby. If it was Josh who took Ethan, this was about *her*.

'Would he do this to hurt you?' I asked.

Maddy's eyes widened. Something hit home. 'Our last argument. He said, "You love the baby more than me," and I said, "No shit, Sherlock!"' She put her cup of tea down and her hands flew to her mouth. 'What have I done?'

At that moment, Maddy's phone pinged. A text. She picked it up from the table and swiped the screen open. 'It's from Mum. I called her and Dad right after I called you. They're on holidays up in Mildura but as soon as I told them about Ethan, they said they'd pack up and head down here straight away.' She paused and read the text. Muttered, 'Oh no, oh no,' over and over while she frantically swiped at the screen.

'What is it?' I hurried around behind her to see what she was doing.

'Mum just saw a notification on Insta. Josh posted a picture of Ethan.' She opened the app and scrolled down until the baby appeared. Ethan in a car, lying on the front passenger seat. There was a one-word caption written underneath the picture.

Revenge.

CHAPTER 3

BREWING TEMPEST

We stationed uniforms at Maddy's house in case Josh McCreedy returned with the baby, then we drove Maddy to the Deception Bay police station to get her statement. By phone, we'd co-ordinated the search for the baby and contacted the Search and Rescue Squad in Melbourne. Wozza had also called in a favour from a mate at the Air Wing, so a helicopter was on its way too.

Maddy had packed a baby bag in anticipation of Ethan's return. He'd need nappies and a bottle. She sat in the interview room with the bag on the floor beside her. Ready.

'We need as much detail as you can give us,' I said, opening my laptop to take down her words. 'Any places you know Josh likes to go. Friends. Anything.'

Maddy had a look of steely resolve. Wozza left us to it and slipped out of the room. He would head back to the house to co-ordinate the crime-scene examiner and the SES. He also had the tech department monitoring Josh's Instagram feed, looking for locations and clocking the times he was posting. Of grave concern was the fact that the photo showed baby Ethan lying on the front passenger seat. There was no sign of any kind of baby seat or child restraint. An angry ex-boyfriend, a stolen baby. Josh clearly wasn't concerned about his son's safety. But how far would he go to hurt Maddy?

Another selfie appeared at 10.47 am. It had been taken at the top of the Devil's Corner, a convergence of cliffs on the coast of Deception Bay. The image showed Josh grinning and the baby crying. The caption read: *I hope you enjoy your independence!* In both photos, Ethan was wearing the same jumpsuit as he was in the baby-monitor video, so it looked like they were taken today.

'He's hungry,' said Maddy, when the second picture dropped. 'He's an hour overdue for his feed.' She clutched at her stomach, like the pain was too much to bear, then leaned forward until her forehead was almost touching the table we were sitting at.

'What do you think Josh means by the caption?' I asked.

Maddy sat up again and rubbed her face with her hands. 'It sounds like he's not going to bring Ethan back, doesn't it?' Her lips quivered as if she was trying not to cry.

She was right. It did sound like that. I didn't say it out loud though. I moved between Maddy and the muster room, which had been hastily converted into a command post. More pictures appeared. One posted at 11.36 out by the old roadhouse that had shut down. The caption for that one was *Payback's a bitch. How does it feel?* Then a time gap, and a new one at

1.35 near the silos on the edge of town. The caption for that was especially worrying: *It's over. I'm gonna end it.*

'He's threatening to kill Ethan!' Maddy screamed when the last one came through.

She was right.

Each time another photo dropped, our new senior sergeant, Amanda Filipovic, directed two uniformed members who'd arrived as reinforcements from neighbouring towns to the sites in the hope Josh and the baby were still there. It was a vain hope. The techies decoded the time stamps on the photos and checked them against the time of posting. There was a consistent delay. Josh was taking photos, then moving on before he posted them.

Returning to the interview room with some tea for Maddy, I found her sobbing. I sat down next to her. 'We're in the process of tracking his phone.'

'You won't be able to.' Her voice hiccoughed from crying. 'He turns off his location services. He always boasts that he can't be tracked.'

'Maddy,' I said, trying to reassure her, 'that makes no difference to police. If he has the phone on—and clearly he has because he's posting to Instagram—then it's pinging off towers.'

A glimmer of hope. 'So you can find him?'

'We're just getting the search signed off. A senior officer needs to authorise it, but in a time-sensitive case like this, it shouldn't take long. Once the request is logged, it should take about half an hour and then we'll find him.'

Maddy checked the time on her phone. 'Ethan is completely overdue for a feed.' Her worry was palpable. I could see her screen was filled with messages of support from friends. She flinched every time her phone pinged but she couldn't look away in case one of the messages was from Josh.

I left Maddy in the interview room and made my way to the new senior sergeant's office. My old boss, Bill Wheeler—Wheels—had taken sick leave a couple of months ago. His claim of PTSD coincided with a close scrutiny of his management style, and made a mockery of our many colleagues who were genuinely coping with the debilitating condition. Amanda, his replacement, was a relocation from the city. Unlike her predecessor, Amanda's door was always open. I paused at the entrance to her office. She looked up from her computer.

'Any luck on the phone search?' I asked.

She tapped some keys. 'Yep, it's been authorised by a commander in the city. Paperwork is in. Techs are on it. Shouldn't be long now.'

'How about the roadblocks?'

She shook her head. 'Nothing. Although, from the pictures he's posting, he's staying local.' She looked worried. 'I gotta say, I'm concerned about the revenge messages he's posting with the photos. I saw a case like this before, in Melbourne, and it didn't end well.'

The case she was talking about had made the headlines when a father had taken his small child and taunted the mother on Facebook. At the time, it felt beyond belief that a father would kill a toddler, but now it was sadly believable.

'Did you work the case?' I asked Amanda.

'Not directly, but I knew people who did.'

'We just need to keep looking.' I took a deep breath.

'I don't know Deception Bay well enough yet to contribute much in the way of suggestions for where to look.' Amanda glanced out her window at the storm sky outside.

'Once we get his phone location, it won't matter. We'll know where to look.' I clenched and unclenched my fists, trying to set aside any thoughts about getting my hands on Josh McCreedy. It was hard to fathom a man who valued terrorising his ex more than he valued his own baby.

'Air Wing is sending a helicopter,' said Amanda. 'Impressive.'

'It was Wozza—reckons he has friends in high places.'

'He's talking about the Air Wing, right?' Amanda's voice held a faint trace of amusement, the best she could muster under the circumstances.

I nodded. 'Correct.'

'Their ETA is ten minutes. They're going to do a sweep from the air. Bit hard to hide a lime green car. They're worried about the weather though.'

I followed her gaze out the window. No rain yet but the sky was dark and the clouds hung over us like the Sword of Damocles. I hoped that by the time the helicopter arrived, we'd have the location of Josh's phone and we could point them in the right direction before the storm. Once they got a visual from the air, the Air Wing could direct us on the ground. Wozza and I would meet up for the arrest and retrieval stage once Josh was located. And hopefully get baby Ethan back unscathed.

'Get Randall to sit with the mother until her parents arrive,' Amanda said. 'Jane can chase up any intel you got from speaking to her.'

I nodded, then made my way to the muster room to seek out Jane and Randall, the station's youngsters.

Jane was sitting at one of the office computers. I gave her a list of things to do, the first of which was to call the uniforms who'd been around to Josh McCreedy's house to find out what his parents knew.

'Done it,' she said, reaching for a piece of paper on which she'd scribbled some notes. 'I was just about to bring this to you. Stu went round there. No one home. Neighbour said his dad works out at the abattoir and his mum's a secretary at Webster's Real Estate in the main street. No sign of the green Gemini at the home address.'

Jane was going to make detective one day. She had good instincts.

'Where's Randall?' I asked, looking around the space.

'He's taking Maddy a cup of tea.'

Randall had good instincts too.

When I walked back into the interview room, Randall was sitting at the table with Maddy. Both looked up as I entered. It only took me a moment to fill Maddy in. We didn't have much yet, but I reassured her that with the imminent arrival of the helicopter, as well as our being able to access Josh's phone location, it shouldn't take too much longer to find Josh and the baby. I told Maddy I was going to head off and join up with Wozza.

'I want you to stay here till your parents arrive,' I said to her. 'Randall will keep you in tea and biscuits while you're waiting.'

En route to Maddy's place to get Wozza, I decided to pick up Waffles as well. He's a black German shepherd I bought from the Dog Squad when he didn't make the cut. He was a great tracker, and might come in handy if Josh had abandoned the car and set off on foot. Even though I wasn't a trained dog handler, when Waffles and I were on a run he would often pick up scent trails. Lately I'd been running with Crystal, a local teen I'd met on a case last year, and her uncle Russell. For fun, Crystal would run and hide and I'd send Waffles off to find her. So far, it was Waffles 38, Crystal 0.

At the gates of my farm—actually my nan's farm, which I'd been living in since she'd gone into the local nursing home—I whistled. My big black lion of a dog came bounding down the driveway, tail wagging.

Ten minutes later, I pulled up at Maddy's house. Wozza was on the street out the front, talking into the police radio. He came straight over.

'Air 491 arrived. They spotted the car from the air using the location data.'

'That's great . . .' I said but stopped when I read his expression. *Not great*. 'What's happened?'

Wozza shook his head. Took a deep breath. 'Phones have just gone nuts,' he said. 'Motorists and a couple of neighbours have called it in. Collision. Car's rolled a bunch of times into a gully. Helicopter's landed. They're trying to get close enough.'

A bright, jagged streak of lightning flashed, followed almost immediately by a boom of thunder so loud it felt like end-of-days. The storm was nearly on top of us now.

My mind flashed to Maddy waiting for her baby to come home. 'Are they sure it's his car?' The brain can't help but scramble for an escape hatch.

Wozza nodded. 'Green Gemini. Plates match. It's him. *Them*.'

■●■

Lights and bells as every available police car sped towards the gully on Birchip Road. The sky overhead was ominous; it looked like a huge, black, metallic UFO covered the bay. The reports coming from the Air Wing and the uniforms ahead of us were not good. From half a kilometre away, I could see the flashing lights and the helicopter sitting in the paddock opposite the gully. Parking behind the marked car from Deception Bay, Wozza and I left Waffles in the car with the windows down and approached the scene.

Stu from the station was leaning in his car window, talking on the radio. He was calling for the Major Collision Investigation Unit to come out. My heart sank. The police crash investigators specialised in fatalities.

'Oh god, poor Maddy.'

'Bloody hell,' Wozza murmured.

Stu finished with the radio and stood up straight. Glanced at the sky. Mouth set in a grim line.

Wozza did that thing where a raised eyebrow asked the question. Stu did that thing where a slight shake of the head told us that the worst had happened.

I used words instead. 'Driver?'

'Deceased,' said Stu.

'Baby?'

'We haven't been able to find the baby. The Air Wing blokes are down there now. I'm heading back to help them look. Car's crushed.' He turned and began walking.

Wozza went to follow him. I touched his arm and he gave me a look of such desolate sorrow. Babies were the most innocent of victims.

'I'm going to get Waffles on the harness. He might be able to help.' I turned back to the car.

A crack from above and a blinding flash. The crisp smell of ozone. The very air was fizzing with the oncoming storm.

■●■

I manoeuvred myself down an incline into the gully where the car was crumpled so badly that it looked like something had taken a bite out of it. Even though it was obvious the car had rolled, it had landed upright. Parts of the roof had been pushed in. The section over the driver's seat was the worst; it was nearly level with the door. My heartbeat drummed as Waffles and I drew near. How could a baby survive that? Especially one who had been lying on the front seat.

Wozza was bent down, peering in the passenger-side window, which had smashed with the impact. There was a smell of dust and blood and storm. Flies were gathering. Wozza straightened.

'McCreedy's dead but I can't see the baby.'

'Can we get the doors open?' I led Waffles around to the passenger side.

'Nah,' said one of the Air Wing blokes, 'crash impact's squashed 'em shut.'

I bent over to see what Wozza had seen. Deceased driver slumped in the driver's seat. Far as I could tell, severe head trauma, neck at an angle to suggest it was broken. In hair colour and build, the body resembled the picture Maddy had sent of Josh McCreedy, but apart from that, identification might have to be DNA, dental or fingerprints. There was a lot of damage.

With nothing to lose, I tapped the Gemini's roof and said to Waffles: 'Find!' He sniffed at the car, tail wagging, and ran around to the other side, where McCreedy was. I followed. Waffles barked and sat next to the driver's-side door, telling me he had found Josh McCreedy. I tapped the roof again. 'Find!' Waffles took off around the car for a second time, sniffing at the front, crawling underneath the gap where it was wedged into the gully. My heart was in my throat as I had no idea of the stability of the crushed Gemini. But moments later, Waffles emerged at the other end and kept sniffing, his nose almost touching the car as he made his way around. At each of the other smashed windows, he rose up on his hind legs and rested his front paws on the door. He poked his nose inside the gaps, sniffing the interior of the car. Finally, he jumped onto the bonnet of the vehicle. His claws click-clacked as he followed his nose to the gap where the windscreen had been. I watched him carefully to see if he lifted his head to air-scent, which might indicate the baby had been thrown from the vehicle. Nothing.

Once he'd been around the car, he returned to the driver's-side door, barked, and sat down again. His way of saying: *Just one, Boss*. I hoped.

'I don't think the baby's here,' I said to Wozza.

He looked strained. 'Then where the bloody hell is he?'

CHAPTER 4

THE DEATH-KNOCK

The first drop of rain fell. It was followed by a million others as I ran for the car with Waffles. Wozza panted behind us. I'd never seen rain like it. It was so loud, drumming on the roof, that we had to raise our voices to be heard. Visibility was not much better than zero. I was reluctant to start the engine as I couldn't see the road, let alone anything that might be coming from the other direction.

'Should ease off eventually,' said Wozza, looking left and right. 'Too dangerous to drive at the moment. All you need is a semi-trailer coming either way and you're gone . . . which would be a pity because I'm only halfway through *The Rosie Project* and I'm really enjoying it.'

'I've read it,' I told him. 'If I see a large truck coming, I'll let you know how it ends.'

'Thanks.'

I saw through Wozza's attempt at humour. I felt it too. I reckon if cops could really unleash our feelings when something like this happened, collectively we'd be wolves howling at the moon.

With one last whole-body shake, Waffles settled himself on the back seat and the smell of wet dog permeated the car.

'Do you reckon the baby's there'—Wozza nodded towards the wreck—'and we just didn't find him?'

I shrugged. I knew Waffles was a good tracker, but I wasn't experienced enough to totally trust my ability to read him. Still, I didn't think he'd found anything, which was a good indication that the baby wasn't there. But there was no way to know for certain until the car was pulled out of the ditch and the area was examined thoroughly.

I checked my phone messages. 'Tow truck's on the way. We'll know soon enough.'

As we sat in the car, unable to move, I turned off the automatic windscreen wipers. They weren't doing much anyway. In the back seat, Waffles settled in for a nap. While we waited for the rain to ease off a bit, we strategised. We needed to trace the location data of Josh McCreedy's phone to see which towers he'd pinged off. If he'd left the baby somewhere, we needed to know the possible locations. We needed to compile a list of friends and relatives, anyone he might have handed the baby to, and then see if any of their phones pinged at the same locations. We needed to speak to Josh McCreedy's parents to see if they a) had the baby; b) knew where the baby was; or c) could suggest places where Josh might have left the baby.

This conversation was going to be difficult since we also had to do the death notification at the same time.

Finally, the pounding rain eased off and some visibility returned. I started the car and pulled out onto the road. The reprieve didn't last long, and when the rain began again we snail-paced it to the McCreedy house via my farm to drop Waffles off.

■●■

No cop likes a death-knock—the heartbreaking moment when you tell a person that a loved one they cherish is no longer alive. Death-knocks, by their very nature, mean the death was sudden and unexpected, a life cut short, usually by tragedy. And this one was going to be even worse than usual. Maddy said Josh McCreedy had lost a brother last year. She hadn't said how he'd died, but this would be a double blow to the family. In my experience, death-knocks could go a number of ways. Usually, there was shock, followed by tears, followed by us trailing a distraught family member through the house to a lounge room or kitchen table to be inundated with questions we didn't know the answers to. *How? What?* And the hardest one of all: *Why?*

Sometimes when we knocked, we might have the door opened to us by someone who knew something important. And that could certainly be the case here. We'd have to tread carefully.

We had sent uniforms to the McCreedys' house, keeping watch for anyone arriving there with a baby. They'd just radioed D24 to say the McCreedys had arrived home.

'Roger that,' Wozza said into the radio. 'Don't approach. We'll be there in five.'

'Strategy?' I asked him.

'We'll have to search the house for the baby,' he said, 'but that's going to be hard to do when they're all . . .' His voice trailed off.

I knew what he meant. 'We're going to have to tell them *after* we search the house.'

'Shit,' said Wozza. 'I frickin hate these things.'

This was going to be hard and we both knew it. I realised we needed to shift our energy. 'Worst death-knock?' I said in a deliberately lighter voice.

He let out a small laugh. 'By far the worst was when this young guy had died in a motorbike accident. Pinging through an intersection, doing a hundred in a sixty zone. Came to grief with a car making a right-hand turn.' Wozza made a whistling sound and moved his hand in an arc to suggest the motorcyclist had catapulted through the air. 'Headbutted a power pole. That's never going to end well. Anyhow, we got his ID and located the next of kin; his mother. We get to her house, do the death-knock. She answers, and as soon as she sees we're coppers, she goes off her nut.'

'Was it your cologne?' I asked.

Wozza shrugged. 'Could have been, or she really did not like police. So there she is saying, "Piss off, you effing coppers! You pigs have no right to come round here. You filth." She even spat at us, but we had a good couple of decades on her and jumped out of the way in time.'

'Geez, how did it end?'

'We had to stand on the footpath outside her house and yell, "Your son is dead."'

'Oh god! That's terrible.'

'What's your worst one?' he asked.

There was a very easy answer to this. It was a memory that made me cringe even now. I told Wozza the story of how I was a fairly new recruit when my partner Suzi and I were first on the scene at a supermarket where an elderly man had suffered a heart attack and couldn't be revived. Me and Suz—who was senior to me by a couple of years in the job—were tasked with alerting his wife.

'At their house, I rang the doorbell and Suzi leaned back on the porch railing while we waited for someone to answer the door. Suddenly, the rusty old railing gave way and Suz fell into the garden bed below, sprawled among the azaleas, just as the new widow answered the door.'

'I hate it when that happens,' said Wozza.

The distracting banter was good. Wozza kept it going.

'What do you think Maddy meant by the whole *value-add* thing when she was talking about Josh?'

I shrugged, but then tried my best to answer him. 'In the days of my grandparents, men were providers. The women did everything else, but the men earned the money and got all the accolades. I couldn't count the number of women who sat at my nan's kitchen table, unhappy, crying, wanting to leave . . . but in the end, there'd be sighs of resignation, and conversations would usually end with, "Oh well, at least he's a good provider." But times have changed. Women provide for themselves. So, what they want from a relationship has changed.'

I paused. 'Not that I'd know.' I laughed without mirth. 'And don't forget, my mum was a single mum. She never even told me who my dad was. Always said she didn't need a man except for the first five minutes.'

'I think one of ours only took three minutes,' said Wozza. 'Where's your mum this month?' He loved hearing stories of my mother.

'She's been running health clinics in a detention centre up north.' I had last seen Mum when she'd blown into town for a couple of days at Christmas. 'You know Mum, constantly off fighting for something.'

Wozza nodded. 'Apple didn't fall far from that tree.' He fell silent. Then, after a moment, he said, 'I can't even imagine sitting on the couch demanding Jess get me a beer.' He shuddered at the thought. Wozza's wife was bright and smart and in all the times I'd visited the Harvey household, things seemed as equal as you could get.

The rain eased off as we turned into the McCreedys' street and cruised slowly up to the marked police car parked a little way up the road. I wound down my window. It was Jane. She must've been called to relieve Stu when the crash happened.

'Any movement?' I said, looking up towards the house.

'No.' She checked her watch. 'It's a quarter past four now. They came in about ten minutes ago. Tamara and Keith McCreedy, I assume. They looked like their licence photos. Parked in the driveway there.' She pointed out a silver Ford sedan. 'They didn't look like they were in a hurry. And they weren't carrying a baby.' Jane looked worried. She had spent time with Maddy at the station. Felt the connection. She handed me a piece of paper. Search warrant. Signed.

I hoped we wouldn't need it. Salt in the wound and all that. We drove on and pulled up outside the McCreedy house.

It was showtime.

Wozza's knees clicked as he climbed out of the car and straightened himself. Brushed dust off his trousers that probably came from the car Josh McCreedy had died in. He sniffed discreetly at an armpit. Didn't screw up his face, so it must've passed muster.

'You good to go?' I asked, looking up at the sky. It was still shades of black and grey I'd never seen before. The storm had not finished. It was just taking a tea break, leaving a steady drizzle in its place. We hurried up the front steps.

From that moment on, it was all about reading what the McCreedys knew. Facial expressions. Body language. The baby was our priority. The death notification came second.

It was Tamara McCreedy who answered the door. She looked about forty-five, had a blonde pixie cut and wore a neat blue and white striped top and white pants. She smiled at us, a smile that faltered when Wozza and I showed her our badges.

'Is there something wrong?' she asked, her brow furrowing.

Either Tamara McCreedy was a really good actor, or she genuinely knew nothing about the drama that had unfolded over the last couple of hours.

'I'm Senior Detective Antigone Pollard and this is Senior Detective Warren Harvey.' I gestured at Wozza. 'May we come in?'

'Of course.' Tamara McCreedy stood back like she had nothing to hide.

We followed her down a passageway that led to a bright, neat living room. Keith McCreedy sat in an armchair with a glass of beer next to him, and a newspaper open on his lap. He looked up. Mild curiosity in his face, nothing else. My ears pricked, listening for sounds of a baby. Nothing.

'They're from the police,' Tamara said, looking from us to her husband.

Keith folded his newspaper and set it on the side table, next to his beer. Stood up. He was wearing one of those orange and navy high-vis polos and I wondered what he did at the abattoir.

'What can we do for you?' His voice was gruff.

I took a step forward, taking the lead. 'Mr McCreedy—'

'Keith.'

'Um, Keith, there's been an incident earlier today. Josh took his baby son from his cot at Maddy's house.'

Tamara's hands flew to her mouth. 'No!'

I pushed on. 'We have been unable to locate the baby—' And that was all I had to say.

Tamara dashed off. 'Come with me,' she said, 'in case he left Ethan here.'

From room to neat room, we followed her as she looked everywhere a baby could possibly be. Nothing. Keith didn't accompany us. As we made our way back to the living room, we found him standing where we'd left him, looking down at his phone. He made eye contact with his wife and shook his head. 'Josh isn't picking up. It's going straight to voicemail.'

'Mind if we check outside?' Wozza asked.

Tamara was on the move again. She grabbed an umbrella from beside the back door, then clicked a lock, and we followed her, checking in the shed and around the yard. Nothing.

'Is there anyone he might leave Ethan with?' I asked.

Tamara stopped and looked at me, the penny dropping. 'If he took the baby, why wouldn't Ethan be with him . . .' She broke off. 'Where is he?' There was a tremor in her voice.

Wozza took her arm. 'I think you'd better come back inside,' he said, his voice gentle.

Tamara McCreedy's lips quivered. With some death-knocks, you don't need words. Keith McCreedy was still pushing the call button on his phone when we came back inside. Tamara rushed to him and buried her face in his chest. He looked at us, confused.

'I'm sorry to have to tell you that there's been an accident involving your son's car. We believe he was the driver . . .'

Tamara let out a primal cry and slumped in her husband's arms. He struggled to hold her as she sank to her knees. He followed her down so they were both kneeling, wrapped together in a monolith of grief. We took a discreet step back to give them this moment. Wozza sniffed. Swiped at his nose with the back of his hand. I pulled a tissue from my sleeve and handed it to him.

'Bug in my eye,' he murmured, taking the tissue.

I looked around the room, anywhere but at them. A sideboard next to the dining table was covered with picture frames. Tamara and Keith with three children. Stepped boys, each one a head taller than the next, with maybe a year or two between them. The boys in the pictures along the sideboard got older and taller until they were young men. One was Josh; I recognised him from the photo Maddy gave us, rather than from what I'd seen in the wreck. At the end of the line of photos was one with Maddy and Josh holding a tiny baby. Both smiling. Happier days.

It took some time for the McCreedys' immediate reaction to expand and then deflate. Wozza stepped discreetly outside to let D24 know that we'd found no sign of the baby.

'C'mon, love,' said Keith after a long while. 'Up you get.' Without letting go of his wife, he leaned backwards on his heels and stood up, then pulled Tamara gently to her feet and led her to the armchair where he'd been sitting when we came in. Once she was settled, he turned to us, his hand still on her shoulder. His mouth moved to form words—the o-shape of a w-word—*where*? *when*?—but nothing came out.

My turn. 'Your son's accident happened on Birchip Road, out by the gully.'

Keith shook his head, as if denying the information would make it untrue. I wished it could. Then he finally found words. 'Did . . . someone run him off the road?'

Wozza came in from outside, tucking his phone into his pocket. 'Let's all sit,' he said, and made his way to the couch opposite the armchair where Tamara had settled. Keith took the twin chair next to his wife, and together they listened to the sorry tale that had brought us all to this moment—Josh taking the baby, posting his revenge-captioned pictures on Instagram from all around town, the crash, the missing baby.

Their predominant look was bafflement. In unsteady voices, they told a story in tandem, finishing each other's sentences.

Josh had fallen for Maddy and moved into her house. Then there was the pregnancy that the McCreedys didn't think Josh was ready for. He'd lasted two months before Maddy had sent him packing.

'He didn't know what to do with himself,' Tamara said, plucking a tissue from a box on the coffee table. 'He lay there,' she pointed to the couch Wozza and I were sitting on, then the TV, 'and he binge-watched Netflix and played video games for weeks. Couldn't shake the funk.'

'And then,' said Keith, 'slowly, he seemed to come out of it. We encouraged him to visit the baby. Ethan.'

'And sometimes, he did. But . . .' Tamara shook her head.

'Our son wasn't the most mature young man,' Keith finished.

Wozza leaned forward. 'Did you both visit the baby?'

Keith reached over and took his wife's hand. Glanced at her. 'Josh didn't want us interfering. We did go round a couple of times, but he saw it as a betrayal, like we were taking Maddy's side.'

Tamara nodded. 'I don't think he understood that Ethan is *our* grandchild. Such a beautiful little baby.'

We let the silence hang in the air while we all contemplated the beautiful little baby who was still missing. And their son who had taken him and was now gone.

Wozza stood up. I followed. 'I know it's a horrible time to do this, but to give us the best chance of finding baby Ethan, we'd like you to come with us to the station so we can get statements.'

'Now?' Keith said, his eyes red-rimmed.

But his wife was way ahead of him. 'Anything we can do,' she said, steeling her voice, 'to find the baby.'

Minutes later, driving through the rain with the McCreedys in the back seat, Wozza and I headed for the Deception Bay police station. No banter this time. Just sad silence filling every space in the car. Grief and sorrow weighed heavily on us all.

I parked around the back and we led Tamara and Keith in through the rear door at the station. We were all polka-dotted with rain by the time we got inside. Just as we entered, we almost ran into Randall, who was waiting outside the women's toilets. We stopped as Maddy came out the door. As soon as Tamara saw her, she rushed over and hugged her.

'I'm so sorry,' she said.

I was relieved to see Maddy hug her back.

'Have you seen Josh and Ethan?' said Maddy, the moment the hug was over.

She didn't know. Of course she didn't know. She had been in the room with Randall since I left.

Wozza picked up on it too. But before the conversation could go anywhere, I sensed a change in Keith, who charged towards Maddy before I could stop him.

He grabbed her by the shoulders and shook her like a rag doll. 'What did you do to make him take the baby?' His voice was loud and angry.

I grabbed him and forced him to let Maddy go.

At first, she looked lost for words at the attack. Then she spluttered, '*What*?' Her voice was indignant. 'How dare you make this my fault! He took my baby!'

I stepped between them and Wozza quickly ushered the McCreedys in the direction of our CIB office while I led Maddy back to the interview room. It took her a couple of seconds to shift her focus from Keith's anger back to me. Then the questions came thick and fast. *Did you get the phone location? Did you find Josh? Where's my baby?*

I gestured for her to sit. 'We found Josh,' I said.

'And Ethan?' she cried.

'No. There was no sign of Ethan.'

Maddy looked confused. 'Where did Josh say he was?'

'Maddy, I'm really sorry to tell you that Josh's car ran off the road . . . and he didn't survive the crash.' I waited for her reaction but there wasn't one. It was like she was frozen, and the information might take a moment to work through her skin, into her consciousness, into her heart. Then it burst out of her in a rush.

'Oh Josh! Oh god! So, where's my baby?' Her eyes widened with sudden recognition as her mind raced to catch up. She leaned forward, fingers splayed on the table. 'That's why Keith is so furious. Do they know where Ethan is?'

'They don't know,' I said. While Maddy was my focus, I was worried about the way Keith had grabbed her and how he shook her. In my experience any man who laid a hand on a woman as an automatic response to anger was dangerous. Was that the role model his son had seen?

Maddy's voice broke. 'This whole thing is a nightmare.' Tears rolled down her cheek. 'What can we do? We have to do something.'

Her desperation filled the room as the rain began drumming angry fingers on the roof and the windows. There was nothing more agonising than being coiled for action and forced into stillness.

CHAPTER 5

PANDORA'S JAR

The rain came in waves, easing off and then returning, drenching each new arrival to the police station. Maddy's parents, Tilly and Paul Muir, were soaked when they came through the front door after their long drive from Mildura. They were reunited with their daughter in the interview room and there were hugs all round. Questions burst from them; most, we didn't have the answers to.

'No news yet,' I said. The *yet* kept hope alive.

Once everyone settled in, there was a sad bewilderment from Maddy's parents. These things didn't happen to good people. They only happened to other people; the ones you saw on the news. Which effectively meant no one was prepared for anything like this to happen to them.

'Maddy's done nothing to deserve this,' said Tilly Muir.

Paul laid a hand on his wife's arm. She fell silent.

'I know,' I said. The word *deserve* came up a lot in my job. Humans seemed to have a need to weigh each atrocity and attribute probabilities based on what people 'deserved'. But when you see these things day in, day out, you realise that no one deserves the bad things that happened to them. Small words have such big meanings.

Tilly and Paul had only met Josh McCreedy a couple of times, they told me. They didn't like him.

'He was living in our holiday house here and acted as if he owned the place,' said Paul. 'First time we visited, before the baby was born, he was sitting on the couch playing a video game with his feet up on the coffee table. Didn't even get up when we arrived.' Paul shook his head at the memory.

Tilly, it seemed, hadn't liked Josh any more than her husband had. 'And there was Maddy, the size of a bus, making the tea and looking after her visitors.'

'Mum, I don't think I was the size of a bus . . .' Maddy's voice had the tone of every daughter who ever challenges her mother: that rising inflection of a teenager. Then the gravity of the situation returned and settled on her like a shroud.

But Tilly wasn't done. 'And he followed that idiot on Twitter or X or whatever it's called now. What's his name?'

'He followed a lot of them,' Maddy said quietly. 'The hyper-masculine ones who give horrible advice to men.'

I knew the type she was talking about because I followed social media commentators who actively shared and challenged those kinds of posts.

'There was one in particular who was just awful.' Tilly turned to Maddy. 'Remember that day he showed me those tweets because he thought he could convince me to follow that worm?'

Maddy nodded as if that particular memory was just one among many.

I excused myself from Maddy and her parents. In our office, Wozza was busy at his computer.

'Anything?' I asked.

'Nada.' Wozza stood up and stretched. 'Uniforms have checked in with the list of Josh's friends his parents gave me. None of them know where the baby is or knew of Josh's plans to take him. SES are still out searching. Crime techs are done with the house, so Maddy and her family can go home. More comfortable waiting there than here.'

The only bright spot was the call we got from the Major Collision guys. They had expedited the movement of the car wreck from the gully because of the possibility the baby could be at the scene. They'd found no sign of him, though.

Outside, the storm cracked and the sky darkened with the evening as rain pelted the windows. Wozza nodded towards them. 'We'll need to brave Armageddon out there and go look for the baby. I've got a list of all the short-term rentals, hotels and Airbnbs around here. Uniforms are knocking on doors. I figured we could do some of the list.'

'Let's go,' I said, grabbing my waterproof jacket. I knew we would work long into the night; it was crucial to cover as much ground as we could in the first twenty-four hours of any kidnapping.

I updated Maddy and her parents, and they headed home while we joined our colleagues in the driving rain, checking addresses, hotels, outlying farms and local picnic areas. There were two possibilities: either Josh McCreedy dumped Ethan somewhere and left him to the elements, or he had given him to someone.

'There's a third possibility,' said Wozza. 'Josh left him somewhere and someone found him and took him.'

It was a hard one to grasp. 'How could you find a baby and then just decide to keep it?'

Wozza shrugged. 'There are some nutters out there.'

■●■

It was almost 11 pm when I leaned in Amanda's office doorway and brought her up to speed. The three locations of the photos around town had been checked. SES searchers had knocked off for the night and would be back in place at first light. Other storm damage around town was stretching their resources. Maddy and her parents had returned to their house. Tamara and Keith McCreedy had given statements and the names of Josh's friends, who had been contacted but would need follow-up visits to give statements.

'I've written a release for Police Media.' Amanda stood and stretched.

That meant it would be all over the news and local radio first thing in the morning. And that in turn meant everyone would be looking for the baby.

'It's hard to know what to say to Maddy,' I said, leaning on the doorframe. I suddenly felt exhausted.

Amanda looked at me. 'How are *you*? This kind of investigation isn't easy.'

Why did that question almost bring tears to my eyes? Maybe because, aside from my nan, no one ever asked how I was. Not that I wanted them to, I reminded myself. That's what independence was all about. 'It's hard,' I admitted. 'The human part of your brain hopes we'll find the baby, and everything will be all right. But the cop part of your brain is way more cynical. We've all seen too many things go wrong in too many other cases. How do you not bring that accumulation of bad experiences with you to every new case?' I blew out a breath to steady my emotions.

Amanda moved around the desk to where I was standing. Her eyes were brimming with compassion. 'We have to put on a brave face, but behind the mask, we're all scared that the baby is no longer alive.' She stopped talking for a moment, then said, 'Have you heard the story of Pandora?'

'The one with the box, right?' I wondered where she was going with this.

'Yep, although apparently that's a mistranslation and it was actually a jar. According to the story, Pandora was the first human woman created on the instructions of Zeus. He gave her the jar as a wedding gift and told her never to open it, but her curiosity got the better of her. When she opened the jar, she released all kinds of ills on the world. She slammed the lid back on and trapped hope inside.'

'And . . . ?' I was too tired to deconstruct the story.

'When darkness swirls around us, all we have left is hope.'

I nodded, not trusting myself to speak.

Amanda squeezed my arm then continued in a lighter voice, 'I think the other moral of the story is to never give someone a gift and tell them not to open it. Kinda mean, I reckon.' She sighed. 'I just wish there was something more I could do.'

We both looked at the rain lashing the window for a moment and then Amanda took her pink polka-dot rain jacket off a hook on the wall, grabbed her keys and phone from her desk and moved to the doorway. I followed her out.

'Be careful out there,' I said as she headed towards the exit.

I watched her walk a couple of paces away from the station before she was swallowed by the storm.

CHAPTER 6

THE MIDNIGHT VISITOR

To say I was exhausted by the time I opened the gates to my farm just before midnight wouldn't quite capture the feeling: bone weariness combined with a stupor of sorrow for Maddy because the chances of finding baby Ethan alive dimmed with each passing hour. Especially if Josh had abandoned him somewhere. The rain had abated, but if Ethan had been left in the open, exposure to the wet and the cold would kill him. If that's what Josh had done, it would be murder by abandonment, and the irony would be that Josh would have killed the baby after he himself was dead.

The best-case scenario was that Josh had left the baby with a friend who somehow didn't know about the kidnapping. In this scenario, the baby was warm and fed and safe, and when Josh didn't turn up tomorrow, the person would hurry to return the baby to Maddy. Until we knew otherwise, like Amanda said, all we had was hope. As my nan always says, *Might as well imagine the best as the worst.*

As I closed the farm gate, I whistled for Waffles, but he didn't come. I quickly jumped back in my car. The last time Waffles didn't come to the gate, it was because a dangerous intruder had broken into the farm and wreaked havoc, so my heart was in my throat as I drove slowly up the sweeping driveway, through the grove of oaks towards the farmhouse. By now, the rain had settled to a light, steady stream and I scanned the parts of the landscape illuminated by the headlights. No sign of Waffles.

The mystery was solved as soon as the driveway curved towards the house and I pulled up behind the jeep parked in front of the porch.

Mum.

I took the steps two at a time and fumbled with my key. Finally unlocking the door, I entered. Waffles was on the other side, tail wagging so hard, it wagged him. I gave him a quick pat and headed in. The house was warm despite the storm and I knew Mum must have built a fire. I hurried up the long hall, past the stern Pollard family portraits and into the cosy back room. Waffles clicked along beside me.

'Antigone!' Mum put a book down on the coffee table next to her end of the couch and stood up to greet me.

'What are you doing here?' I asked in wonder as I hugged her. 'I thought you were up north.'

'Long story, and one that will keep till tomorrow. Waffles has been keeping me company.' She smiled as he sat down beside her. Waffles wagged his tail, looked at me, but didn't move. His allegiance was usually towards me, but there was something about my mum that shifted it. He had identified the pack leader. The force of nature that she was.

I moved behind the kitchen counter and put the kettle on. I needed a strong cup of tea more than anything right now.

'Tough day?' Mum said.

'The worst.' I took two cups from the cupboard and spooned tea leaves into the teapot. 'Baby kidnapping.'

'Bloody hell. Any leads?'

I shook my head. 'Our only lead is on a slab at the morgue.' That was all I could manage; words felt too hard after the day I'd had. Mum came around to my side of the counter and gently took the tea strainer from my hand. 'Your hands are cold,' she said. 'Go sit by the fire and warm up.'

I moved over to the toasty hearth, too wired to sit. I stood instead, hands behind my back, thawing out. I gave Mum the short version. 'The father took the baby out of his cot, posted pictures on social media of the two of them around town, then was found dead in his wrecked car. Baby's gone.'

Mum handed me a cup of tea. 'How's the mother?'

I pictured Maddy, flanked by her parents. 'What you would expect: shocked, distraught, frantic.'

Mum settled back on the couch and tucked her knees under her, hands wrapped around her mug. 'I can imagine. I would have been beside myself if anything happened to you when you were a baby.'

There was an expression on my mother's face that I couldn't read. She was normally empathetic, but this was next level. Then it occurred to me: in her line of work, she would have seen plenty of mums who had lost their babies.

'What time are you back on?'

I glanced at the grandfather clock, which was approaching 12.30 am. 'Seven,' I said.

'If I can help in any way . . .'

I looked closely at my mother. Saw the worry on her face. 'Mum, what are you doing here?' I kept my voice soft and took a sip of tea. Mum didn't usually drop in like this. She'd visited for a couple of days over Christmas. We'd brought Nan to the house and the three of us and Waffles had spent several really nice days together, relaxing, cooking and reading. Then she was off again.

'I need to tell you something,' she said. 'And it's not going to be easy.'

'Okay,' I said, trying not to panic, trying not to jump from zero to a hundred. *Is she ill? Dying*? 'You're not . . .' I couldn't get the words out.

She looked puzzled for a second, then realised what I was thinking. 'Oh no, nothing like that. I'm fine. I promise.'

It took a moment for my heart to settle in my chest.

'I just need to talk to you and your nan together,' she said. 'I've rung her aged care facility and I'm picking her up tomorrow. Hope you don't mind the company.'

Tomorrow I'd be up before dawn to run Waffles and then I'd be back at work, trying to find baby Ethan. I loved Mum and Nan, but I really didn't have time for them tomorrow. I said as much. A baby's life was at stake. 'You can't give me a hint now?'

She shook her head. 'No pressure. I understand the demands of work as much as anyone. Nan and I can spend some time together while you're working. I won't tell her anything before we all get a chance to sit down as a family. As far as she's concerned, this is just a visit.'

Good luck with that, I thought. Nan might be frail enough for aged care, but she was sharp as a tack.

I hugged Mum goodnight and went to my room. Waffles followed, climbing onto his fluffy dog bed. Just as I was setting the alarm on my phone, I scrolled quickly through my messages. I had been so busy with the case I hadn't had a chance to look at any of them earlier. My heart skipped a beat.

There was one from Daniel. The man I had loved more than anyone. The man I had left to come to Deception Bay. The man, it seemed, who was not quite out of my system—not if my heart rate was anything to go by.

I'm headed your way on the weekend.

Thought I could swing by, and we can talk.

D x

It was too late to respond so, instead, I tumbled into bed and fell into an uneasy slumber.

CHAPTER 7

THE BABY

She had never even held a baby before her husband arrived home with one.

'Where did you . . . ?' The words escaped her lips before she could stop them, but she quickly checked herself and repeated the mantra in her mind. *Don't ask questions, don't ask questions, don't ask . . .*

But he either hadn't noticed or had decided to let it pass in his excitement about the baby. 'Just look at him!' he said with pride, as if the baby boy was his. He handed her the bundle.

The baby was beautiful.

She ran her fingers along his forehead. He felt like a warm, delicate peach. Her arms felt full, like this baby belonged in them. She looked up at her beaming husband, not daring to voice the questions flooding into her head. She had perfected the look over the years. The look that made him talk.

'My dear, sometimes providence grants your heart's desire. There you are, minding your own business and . . .' He smiled down at the baby.

The baby stirred but didn't wake.

Her husband turned and headed out of the room. She heard the front door and then the car door, then the front door again. He appeared with two shopping bags filled with what looked like baby paraphernalia. 'I went by the supermarket in Bellanook and got everything you'll need. I've fed him already. A full belly put him right to sleep.'

'But how?'

His expression hardened. 'No need for questions,' he said. 'All you need to do is look after him.'

And then he left her holding the baby, wondering what the hell had just happened.

CHAPTER 8

THE FORK IN THE ROAD

It was a little before six in the morning when I stood with Waffles on the verandah of the farm, stretching for our run. Waffles did one downward dog and he was good to go. My routine took a little longer. When I was done, I stood up and took in the view. I had tossed and turned most of the night. The missing baby, Mum, the message from Daniel. I had no hope of sleeping properly. The sun had yet to rise, and the paddocks stretched out before me in shadow. Up here, the air was crisp and clean; every now and again, a hint of sea breeze. It was hard to imagine living anywhere else. I strapped on my armband phone holder and opened the podcast app. Wozza's wife, Jess, had got me addicted to true-crime podcasts. I pressed play on *Casefile* and let the anonymous host's voice tell me stories of murder as I sprung from the porch and set off over the back paddock. Waffles galloped next to me.

Waffles always reacted when we hit the spot along the stretch of road adjacent to the farm where, last year, we'd located the vehicle of an intruder he'd bitten. No doubt he revelled in the happy memory of the scent trail. He barked, tail wagging.

'I know, buddy,' I said and kept running. I figured a couple of kilometres would do the trick. We would take the back road towards town and take the turn at the fork in the road that led back to my farm. The earth was still damp from yesterday's downpour and puddles remained on the side of the road. Waffles ran through several of them and I factored in some towel-drying time when we got back to the farm.

Rounding the bend in the road near the turnoff, it took me a second to process what I was seeing. Instead of undisturbed countryside, I saw a car smashed into a giant eucalypt on the bend.

'Bloody hell!' I cried, running over to the wreck.

Waffles was way ahead of me. He reached the maroon SUV before I did. He put his nose to the ground and did a quick sweep of the area. He stopped at the driver's door and sat down, so before I reached the car, I suspected someone was still inside. There was a settled look to the scene, like it had happened a while ago. If someone *was* still inside, they were too injured to get out. I scanned the road for skid marks. One set from the road to the tree. The driver had hit the brakes. Probably avoiding a roo. I looked for any signs of injured wildlife and found none.

I put my hand on the bonnet as I moved towards the driver's door. It was cold. The wreck had probably been here all night.

The windows were tinted and streaked with dirt so it wasn't until I wrenched open the door that I saw the driver.

It was Amanda. My boss.

The pieces clinked into place. Maroon SUV. I saw it every day in the station car park. Amanda picking up her keys to go last night, putting on the pink polka-dot jacket. Me telling her to drive carefully in the storm. My thoughts raced. She was still in uniform but she wasn't wearing the pink jacket now. I couldn't see it in the car.

Did this happen last night?

Amanda lay back against the seat, dried blood underneath her nose. The airbag hung limply from the steering wheel. Leaning into the car, I tentatively touched her face. Warmth radiated into my fingertips. I blew out a breath of relief; she wasn't dead. I reached to check her pulse. Alive but unconscious. I called D24. I needed an ambulance, and backup from the station.

Despite the shock of finding my boss in a wreck, my training kicked in. Check for danger. I stood straight and took a quick look around. Aside from the skid marks, I couldn't find anything to suggest what it was that had made her swerve off the road. The fact that no one had come upon the wreckage before me demonstrated just how little this back road was used. Two roads from town led out to our farm. This was not the one I took last night.

Leaning back into the car, I squatted down and tried to get Amanda to respond. I shook her shoulder gently. 'Amanda? Can you hear me?'

There was a slight stirring, but she didn't open her eyes. Her skin was pale and I wondered if she was bleeding somewhere. I thought of my mum. She was just over the paddock. She answered on the second ring—a lifelong habit of being on-call.

'Mum!' I could hear the shake in my own voice.

'Antigone? What's wrong? Where are you?' Her voice switched from sleepy to calm and in charge.

'I'm out on the road behind the back paddock. There's been a car crash—' I drew in a deep breath to keep my voice steady. 'It's my boss. Amanda.'

'What do you need?' No preamble.

'Can you drive around here? She's unconscious. You'll be quicker than the ambulance.'

'On my way.' And then the line went dead.

I felt a lump in my throat; my mum was coming. I tried to think of the last time I'd called on her in an emergency and came up blank. I crouched down next to Amanda again. There was considerable damage to the front of the car, which was partly folded around the tree. I knew from experience that front-seat occupants could become trapped if footwells collapsed. I reached for her right knee, the one closest to me, and gently ran my hands from the knee down towards the foot. It seemed clear. There was no blood when I checked my hands. I tried to repeat the process with her left knee but couldn't move my hands down very far. Her lower leg was jammed against something and then . . . I could feel the break. I jerked my hands away. And there was blood. My stomach lurched; there was something about bones that weren't pointing in the right direction . . . I stood up and wiped my hands on my running pants, then checked again that Amanda was still breathing. She was.

Waffles stood next to me, on alert. He sensed my tension. Then he did something strange. He put his head down and sniffed as if he was picking up a scent trail.

'What is it, buddy?' I watched as he walked to the road diagonally from where we had come. I couldn't follow him because I couldn't leave Amanda. I took her hand and felt the warmth again, which gave me hope. 'Please be okay,' I whispered. I heard Mum's car approach and I waved her over to park next to the wreck.

Mum got out of her car with her medical bag and headed straight for Amanda. She put on disposable gloves and got out a stethoscope, listening for a heartbeat, releasing a slow, steady breath when she found one. She then began checking for injuries, starting at the top.

'Nasty bump here,' said Mum, gently probing the back of Amanda's head with her gloved fingers. As she moved to her neck, Amanda made a noise that wasn't quite a moan, more like the whisper of a moan.

Faint sirens in the distance.

'Her leg is broken,' I offered as Mum moved down to Amanda's arms.

Mum nodded, then she kneeled down and felt what I had felt minutes earlier. 'She's lost a lot of blood. There's no time to lose.'

The sirens got louder. I walked out onto the road so they could see me from around the bend, careful to avoid the evidence of tyre marks stamped into the muddy clay surface.

First the ambulance, then the squad car, then Wozza in the unmarked car. I directed them all to pull up short of the path of Amanda's car.

I radioed D24 again and requested the Major Collision Squad, on the chance that the investigators had stayed in town overnight after processing Josh McCreedy's fatal. I was hoping they'd help out since this collision involved a police officer.

Jane and Randall were in the squad car. I instructed them to put cones around the skid marks.

'Sure thing,' said Jane, opening the boot of the car and removing traffic cones and crime-scene tape. 'Major Collision are on their way too. They weren't happy being woken up so early.'

'Big babies,' said Wozza, walking over to join us, looking like he wasn't happy to be up so early either. He glanced over to Amanda's car with a worried expression.

We moved closer to the car as the ambos unloaded their kit and met with Mum. She introduced herself and greeted Wozza. He nodded back, but his eyes were on Amanda. He winced.

'Geez.' Wozza took a step back. He was a fainter so it was just as well.

One of the ambos went around to the other side of the car and was able to wrench the door open. From the screaming of metal while she did it, it sounded like the structure of the car had been compromised. She moved onto the passenger seat and attached a blood-pressure cuff onto Amanda's limp arm. She called out a number and the other ambo made a note of it. We stepped further away to let them do their job.

Wozza looked up and down the lonely back road. 'What the hell was she doing out here? If I didn't know better, I'd say she was on her way to your place.'

'Engine's cold,' I said. 'She's been here all night. We both left late and she was headed home. Why would she come out here?'

More sirens told us the Major Collision Squad was on its way.

'Hey!' One of the ambos called us over. She had climbed out of the passenger seat with the blood-pressure cuff. She had something in her other hand. 'Do you want this?'

It was Amanda's mobile phone. Wozza took it from her. 'Where was it?' he said.

'In the passenger-side footwell,' said the ambo. 'Probably flew off the seat in the crash.'

He turned it over in his hands. I looked on. Definitely Amanda's. It had the distinctive sparkly cover we saw daily at the police station.

The Major Collision guys pulled to a halt behind the station sedan and got out. I hurried over to them and pointed out the area Jane and Randall had just roped off with crime-scene tape.

One of the crash investigators, who I recognised from Josh McCreedy's wreck, pointed to the set of skid marks on the road. 'She's swerved to avoid something. Hit the brakes, then hit the tree. Not much time, maybe a second to react. Then . . . bang.' He turned and gestured towards another tree near the skid marks. 'There are some shoe impressions between there and the wreck. Did anyone walk over there?'

'I kept everyone away,' I said, remembering how Waffles had headed in that direction. Maybe he'd picked up a scent.

The crash investigator looked distracted as Wozza and I followed his gaze to the tree and the wreck, where the ambos and Mum were extracting Amanda from the car.

We all went over to see if we could help.

'Oh geez,' said Wozza as he caught a glimpse of her bloodied leg and quickly looked away. Waffles, who'd been sniffing around the scene, came and sat next to his leg and leaned on him. Wozza patted his head. 'Thanks, buddy.' He blew out a calming breath and then looked at the phone in his hand. He poked at it and the lockscreen came to life. The wallpaper was a picture of Amanda in a wetsuit, sitting on the deck of what looked like a dive boat. She was smiling broadly.

I looked at Amanda, who was now loaded onto the stretcher. Didn't look like the same person. The screen went black again. Wozza poked it and the picture came back. It gave me an idea. I took the phone from him and moved closer to Amanda. One of the paramedics was inserting a cannula into her arm while the other was unwinding a tube connected to a bag of fluid. I touched the locked screen and flicked up from the bottom, holding it over her face for long enough for the facial recognition software to recognise her, then quickly stepped back out of the way.

The screen came to life and I immediately felt guilty for intruding. It was like I was spying on my boss. 'Should I do this?' I asked Wozza. I needed a second opinion.

'You're trying to find out why she was out here last night?'

I nodded.

'Go for it.'

I shook aside my reluctance and tapped on the Messenger app. There were messages from a whole list of people: some I'd heard her mention, most I hadn't. None were from yesterday. Next, I tried recent calls. Nothing from after I'd watched her leave the station last night. Then I tried text messages. There was one from a mobile number that had come in at 11.30—about half an hour after Amanda left work last night. I tapped on it.

'Bloody hell,' said Wozza, looking over my shoulder.

'Bloody hell indeed.' The message didn't make sense. It read: *Emergency! I need you out at the farm asap!—Antigone*

'It's not your number,' said Wozza, pointing to the screen. 'But she must have come out here to get to you.' He looked around the lonely narrow road. 'She hasn't been in town long enough to know to take the better road.'

Suddenly, it dawned on me. 'If you put my address into any sat-nav, it takes you via this road because it's technically the shortest route. So that means this accident is . . .'

'Probably not an accident,' Wozza finished.

CHAPTER 9

THE HUNT FOR THE MISSING BABY

By the time Wozza and I got to work, around 9 am, there was a handful of reporters waiting at the station. Too late, we remembered Amanda's missing-baby media release from the night before. It had had time to wing its way to Melbourne and gather forces that had made a beeline straight for the station. Normally, cops of our rank did not front the media but, given that our senior sergeant was lying in a hospital bed unconscious, we had to provide something if we wanted to get the story out there. The more people looking for the baby, the better.

I glanced at Wozza, who suddenly looked pale.

'Give me an autopsy any day over public speaking.' He nodded his head at the cluster of reporters.

Given how much Wozza hated the morgue, I figured I'd be the one to talk to them. He drove the car around to the rear of the police station and we both got out and entered through the back door. We walked through the station and found Stu on the front desk, leaning on the counter. He looked at me and then to the front door. Several cameras were pointing in our direction. He shrugged the kind of shrug that said: *above my pay grade*.

Wozza and I went into our office to prepare for the media statement. We'd had photocopies made of several pictures of baby Ethan that Maddy had taken just yesterday morning before his nap. We strategised about the information we would share.

'They'll be all over Josh's death,' said Wozza. 'And the social media stuff won't take long to leak, if it hasn't already.'

He was right. We'd both been tied up since before dawn with Amanda's collision. Neither of us had checked the socials. Wozza's kids had got him onto Instagram and he seemed to watch a lot of furniture-restoration videos, and ones of sea creatures being cut free from nets by kind passers-by.

When we were ready, we made our way outside. Walking towards the journalists was like walking on the red carpet for the Academy Awards, with cameras clicking in our faces and reporters calling out questions as soon as they saw us. I held up a hand, like I'd seen my friend Pip do when she did press conferences as the Chief Commissioner. It worked—everyone fell silent.

'I'm Senior Detective Antigone Pollard. Yesterday morning, a baby was taken from his cot at his mother's home in Deception Bay. The person we believe took him is now deceased, but the baby is still missing.' Beside me, Wozza held up a picture of baby Ethan in his little animal-print jumpsuit. There was a moment of silence among the journalists. It was the baby.

I could see it in their faces. I went on. 'We have SES searching around town, but we would like people with properties to check around. Please be vigilant as you move through town. We don't know if the baby has been left somewhere or with someone. If you have any information, I urge you to call Crimestoppers as soon as possible.' I paused and took a breath, bracing for questions.

'Senior Detective Pollard,' Tammy Millhouse, a journalist I recognised, called from the left side of the throng, 'is it true the baby's father took the baby?'

I had expected this question. The information we give to the media is always so vague, but I understood the importance of admitting that it was Josh McCreedy. People watching who knew him might have the baby, and the life of the baby was more important than his dead father's reputation.

'At this early stage, we will be making enquiries with anyone who knew Mr McCreedy and has any knowledge of the whereabouts of the baby.' It was a not-quite-yes answer but close enough for people to make the connection.

'Senior Detective, can you comment on the social media posts made by Josh McCreedy before the collision?'

I took a deep breath and thought about an answer that would seem impartial, as if Josh McCreedy hadn't taunted poor Maddy with pictures of her distressed baby. 'When people don't utilise privacy settings on social media, what they write can be viewed by anyone.' I stopped. The reporter nodded as if satisfied. Answering without answering is a thing.

'I'm Lincoln Steele from The Drew Nayle Show on Three Triple P.' The man who was speaking paused and smoothed his hair. 'Does the mother take some responsibility for what's happened?'

Several female journalists near him gasped at his question.

The counter-narrative that everything the offender does is somehow the fault of the victim is truly exhausting. I decided not to pander to it. 'That question,' I said, 'is profoundly unhelpful; our focus is finding the baby.'

'Senior Detective Pollard,' another reporter called out. 'We are hearing reports of a second accident site, one that was discovered this morning.'

Bugger. They knew. I needed to pull the pin.

I leaned into the microphones. 'I'd like to thank you all for coming to cover this story. Please keep your eyes and ears to the ground while you're here. We need to do everything we can to locate the missing baby, Ethan Muir.' Then Wozza and I hurried back inside and closed the station door against the barrage of questions.

■●■

No sooner were we safely back in our office than stories began popping up on news sites everywhere. Media interest in a missing baby was always going to be huge. Wozza and I fuelled up on a quick cuppa and banana cake while we strategised about the investigation.

An email pinged. It was a report from our tech department on Josh McCreedy's phone data. I printed it out for our rapidly growing file. 'Let's retrace his steps from yesterday.'

Wozza rummaged in a desk drawer for a notepad.

'Maddy called us at nine forty am.'

He made a note of it.

'According to this . . .' I said as I scanned the data, 'Josh took the picture of Ethan in the car at nine twenty-four am. Before Maddy discovered the baby missing. Can't tell where the photo was taken, but I'd guess outside Maddy's house.'

'That fits with the time Maddy said she took a shower,' said Wozza.

'It says here that the picture from the Devil's Corner was taken at ten thirteen, four minutes after the picture on the car seat was posted. The location data supports that.'

Wozza continued scribbling notes. 'So he stops at the Devil's Corner and posts that picture he took earlier, then takes a new picture of him holding the baby near the cliffs.'

'But he doesn't post the Devil's Corner picture until ten forty-seven, when his phone is no longer pinging in that location.'

'Next stop was the abandoned roadhouse,' said Wozza. 'What time do we reckon he got there?'

I scanned the data. 'Picture taken at eleven fifteen but not posted till eleven thirty-six.'

'Let me guess,' said Wozza, pressing fingers to his forehead, 'our kidnapper was long gone.'

'That's weird,' I said when the next line of data registered. 'The final photo, the one at the silos, isn't taken till nine past one, and it was posted at one thirty-five. That leaves a pretty big gap between the roadhouse posting and when he gets to the silos.'

'If you're gonna make me do maths, I'll need a pastry,' said Wozza.

'From eleven fifteen till nine past one, from the roadhouse to the silos, there's almost two hours.'

'So where's his phone pinging during those two hours?'

I checked the records. 'In town.'

'Bloody hell,' said Wozza.

'You took the words right out of my mouth. He could have been walking around town with the baby while we were searching for him at the sites of all the photos.'

'And no one would have realised,' said Wozza, a note of wonder in his voice. 'They wouldn't have looked twice.'

I stood up and pocketed my phone. 'Time to talk to the townsfolk.'

'And check CCTV.' Wozza stretched out an ache in his back with a groan.

■●■

Wozza looked contemplative as he started the police car's engine. 'What do you reckon Josh McCreedy's endgame was when he took the baby?' he said.

I always find it difficult to step into the shoes of someone who does something unthinkable. 'It's hard to tell. He said *revenge* in his message. Did he want to keep Ethan for himself? Or to kill Ethan? Or just scare Maddy?'

Wozza picked up the point. 'Because if he just wanted to scare Maddy and not hurt the baby, he would have had a baby seat at least, but he didn't. There was also no sign of a baby bag in the car. What kind of parent goes anywhere with a baby without a bag full of baby stuff? Even if he hadn't done much of the parenting, every parent knows babies need stuff.'

I pulled the preliminary report from the Major Collision investigators out of the manila folder on my knee. Scanned it for mentions of anything a baby might need. There was only one thing in the car: a baby bottle that looked like it had remnants of formula in it.

'He didn't have anything else with him,' I said, 'but what if he intended to take the baby somewhere that did have baby stuff?'

Woz looked thoughtful. 'If I wanted to drop my kids off somewhere, I've got thirty-five friends who I could call on in an emergency and they're all equipped for kids.'

'Thirty-five people want to mind your kids? They're kind of wild.'

Wozza considered this and recalculated. 'Okay, maybe three or four friends. But would Josh McCreedy have mates who he could drop a baby off to? People who would have all the things you need? You saw Maddy's place, right? Babies need mountains of stuff.'

I sighed. 'Do you think he could have killed the baby and hidden the body somewhere? Could that have been his plan all along? Then run his car off the road to take his own life?'

Wozza pulled up on Main Street. 'If he did, then the baby is going to be really hard to find.'

Before we had a chance to get out of the car, I received a panicked call from Maddy.

'Antigone, my house is surrounded by reporters! What do I do?' Her voice trembled with fear.

Oh no! I should have anticipated this. It was hard enough for us to face the media. How hard would it be for a young mother who was already traumatised by her baby being missing?

'We'll be right there,' I told her.

Wozza, who'd gathered there was something wrong, turned the car back on and we headed towards Maddy's house with lights and sirens on. He switched them off when we turned into her street. No sense adding to the circus. Sure enough, there were media vans everywhere. I cursed inwardly. Amanda would normally have dealt with this but she was unconscious in hospital, battered and broken.

'I'll turn into the driveway,' said Wozza. 'That way, we won't have to run the gauntlet.'

He pulled up behind Maddy's parents' car. Her mum met us at the door before we had the chance to knock.

'Thank god you're here,' she said, closing the door behind us to the sound of camera clicks. 'They started ringing on the bell half an hour ago.'

Maddy was sitting at the table in the back room where we had sat yesterday. It had now been cleared of folded baby clothes. The rest of the house also looked much neater. I'd seen this kind of cleaning before. People thrust into chaos trying to restore order where they could. Maddy seemed smaller than she did yesterday. She hugged her arms around herself and looked at us with such profound sadness it was hard to meet her gaze. I heard Wozza let out a breath. I couldn't imagine what it would be like to lose a child, but he had three daughters and his response was palpable. Maddy was going through every parent's worst nightmare.

'Maddy, I know this is hard,' Wozza said, 'but the fastest way to make the media leave is to give them a statement. An appeal by a parent can reach people in a way that a police media conference can't. But only if you feel up to it.'

Maddy's mum turned to me. 'Do you think it will help find baby Ethan?'

'It can't hurt,' I said. 'We won't advise you one way or another, but if someone does have him and they see Maddy's distress, they might be moved to return him.' Even as I said it, I wavered. If any reasonable person had the baby, they would have returned him by now. But there was a more profound truth at play here: the family had to feel like they had done everything they could to find Ethan. If it turned out badly, they needed to move forward believing they'd left no stone unturned.

When the family agreed to speak to the media, Wozza went outside to let the reporters know. From the length of time he was gone, I guessed he'd given them some rules to abide by about respectful behaviour towards the distressed mother.

'Are you ready?' I asked Maddy when Wozza came back inside.

'No . . . but I'll do it anyway. For Ethan.' Her lip trembled and her parents walked with her to the front door.

Wozza had invited the media up to the front lawn and the bed of flowers lining the porch put a barrier between Maddy and the journalists. Her parents stood on either side of Maddy with their arms around her. She stood there uncertainly as a dozen microphones were held out in front of her.

Tammy Millhouse asked the opening question. 'Maddy, we are so sorry for what's happened. I hope you're holding up okay.'

Maddy looked grateful that someone had acknowledged the horror she was going through.

Tammy continued. 'If someone out there has baby Ethan, what do you want to say to them?'

Maddy didn't hesitate. 'Please, please, please bring him home to me. He is my beautiful baby and we just want him back safely.'

A second reporter: 'Maddy, what is the best-case scenario here?'

The young mother focused her gaze on the reporter and appeared to draw on all her strength to speak. 'The most heartbreaking thing is that I hope someone has Ethan because at least that means he is safe and someone is looking after him. I can't even imagine the possibility that Josh has left him somewhere. It's too hard.' Her eyes filled with tears. 'But if people could check their sheds and farms, we would be so grateful.'

Lincoln Steele, who had asked the offensive question at the earlier media conference, nudged another reporter aside and stepped forward. 'Maddy, would you like to comment on what made Josh take the baby? So many fathers don't get custody and are forced to take desperate measures.'

Maddy's forehead creased in puzzlement, then colour rose in her pale cheeks. 'What kind of question is that?' she spluttered.

Steele looked momentarily perplexed that she hadn't answered his question, but quickly tried to regain his position by going on the attack. 'Come on, it takes two to tango.'

There were gasps again and I could see Tammy Millhouse nudging her cameraman to catch the appalling treatment.

I hoped it would trend on social media and Steele would be shamed. I turned back to Maddy, ready to intervene if she needed me to. She didn't.

'Firstly,' she said, eyes ablaze, 'to ask if I provoked Josh to kidnap my baby is victim blaming at its finest because then you put the focus on me and my actions and not on the person who we all know took my baby. And second'—she paused for breath—'how the hell did you ever pass journalism school?'

A round of spontaneous applause broke out, which quickly subsided due to the sobering circumstances.

Maddy's mum stepped forward. 'I think that's enough for now,' she said, moving her daughter towards the door.

THE DREW NAYLE SHOW, THREE TRIPLE P

Tuesday, 14 January

Drew Nayle: *This morning we have Lincoln Steele reporting on the terrible situation playing out in the small coastal town of Deception Bay. Yesterday morning, a young single mother reported her baby missing. She said she put him down in his cot and then, listeners, she said her baby was kidnapped. The young lady called the police and dobbed in the father—a man she'd dumped soon after the baby was born. Lincoln, what is the latest?*

Lincoln Steele: *Good morning Drew. You can hear the words from Senior Detective Antigone Pollard herself. Here's an exchange we recorded earlier, outside the Deception Bay police station.*

Lincoln Steele: *I'm Lincoln Steele from The Drew Nayle Show on Three Triple P. Does the mother take some responsibility for what's happened?*

Senior Detective Antigone Pollard: *That question is profoundly unhelpful; our focus is finding the baby.*

Drew Nayle: *Geez, she's quick with a serving, isn't she, mate? And she doesn't even answer your question.*

Lincoln Steele: *I tried to engage the baby's mother in a similar conversation, but she shut me down too. She was quite nasty about it, if I might say so.*

Drew Nayle: *Are you all right, Steely? We are seeing this kind of thing more and more. If men spoke to women like that, we'd get #MeToo'd.*

Lincoln Steele: *That's exactly right, Drew. A good honest bloke can't even talk to a woman anymore.*

Drew Nayle: *Tell me about it! In the good old days, you could compliment a lady on her outfit and, I tell you, they loved it!*

Lincoln Steele: [laughter] *You can't do that anymore, Drew! They'd have you in court. Men are too scared to even talk to women these days lest we're accused of assault.*

Drew Nayle: *I miss the old days. I remember going up to women and saying, 'I think your dress is sexy.' You could see the ladies stand up a bit taller. It's a gift men can no longer give. Actually, bugger it, I'm going to do it now. My assistant Anita is looking particularly lovely today in a figure-hugging shirt and pair of trousers. Va-va-vroom!*

Lincoln Steele: [laughter] *Watch those censors, mate! Next thing you know, the lawyers will be chasing after you.*

Drew Nayle: *The censors can't take a joke. Lucky Anita can, can't you, love? Don't you worry about that. Ladies and gentlemen, that was Lincoln Steele reporting live from Deception Bay where a young man has died after trying to assert his parental rights in a custody dispute. Yes, I know, these women get pregnant and then want their . . . how shall I put it . . . independence. Kick out the man. The father. Keep him away from his flesh and blood. And they wonder why men are pushed beyond reason. And, listeners, this has resulted in the death of the baby's father. He paid with his life. We are taking your calls.*

Wayne from Chelsea, what are your thoughts?

Wayne: *Geez, mate, happens all the time. What are men supposed to do? My missus kicked me out 'cos I didn't have a job. Reckons if I don't pay her child support, I can't see my kids. Bitch.*

Drew Nayle: [laughter] *Okay! Keep it clean, Wayne. You'll have the fun police down on us. But I get your point, mate. The bloody bleeding-heart judges give kids to mothers and cut fathers out completely. I'm sure when you get a job, you'll pay your fair share.*

Wayne: [laughter] *Mate, I got a job! I just got tired of her spending my child support on whatever she wanted. Once I saw her at the hairdressers. I thought to myself, that's where this month's seventy-five bucks is going. Never paid another cent after that. There are ways around the system, mate. Work for cash.*

Drew Nayle: *Woah! Say no more, my friend. We now have Kyle on the line. Go ahead, mate.*

Kyle: *So one guy does the wrong thing and now the feminists will want to throw all men under the bus. What about all those predatory women that go out and get pregnant with a guy so they can get him on the hook for child support?*

Drew Nayle: *Ho! Yes! I'm glad you brought that up, Kyle. This is part of the resentment, I think. Now I'm not saying the mother in this case is predatory, but it certainly seems like Josh McCreedy was a man who was pushed beyond his limits. And now he's been killed in a car accident, so he's paid the ultimate price.*

Kyle: *Yeah, well the joke's on her. You can't get money from a dead man.*

Drew Nayle: *Next up, we have Margaret from Epping on the line. Go ahead, Margaret.*

Margaret: *Drew, why do you always blame women for the actions of men? Nobody made that young man kidnap that baby. Why turn on the mother?*

Drew Nayle: *Oh, Margaret, it's you again, trying to tell us our opinions aren't valid. You're a misandrist, aren't you?*

Margaret: *You didn't answer my quest—*

Drew Nayle: *We're out of time. We'll be back for more after a word from our sponsors.*

CHAPTER 10

THE PYRAMID CLUE

After we cleared Maddy's place, Wozza and I headed back into town. We needed to check CCTV from the shops to see what Josh McCreedy was doing for those two lost hours yesterday. The summer sun had regained its strength and evaporated evidence of yesterday's storm. It was lunchtime and holiday-makers were heading up from the beach at the bottom of the cliffs. There were lines at the charcoal chicken joint, the fish and chip place, and of course, the bakery counter of Angie's Cafe. The smell of sunscreen battled with the sea breeze and someone in one of the nearby houses was cooking a barbecue.

Wozza's stomach growled. We would have to address that, but first, we headed for the supermarket—the first logical stop. At the service counter, we asked to see the manager. A man called Rory eventually approached us. He was early forties and officious. Wozza explained the situation to him and asked if there was CCTV footage available of the street and the baby aisle.

'It's awful,' said Rory. 'I saw the story on the news. Maddy shops here.'

'Do you know her?' I examined his face for signs of a connection.

Rory shrugged. 'Everyone knows everyone in a town like this. She taught my nephew last year and I know her well enough to say hi when she's shopping.'

'Do you know Josh McCreedy?' I asked, ready to pull a photo out of my police notebook in case he didn't.

'Yeah, the McCreedys shop here too. Tamara more than the male McCreedys.'

It might have been my imagination, but Rory didn't look like a fan of the male McCreedys. 'Not a fan?' I was blunter than I might usually have been.

He shrugged. 'Some customers are nicer than others.'

'Any sign of Josh in here yesterday?' Wozza asked.

Rory shook his head. 'Not that I saw.'

'So what cameras have you got?' Wozza said.

'Several external cameras,' said Rory, 'and every aisle has cameras too. We are on constant alert for shoplifters.'

'What about sales records?' I asked, my eyes sweeping the rows of checkouts and self-checkouts. 'Could we track any purchase of baby paraphernalia?'

'We have records of all electronic transactions, and if a person used the self-checkout, there are photographic recordings of their face.'

Wozza looked at him, brow furrowed. 'You take pictures of all your customers?'

'You can see it when you shop,' I cut in. Maybe Wozza didn't notice, but I always caught my reflection in the camera when I used the self-checkout; I usually looked annoyed because of the constant need to summon the checkout assistant when I did things the machine didn't like.

The manager nodded. 'The only way we wouldn't have an electronic record is if the customer paid cash and wore a hoodie when they were in sight of any of the many cameras.' He looked up and our eyes followed his.

There were cameras everywhere.

'We would really appreciate you giving us access to the footage you have—from yesterday afternoon till now,' I said, hoping Rory wouldn't demand a search warrant.

He didn't. 'Anything we can do to help find that baby,' he said with a catch in his voice.

▪•▪

With the CCTV footage on a USB in my pocket, Wozza and I made our way to our next stop. The chemist shop—Filmore's Pharmacy—in Main Street was the only other place in town that sold the things a baby might need. A bunch of young children were sitting on the bench seat outside the shop. They looked hot and cranky. I was about to stop and ask where their parents were, when Dawn, the pharmacist's assistant, appeared with a handful of icy poles and grinned at the kids. 'I checked with your mums and they said it was okay.' She held out the coloured icy poles like playing cards. The kids all scrambled for their favourites and then sat back, happily slurping.

'Looks like you're their favourite person in the world,' said Wozza.

Dawn blushed. 'We keep a stock of them in the freezer inside. I used to hate it when my mum left me and my brother outside the shops. I'm righting the wrongs of the world one icy pole at a time.' She laughed.

We all headed into the pharmacy together. Dawn made her way to the back of the shop, where two women were sitting on chairs near the prescriptions counter, waiting for scripts to be filled, presumably the mothers of the kids outside. Over the top of the high counter, I could see Mr Filmore, the pharmacist, head bowed and concentrating on whatever he was doing.

Norma O'Mealley, part-time pharmacist and maker of prize-winning banana cakes, was working behind the counter, and as I waved at her, my running pal Crystal also appeared from behind a display of diet powders. I knew she was taking full advantage of the summer school holidays to work as many shifts as she could. She was saving for a new saddle for her horse, Black Beauty, and avoiding her holiday maths homework at the same time.

'Hey, Antigone!' she said, approaching us with a big smile. 'Hey, Wozza.'

'Hey, Crystal,' said Wozza.

Her smile faltered. 'Are you here on official police business? Is it the baby that's all over the news?' She paused as an idea struck her. 'Do you need to show me your badges?'

'Yes, yes and no,' said Wozza.

When Crystal was too young to remember, she had lost both her parents in a brutal murder that Wozza and I had solved a couple of months back. She was tough on the outside, but there was a fragility lurking beneath the surface. I hastened to reassure her. 'Yes, we are here about the baby. The father took it, but he's been in an accident. There's a possibility he might've left the baby with someone, and if he did, they would need baby supplies.'

'Unless the person he gave it to had their own baby,' she said.

The kid was astute.

'You're right. But if they didn't have their own baby, we are checking places that might have sold supplies to someone who doesn't normally buy baby supplies. And checking places the father might have come himself yesterday. His phone data puts him in town for a couple of hours. He would have had the baby with him and needed supplies.'

Wozza checked a list off on his fingers. 'Formula. Bottles. Dummy. Nappies. Nappy poo bags. Nappy cream. Wipes. Bibs. Baby food. Baby change mat.' He ran out of fingers.

We all moved towards the section with the big sign that said 'Baby' and stood in front of the well-stocked shelves. Norma joined us. She offered to check the electronic records for recent baby-supply purchases.

Wozza asked if she'd seen Josh McCreedy and the baby yesterday.

Norma shook her head. 'I know all the McCreedys. They get their prescriptions here. But I didn't see Josh.'

'Someone's bought formula,' said Crystal, pointing to a pyramid of tins. 'I just stacked these this morning. The top one is missing.'

Norma went back to the counter, tapped on the keyboard and peered at the screen. 'Not according to the records,' she said.

'There was definitely another tin there,' said Crystal, a little defensively. Sometimes, she let her teen show.

'I believe you,' I said, looking up at the ceiling, corner to corner. No cameras. 'If there's no record of a sale, then someone may have taken the formula . . .'

Wozza made his way over to the counter where Norma was looking at the computer screen. He pulled out his notebook and flipped to a clean page. Crystal and I joined them while Wozza began writing down a list of the locals who had come in that morning. There were around a dozen people. We would have to run checks on the ones we could identify, knock on doors and listen for a baby.

'What about customers you didn't know?' I glanced out at the popsicle children on the bench.

Norma nodded. 'A lot of holiday-makers. Most buy sunscreen and Panadol.'

And that was the problem. Deception Bay's numbers swelled by thousands over the summer.

Even so, the missing tin of baby formula gave me a glimmer of hope.

Wozza finished writing the list of names and put his notebook back in his pocket.

'How's the banana cake going?' Norma asked him.

Wozza blushed. 'It's great . . .' he said.

She looked at him, eyes narrowed. 'But?'

In a rush, Wozza asked her if sometimes she could make it chocolate.

Norma leaned forward and patted his hand. 'I'll see what I can do.'

Wozza's blush turned into a beam as we left the pharmacy and stepped back out into the sunshine. Crystal ran after us with a bulky paper bag.

'We have samples of formula out the back,' she said, handing me the bag. 'Norma and Dawn give it to mothers to see if their babies take to it. I thought maybe you could take some . . . you know, just in case you find little Ethan and he's hungry.' Her eyes were earnest.

'Thanks, honey,' I said, taking the bag from her.

She gave me a small smile. 'I can ask the rep for extras when he comes in next.'

I thanked her again, hoping that by the time the rep visited again, we would have found the baby.

Wozza and I went up and down the street trying to find people who remembered seeing Josh McCreedy and the baby in town yesterday. We showed his photo to shop owners and tourists but didn't have any luck. Looking around at the hundreds of holiday-makers, most of them parents with kids, I figured it was no surprise Josh hadn't stood out. We gathered CCTV from the supermarket, the hardware store, the bank, the jewellers and the dry cleaners. The cameras were spaced out enough to give us a good view of the whole street.

By the time we were finished, Wozza declared he was going to pass out with hunger, so we stopped at Angie's Cafe to grab some takeaway. Inside, I let the cool air-conditioning wash over me as I studied the takeaway menu. Someone called my name from a nearby table and I turned to see who it was. It was Crystal's uncle, Russell.

'Hey, Russell.' I was relieved to slip back into the ordinary world for a moment, where babies were safe and mothers were just enjoying the summer. I walked over to his table. He was sitting with a man I'd never met before.

'Hey, Antigone! Fancy bumping into you here.' Russell beamed and stood up. His chair scraped against the rustic floorboards.

'Sit, sit,' I said. 'I'll join you for a sec.' I glanced over at Wozza, who was in a deep discussion with Angie about today's pastry offerings. I figured I had a couple of minutes before he even noticed I had moved. I pulled out a chair and, to my relief, Russell sat down again. He always seemed a little nervous when we met.

'Antigone, this is my long-lost buddy Andy Gilbert,' Russell said, gesturing to the man at the table. 'We went to school together and then he left for the big smoke. Now he's back.' Russell sounded very pleased.

Andy blushed slightly and offered his hand. 'Nice to meet you, Antigone,' he said. 'And I'm not technically back. Just minding my dad's place while he's visiting relatives in the UK.'

I searched his face for signs of familiarity. I had spent a lot of my childhood in Deception Bay while my mum worked in remote locations and I had sporadically attended the local school. But I didn't recognise Andy, probably because he looked a bit older than me. There was something familiar about him though. I just couldn't put my finger on it.

'Can you join us for lunch?' Russell asked, holding out a menu.

'Afraid not,' I said, getting to my feet. 'We're working.'

Russell's face clouded and he lowered his voice. 'The missing baby? I heard the story on the news.'

I nodded. 'We were just in the pharmacy talking to Crystal about it so I guess you'll hear more soon.'

His smile was rueful. 'She already sent me a string of texts.'

'She was really helpful. I think that job was the best thing for her.' I saw Wozza paying for his pastries. It was time to go. I turned to Andy. 'Enjoy your visit.'

I stepped away from their table and back into the heaviness of our investigation.

■●■

Back in our office, the day felt too full, too wrought with horror. Maddy's grief, the press conferences and a ghostly-white Amanda being loaded into an ambulance. It had been a long day. But with a missing baby, we needed to keep our heads in the game.

As soon as I got the preliminary report on Amanda's accident from Major Collision, I called the divisional district inspector and updated her.

'Do they know what caused it?' she asked, concern in her voice. The DDI and Amanda were friends.

I scanned the report. 'The crash squad blokes have documented the scene and they've photographed the tyre marks and worked out the exact moment she swerved, but they can't tell what made her swerve.' I told her about the text that was supposed to be from me.

'Did you check the number the text came from?'

'First thing this morning. It was from a burner phone, one of those ones you buy from the supermarket.'

'So someone texted her to come out to your farm and then she crashed. It seems very bizarre. I know you and the whole Deception Bay team are tied up with the baby kidnapping so I'm going to pass this one on to Major Collision. See if they can come up with something more concrete than skid marks.' The DDI paused. 'I will be briefing the Chief Commissioner as well. No doubt she'll pay you a visit to check on Amanda.' There was a catch in her voice as she said Amanda's name.

'Let's hope she's okay,' I said, and ended the call. Our regard for Amanda notwithstanding, it felt like a relief to hand the investigation over to Major Collision. There was no way we could handle it on top of looking for baby Ethan.

As soon as I got off the phone, Wozza came over to my desk with a handful of papers. He spread them out in front of me. 'Here's where the searchers have been,' he said, pointing to a map of the district. 'And here's where the door-knockers got to.' He indicated several streets fanning out from Maddy's house. 'We have to figure out the best use of our resources and personnel from here.'

I pulled the USB from my pocket. Wozza groaned. Looking at CCTV footage was one of his least favourite things to do.

'We can each take half,' I said, plugging it into my computer and copying half the files. I took out the USB and tossed it over to Wozza.

Then, I clicked one of the supermarket's external-camera files and pressed play. I glanced at the photos on my desk that

Josh had posted of him and Ethan at the Devil's Corner and at the roadhouse. In the photos, Josh was wearing stovepipe black jeans and a rainbow patterned T-shirt that looked like it was tie-dyed. He also had a hoodie wrapped around his waist. I took a guess that if Josh McCreedy had posted pictures till around midday, then headed straight into town like the phone data suggested, he might appear on footage around 12.10 pm, or thereabouts.

'Bloody hell!'

'Find him?' Wozza paused the film he was checking.

'He's carrying Ethan and going into the fish and chip shop.' I couldn't believe the proprietors hadn't come forward.

'We need to go and talk to them,' Wozza said, reaching for his keys.

I stopped him. 'We need to see where else he went or see if he spoke to anyone first.'

Wozza grumbled and went back to checking his footage.

'There he is, walking past the pharmacy.' Woz turned his screen around so I could see Josh McCreedy with the baby in one arm and a bag of takeaway in the other.

The footage was a little grainy, but as soon as Josh walked out of the frame, Norma and Dawn emerged from the pharmacy. 'Gee, they just missed him,' I said, wondering how many others narrowly missed the chance to intervene that day.

'No one said they saw him, but these images might jog some memories.' I took some screenshots of Josh and Ethan and sent them to the printer.

'Hey, check this out.' There was a note of excitement in Wozza's voice. He swivelled his screen and we both watched

Josh McCreedy, with his stolen baby and his takeaway food, stop and talk to another man in the street. The man was of medium height and build, dressed in jeans and a white T-shirt. Fair hair. The clock on the screen clicked over as the two stood together. One minute. Two minutes. Then Josh adjusted the baby on his hip and the two men walked off in the same direction.

We printed a picture of the man talking to Josh and headed back to town to try to find out who he was, and to canvas who had seen or talked to Josh McCreedy at lunchtime yesterday.

'It's a good sign,' said Wozza as we trawled down the main drag looking for a place to park.

'What is?' I spotted a car park up ahead and pointed.

Wozza hit the indicator and headed for it. 'That he bought fish and chips. I mean, if you were planning to murder your baby, would you really start with fish and chips?'

'I hope you're right. At the very least, it's a delaying tactic.'

'We know he didn't pass the baby on to someone else at lunch, because the photo at the silos was taken after this.'

The picture of Josh talking to the man in the white T-shirt lay in my lap. I had no idea who he was but I hoped he had talked Josh out of doing anything stupid.

■●■

First, we headed to the fish and chip shop. When we'd visited earlier, the small Greek woman behind the counter had said in broken English that she hadn't seen Josh. But now she was gone and in her place was Nick, the Greek owner.

'G'day, Nick,' said Wozza.

'Wozza!' said Nick as if he was greeting a champion. 'How's my favourite customer?'

Wozza looked a little embarrassed and quickly asked about Josh McCreedy, showing Nick the photo of Josh.

'Sure I remember him,' said Nick. 'He come in here all the time. What you say his name is?'

'Josh McCreedy,' I said.

'Sure. He was here yesterday. But until then, I never knew he had baby.' He gestured a stubby finger towards the photo I held up.

'Have you heard that the baby is missing?' I asked. Nick's body language and tone suggested he hadn't.

Nick looked shocked and clapped a hand to his mouth. 'No! Not the one they talk about on the radio? Is this him?'

'Yeah, mate,' said Wozza. 'That's him.'

Nick shook his head in wonder.

'Do you remember what Josh ordered?'

'Two hamburgers, chips, four dimmies.' Nick counted the items on his fingers. 'Two Cokes. And milk but I not let him buy.'

'He wanted to buy milk?' I asked.

'For the baby. He had a baby bottle in a pocket of his hoodie and he wanted to buy milk.' Nick looked over at the fridge on the customer side of the counter. In among the array of soft drinks was a section with bottles and cartons of milk. 'But I say, "Your baby too young for milk. Hurt his belly." I have grandson. I know.' Nick pointed to the corkboard on the bench next to the fryer. There were several pictures of a round-faced, dark-haired baby who was clearly adored.

'So what did you do?' asked Wozza.

'I make him a bottle,' declared Nick proudly. 'We have formula here. His baby was hungry. He sit there and feed him.' Nick pointed to the bench seat behind us. 'By the time I cook his lunch, the baby drank bottle.'

An enormous feeling of relief almost overwhelmed me. To know that Josh had made an effort to feed the baby was another good sign.

'Did he say anything to you about the baby?' I asked.

'I ask him questions while I was cooking. But then more customers came in and . . .' Nick shrugged. 'I get feeling he not know a lot about baby. But I also get feeling he love baby.'

'What made you think that?' There was a glint of hope in Wozza's question.

'Tenderness,' said Nick. 'I watch him sit and feed baby and smile and coo. Just like I do with my grandson.'

■●■

Next stop, Filmore's Pharmacy. Norma and Dawn were at the front counter, helping holiday-makers choose sunscreen and jellybeans from the display. Wozza eyed the jellybeans keenly. I knew chemist jellybeans were a favourite of his. One of many.

As soon as the customers cleared, we moved to the counter and showed Norma and Dawn the screengrab we'd taken of them following Josh McCreedy up the road.

'Oh my.' Norma put a hand over her mouth in shock. 'I didn't notice him. Did you, Dawn?'

Dawn looked horrified. 'We were right there,' she said. 'We could have . . .'

Wozza was quick to jump in. 'You weren't to know,' he said.

'What about him?' I asked, pointing to the man Josh had been talking to. 'Do you recognise him?'

Dawn shook her head, but Norma looked thoughtful. 'He seems familiar but it's a bit hard to see at that angle.'

'Care to take a guess?' Wozza pushed.

'I'll give it some thought,' said Norma. And that was the end of that.

■●■

Back at the office, I rang Maddy. 'He fed the baby,' I told her. 'We talked to Nick at the fish and chip shop and he told us that Josh wanted to buy milk but Nick knew Ethan was too young for milk and made him some formula.' I could hear Maddy burst into tears.

'It's a good sign,' she finally replied. Then her voice sounded a little stronger. 'A very good sign.'

Over a cup of tea, Wozza and I discussed what we had so far. Josh had been attentive towards the baby and had fed him. Then, it appeared, he had walked openly around town.

'How much do guys eat?' I asked suddenly.

Wozza patted his middle. 'A lot, usually. Why?'

'It's Josh's fish and chip shop order. Two hamburgers, chips, dim sims. Two Cokes. Could he have arranged to meet the guy in the white T-shirt? They meet after he comes out with the order, then walk off together.'

Wozza pondered that. 'Nick's hamburgers are monsters. Even I would struggle to eat two. And the chips and dimmies as well. You could be onto something.'

The office phone rang. Wozza took the call, made some grunting noises in response to whoever was on the other end, then hung up and turned to me. 'They're sending reinforcements up from Melbourne. Just what we need—city slickers.'

At the mention of the city, my thoughts turned unbidden to Daniel. I wondered if they'd send him, given Amanda's accident. Daniel was a detective inspector. In our last big case, he had appeared just when we needed him and no one had guessed at our history. No one could see how his presence knocked me out of my orbit. I picked up my phone from where it was charging on my desk and tapped on his message from yesterday, then typed a response before I could stop myself.

Not sure I'll have time to talk this weekend. Baby kidnapping. I pressed send.

Immediately, the three dancing dots appeared. Then my phone vibrated with a message.

Following the case from town. Watched you on the morning news. D

I put my phone face down on my desk.

Wozza looked up. 'Everything all right?'

I nodded but didn't say anything. How did I feel about Daniel following my work? I didn't know. My mind operated with such sharp clarity, except where he was concerned. When we separated, I badly missed his friendship and professional advice, but I did not miss the way he made my head spin.

Wozza brought over printouts of the photos Josh had posted on Insta and added them to the pile on my desk. I studied our aerial map of the town and pointed to the silos, the site of the final photo. Wozza lined up the printouts in order. First there was baby Ethan lying on the front seat of the car. The caption was: *Revenge*. Next there was Ethan squirming as Josh took a selfie of them both at the cliff tops of the Devil's Corner. The caption read: *You want to be independent, now you can*. It was more of a veiled threat than the other captions. Then there was the picture by the abandoned roadhouse. Josh held the baby around the middle, and it looked like Ethan was trying to wriggle out of his grip. The caption was: *Payback's a bitch. How does it feel?* And then the fourth and final photo by the grain silos. That last caption read: *It's over. I'm gonna end it*. The photocopies of the screen captures all showed Maddy's pleading comments as soon as he posted.

Please, please bring my baby back.

We can talk about this.

Don't hurt him.

Please, Josh.

It was so heartbreaking. Wozza stood next to my desk and I could tell he felt it too. There were no quips. No mention of cake. Just a steady intake of air followed by the sound of it sighing back out of him. I studied each photo, remembering that the one near the Devil's Corner was the one Maddy said Ethan was an hour overdue for a bottle, but now we knew Josh was about to head into town to try to feed him. Something didn't fit. The revenge messages didn't mesh with the cooing, attentive father that Nick had seen in the fish and chip shop. Could Josh have been lashing out at Maddy but not intending to harm the baby? Suddenly, I noticed something about the fourth photo near the silo. Sometimes you look at something over and over and don't notice anything. And then you do.

'Look at that,' I said, pointing to Josh holding the crying baby. Unlike in the other two photos that featured him and Ethan, Josh was set back. And, most importantly, one arm was holding the baby and the other was by his side.

'Bloody hell, it's not a selfie,' said Wozza, finally realising. 'Someone else took that photo.'

My finger traced the bottom of the image. There was a dark shadow. 'Look!' I could just make out a silhouette of a hand holding a phone.

'We need to trace any phones that were pinging off the same towers his was.' Wozza picked up his phone, barking orders to whoever answered.

'This is good, right?' I said as soon as he hung up. 'Because if someone was there with him for that final photo, then they could have the baby.' And if they did, then the baby might be okay.

Our jubilation was interrupted by Randall. 'Here are the statements from the two witnesses at Josh's crash scene. There's something weird about what they saw.'

I took a look at them and agreed.

RECORDS OF INTERVIEW

Record of conversation between Senior Constable Stuart James and Kellie Maddox, conducted on Birchip Road at scene of collision, 13 January, 3.11 pm

Oh god! I'm still shaking. Sorry. Um. I was driving down Birchip Road towards town. I needed to get to the supermarket before the storm. I drove over that crest just there . . . and bloody hell, there was this green Gemini headed straight towards me. I swerved. Honked my horn. But you know what? It looked like the driver had passed out or something. I saw him veer off the road and I pulled up over there . . . and he just went spinning into the ditch. It was like watching the whole thing in slow motion. The car flipped and flipped like in the movies. I rang triple zero straight away. I was too scared to go over there. No one could have survived that crash.

■●■

Record of conversation between Senior Constable Stuart James and Sofia Maalak, conducted on Birchip Road at scene of collision, 13 January, 3.25 pm

And yeah, I saw it happen too. I was riding my horse along the gully. Lucky we weren't too close when the car came over the hill. It just flew off the road and kept going then it hit the gully and just flipped. I went over to the wreck to see if I could help. So awful! I think I'm going to throw up. I'm going to need therapy to get that image out of my head. Or maybe beer. That's the last time I ever watch collisions on YouTube. Once you've seen the real thing . . .

■●■

Record of conversation between Senior Constable Stuart James and Senior Constable Charlie Wright (Air Wing), conducted at Deception Bay police station, 13 January, 5.13 pm

At 2.25 pm today, we spotted the wrecked Gemini from the air as we were coming in from the east. We landed the helicopter and provided ground assistance. We were asked to stay around to provide air access to the Major Collision Investigation Unit upon their arrival, which we did. Aerial photographs were taken of the crash site.

CHAPTER 11

THE GRUMPY CAT CALENDAR

When I called the hospital to check who was doing the post-mortem examination—or, more to the point, to check who wasn't—it turned out Dr 'Wonky' George Gilbert, who we always hoped was unavailable, was on holidays, and Doc Caldicott would be responsible for the examination of Josh McCreedy.

While I was on the phone, I asked to be put through to the emergency department, and got an update on Amanda. She was in surgery, they said. I would need to call back later. We went one better and called in to see her on our way to the hospital morgue. Our badges meant we bypassed the usual wait and got a quick audience with the head of the ED. Amanda's surgery had gone well. She was resting comfortably and wouldn't be able to be interviewed for several days. They were still concerned about her head trauma. This meant that the wait to see if she was okay wasn't over. Neither was the worry.

■●■

For Christmas, Wozza had bought Doc Caldicott a new calendar for the mortuary. In the post-mortems we'd been to, last year's puppy calendar was our go-to for line-of-sight adjustment. Wozza had found another funny animal calendar for this year. Ms January was a big tabby cat wearing a pink shower cap. The cat had a grumpy *what-the-hell* look on its face. Wozza nudged me and pointed at the calendar. I had to admit, the funny cat was better to look at than the shattered body of Josh McCreedy.

'Doc, we've got eyewitnesses saying he seemed to be unconscious prior to the collision,' Wozza told Doc Caldicott.

'Interesting,' said the doctor as she ran a gentle hand over the dead man's forehead. 'We'll have a look to see what might have caused that.'

The mortuary assistant had left a pile of torn clothing and some personal items on a large paper bag. Wozza and I gloved up to pick through the pockets and see what Josh had left behind. Wallet. A single key, which I wondered might be the one missing from Maddy's fake rock. No car keys, but they would have been left in situ in the wreck.

An iPhone with a cracked screen. I tapped on the screen and it came to life. I was careful to avoid the lower part of the screen; when the camera app was in use, that's where the unknown person at the silos would have tapped to take a photo. We'd have it examined for fingerprints.

'Is it a face ID?' Wozza asked. 'We can do what we did this morning.'

'Worth a try,' I said as I took it over to the table, tapped the screen again and waved it over the still and lifeless face of Josh McCreedy.

Nothing.

'Might need body heat,' said Doc Caldicott.

I held it close to my own face for a moment then quickly put it in front of Josh's face. Still didn't work. His features were distorted enough to stop the facial recognition software, I guessed.

'Gimme a try,' said Wozza, holding out his hand.

'Just don't touch where the camera button would be.' I knew I sounded anxious.

His forehead creased in concentration as he pressed 123456. The screen sprang to life. 'Yes!' Wozza cried as if he'd kicked a goal. Then he lowered his fist pump and mumbled an apology to Doc Caldicott.

She acknowledged his silliness with a nod, then got down to business. 'A car is a deadly weapon,' she said, looking down at the damaged young man.

Wozza returned the phone to the pile of Josh's belongings. 'If it makes you feel any better,' he said, 'the car didn't escape unscathed.'

'A little,' said the doc. She began her external examination. She noted a lot of damage. Serious head trauma. Legs shattered to the bone. Crush injuries. Broken neck. 'That's interesting,' she said into the small dictaphone she used to record her findings.

'What?' Wozza dragged his eyes away from the cat in the shower cap. 'Oh geez,' he muttered as he looked closely at the injuries.

'There's not as much bleeding as I would have expected. We'll see what it looks like on the inside.' She picked up the instrument that would slice Josh McCreedy open.

Grumpy cat. Pink shower cap.

'Just as I thought,' said Doc Caldicott. 'The lack of internal bleeding . . . maybe your witnesses saw a dead man prior to the crash, not an unconscious man.' She continued to probe and cut.

'If he died before he went into the ditch, what could have caused that?' I asked.

Doc Caldicott paused in her cutting. Her voice a little muffled under her surgical mask, she said, 'Could be any number of things. At his age, heart attack and stroke are less likely. Drug overdose, maybe?' She leaned closer to the body and inhaled. 'There's a faint odour of . . . beer, I think. There's SUDEP . . . do we know if he's epileptic?'

Wozza tore his eyes away from the cat calendar and glanced at Doc Caldicott long enough to ask: 'What's SUDEP?'

The doctor resumed the examination, probing organs. 'Sudden Unexpected Death in Epilepsy. It's rare but we see it from time to time. It means that, as much as we might've looked, there's no definitive cause of death.'

I moved around to be closer to the table, careful not to get too close. I wasn't a fainter, but certain bits always creep through the mental barrier. This time, it was Josh's eagle tattoo. We'd seen a shadow of it on the baby-monitor video as this young man had stolen his son away from the safety and security of his home and his mother before casting him adrift. I remembered Maddy's story about Josh getting the tattoo in memory of his dead brother because birds travel between the land and the sky, between Earth and Heaven. The tattoo was a reminder of how painful his brother's loss was to his family, but Josh had been prepared for Maddy to suffer the same loss.

'Josh lost a brother last year,' I said to the doc. 'Do you know how he died?'

Doc Caldicott's eyes widened over her mask. 'McCreedy . . . oh goodness, yes. I did the post-mortem. Is this his brother? Josh was never a patient of mine. All the older McCreedy's went to Dr Bill Farrow. He's retired now.'

'What killed the younger brother?' Wozza asked, fixing his gaze on the instrument tray beyond the mortuary table.

'Carelessness,' said the doc, taking a sample from the second McCreedy son she'd examined. 'Young Pete McCreedy had anaphylaxis. I remember he came into the clinic for some antibiotics and a check-up. He had the flu and couldn't shake it. His EpiPen was out of date. I told him to get a new one. He was headed off camping with some mates. He wasn't well and I advised him not to go, but he went anyway. Somehow, he had exposure to peanuts on the trip. Expired EpiPen. A bunch of young men in the middle of nowhere, feeling invincible, only they weren't. He might have survived, though, had he been able to get to a hospital.'

'Horrible luck,' said Wozza.

'Indeed,' said Doc Caldicott, cutting out Josh McCreedy's heart and putting it on a scale to weigh it.

'Are you regretting those pastries?' I whispered to Wozza.

'I never regret pastries,' he replied stoically.

'These samples may hold the key to Josh's death,' said Doc Caldicott, writing on the label of a small plastic container and placing it next to several others containing pieces of Josh McCreedy.

At the end of the post-mortem, Doc Caldicott removed her gloves and said that there were any number of injuries that could have caused Josh McCreedy's death, but she had concerns about the lack of bleeding. 'I don't think he was unconscious before the crash; I really do think he was dead.'

'Bloody hell,' said Wozza quietly.

'Indeed,' said the doc.

'Anything to indicate how?' I asked.

'Not yet. Everything looks to be within normal ranges. The answers might be in the tox screen.'

As Doc Caldicott began sewing up the body, we turned our attention back to Josh's belongings. His wallet contained a licence, a couple of credit cards, a gym membership, loyalty cards for several local businesses and twenty-five dollars in cash. Wozza pressed 123456 on the phone again and the screen unlocked.

'First things first. Can you pull up the photos?' I asked, standing next to him.

I think we both braced ourselves for the series of photos from Monday. A father, now dead, holding his baby, now missing. There were more than just the ones he'd posted. At every site—car, the Devil's Corner, roadhouse and silos—there were multiple photos, though he'd chosen just one for each post. I took the phone from Wozza and selected all the ones taken during the kidnapping and airdropped them to my phone. Then I clicked on the one he'd posted from the silos, with the shadow at the bottom. It meant the picture-taker, who was possibly also the baby-taker, had been at the silos at 1.09 pm.

'Now check his call list.'

Wozza tapped the phone icon, then tapped 'recent'. A whole bunch of incoming calls were listed in red. There was the call Maddy made after we'd arrived at her house. Several from Tilly Muir, which must have been made while she and Paul were driving from Mildura. There were the calls made from Keith McCreedy while we'd been at his house. There were a couple from people I assumed were friends: Trev, Christos. Someone called Shags. And someone called Lesley Gillis. I photographed the list with my phone. None of the calls had been answered and only Lesley Gillis had left a message. Wozza tapped the play button and an older woman's voice echoed into the morgue. 'Good morning, Josh, this is Lesley Gillis returning your call about getting some things for your baby. The church charity stall has everything you'll need, so yes, I can help you. Ring me back when you get this message.'

Doc Caldicott looked up from her sewing. 'Not surprising Lesley Gillis would be helping him with baby things.'

'Do you know her?'

Doc Caldicott gave a laugh. 'It's a small town, Antigone. Sneeze and you'll get germs on someone you know.'

'Who is she?'

Wozza cut in. 'She's the one who's always at the church.'

Doc Caldicott nodded. 'Lesley runs the charity stall after church on Sundays. Raises money for the CWA. There are a bunch of them who help out. It's mostly donated clothes, furniture, bric-a-brac.'

'Geez,' said Wozza in a low voice, 'if he rang her to stock up on baby things, then it doesn't sound like he wanted to hurt Ethan.'

My thoughts spun and rearranged from a young father hellbent on revenge, to a young father who took his baby and wanted to keep him. *So how did he come to be dead alone without the baby?* Then another thought occurred. I turned it into a question. 'How would Josh know Lesley Gillis?'

'Remember the sneeze metaphor I just made?' Doc Caldicott removed her gloves and tossed them into a bin. 'Everyone is connected. Before she retired, Lesley used to teach at the local high school. She would know every kid in town. Word on the street is that she was one of those teachers everyone loved. I heard she used an endless store of jellybeans to sweeten the deal. Her students did a guard of honour for her in the main street when she retired.'

'I'm pretty sure she taught my wife,' said Wozza. 'Lucky she retired before my kids come through. They're wild.'

I got my notebook out to add Lesley Gillis to the list of people we needed to talk to.

CHAPTER 12

ANGIE'S CAFE

Wozza has some extraordinary qualities, not least of which is his ability to go from queasy to hungry at the speed of light. When he started audibly hankering for a snack, I pressed my fingertips to my forehead and said, 'Let me guess. Pastries?'

'You're a bloody psychic, Pollard.'

We got in the car and I turned towards Angie's Cafe. Cases like this were intense, and we knew this one wouldn't let up until we found the baby. It was important to snatch a chance to refuel when we could.

Even though it was late afternoon, the main street was still bustling with holiday-makers. Just down from the cafe, though, I saw a carload of kids in their late teens pulling out and slid into their spot.

We ran into Maddy and her mum just outside the cafe. Tilly Muir had an arm around her daughter and Maddy was leaning into her.

'Hey, Maddy,' I said.

'Any news?' Her eyes filled with the hope that this encounter wasn't a coincidence.

'Nothing yet,' I said quickly so as not to get her expectations up. 'We've just come from the hospital where they were examining Josh . . .' I was interested to see how she would respond to that. Unguarded reactions crossed her face. Firstly, distress at the death of Josh, which was quickly replaced with a flash of anger—this was the man who took her baby, and then finally she looked bereft because Josh was dead and little Ethan remained lost.

Tilly Muir hugged Maddy to her. 'I thought it would be a good idea to get her out of the house,' she said, looking at her daughter, worry etched into her face. 'You know, fresh air. Coffee.' She shook her head slowly and her eyes became moist.

'It's hard to know what to do,' Wozza said with sympathy and understanding, 'but coffee and fresh air sound like a good idea.'

Tilly lifted a big white bag from Angie's cafe. 'Angie gave us some crusts to feed the seagulls. Maddy loved doing that when she was little. We're heading down to the beach for a walk.'

'Feeding the seagulls is a favourite in my family too,' I said.

Wozza nodded. 'Take your mind off things for a little bit.'

We all smiled sadly, knowing that nothing would take their minds off a missing baby. Not even for a single second.

■●■

Angie was doing good business. I inhaled the smell of coffee and pies and toast. My stomach rumbled.

Wozza gestured at an empty table near the counter. 'Let's sit down. Take the load off.' He pulled out a chair and plonked himself down.

I joined him, glad to have a quick break. Angie came over to the table with a notepad and pen, ready to take our order. I went for a salad sandwich while Wozza ordered a pie, two pastries and a milkshake.

Angie smiled as she scribbled. 'Good to see the case hasn't diminished your appetite, Woz.' She turned to me. 'Everyone is talking about it. That poor baby. And Maddy . . .'

'We just bumped into her,' I said, nodding towards the door.

Angie's eyes glistened. 'She comes in here all the time, with little Ethan in his pram. He is such a cutie.' She looked over to a table near the bookshelf, which was stuffed with books and toys. I guessed that was where Maddy and Ethan usually sat. With that, she sniffed and returned behind the counter.

Wozza swiped at his eyes. 'Bug in my eye,' he said.

I patted his hand. If Josh had abandoned the baby somewhere, there was a chance that little Ethan Muir was no longer with us. But it was starting to look possible that someone else was involved. We just needed to cling to the hope that someone had baby Ethan. And then find out who they were.

When Angie returned with our food, I pulled out the picture of the man we'd seen talking to Josh McCreedy on the street. 'Ange, do you recognise this guy?' I tapped the image.

Her brow furrowed in concentration. 'Fair-haired, medium height, jeans . . . from the back, he looks like half the young men who work in the hardware store.' She thought for a moment. 'And the ones who work in the supermarket. Pity it's in profile.'

'Yeah,' said Wozza. 'He doesn't turn around in the CCTV footage. This is the best we've got.'

Angie shrugged sympathetically. 'I'll be on the lookout.'

Moments later, we were sipping the best coffee around and enjoying a tiny bit of normalcy.

I finished my latte. 'How many reinforcements do you reckon they'll send up from Melbourne?'

'Dunno.' Wozza looked up as the bell tinkled above the shop door. 'Speak of the devil.'

Two men had entered the cafe. They were both dressed in suits and white shirts, the uniform of the city detective. Not that Wozza and I looked like slobs, but in Deception Bay, we didn't suit up to go to work. These guys wore lanyards with the Victoria Police insignia, too, in case people couldn't tell that they were cops just by their haircuts. Their eyes swept the cafe. Neither gave us more than a dismissive glance.

'Nice swagger,' said Wozza in a low voice as the one in the lead made his way up to the counter to order.

'Matches his fancy suit,' I said.

We both sat back and enjoyed examining our new colleagues without their knowledge. Occupational hazard. They were both tall. One had sandy-coloured hair, the other dark. The dark-haired one spoke first as Angie stepped over to the counter to take their order. He had that easy charm of the good-looking as he spoke. A grin exposed his dimples. While I couldn't hear what he was saying, I could see Angie's welcoming smile fade, followed by an involuntary step back.

'Whoa, what's with Dimples?' Wozza said. He put his hands on the table as if he was about to push his chair back to go to Angie's aid.

I put a hand out to stop him. 'Let it play out,' I said. 'Angie will be fine. Let's get their measure.' I watched Angie move to the coffee machine and begin their order. Every now and again, she glanced over to the two detectives. They were taking up all the space at the counter. When she handed over two takeaway coffees, Dimples swiped a card to pay, then they left. Angie caught my eye and came over.

'Friends of yours?' she said.

'I don't make friends easily,' said Wozza, 'because people don't usually like me.'

Through the window, we watched as they got into an unmarked white police vehicle and drove off.

'What did he say to you?' I asked.

Angie frowned and shook her head. 'It wasn't as much what he said as . . .' She shuddered. 'He just gave me the willies.'

'In what way?'

She looked at me, then rolled her eyes towards the ceiling. 'Oh, you know. Guys that just . . .' She paused then shrugged.

Yep, I knew. Some guys just gave you the willies.

Wozza stood up and pushed out his chair. 'Time to go meet our new Melbourne pals.'

'Hope that works out well for you,' said Angie dryly.

I gestured to the pastry crumbs on the front of Wozza's creased shirt. 'Bit hard to make new friends if they're laughing at your crumbs.'

'Oh geez.' He brushed them away.

■●■

The unmarked white car was parked in our usual spot behind the station. Wozza grunted as he pulled in next to it.

I glanced at him. 'Hope you're going to play nicely.'

He grimaced and got out of the car. I swiped us both through the back entrance and then paused at the door. The place seemed quiet. We headed along the corridor, then through to the muster room. Randall was at his desk, typing in his hen-pecking way. He looked up, nodded, then went back to his work.

'Where'd everyone go?' Wozza said.

Randall lifted one hand off the keyboard and pointed in the direction of our CIB office.

'Those Melbourne cops better not be eating our banana cake!' Wozza hurried up the corridor.

I was close on his heels as he flung the door open. Lucky the newcomers had had the sense to take the two spare desks and not mine and Wozza's. Nonetheless, Wozza looked at his chair suspiciously as he entered the room.

Dimples stood up. 'Ah, the country bumpkins have finally arrived.'

Not a good start.

'She's from Brunswick,' Wozza said too quickly, jerking his head in my direction.

'And Wozza went to the big smoke that one time, didn't you, Woz?' I said in my best country drawl.

'I surely did,' said Wozza. 'Didn't like it and won't be going again.' He sat down.

Dimples looked at the nameplate on my desk. He squinted. 'Anti-gone?'

Wozza sniggered. 'Hey, Einstein, haven't you read your Greek mythology? It's pronounced An-tig-a-nee.'

I smiled. Mostly because Wozza hadn't read any Greek mythology either and only knew how to pronounce my name because I'd told him the first time we met. But I let him have his small victory, particularly because he was still wearing a big pastry crumb.

Dimples coloured with embarrassment. 'Senior Detective Carsten Riggs from Melbourne CI.' He looked over at his buddy, who jumped up from behind the desk.

'Senior Detective Leonard Kasparas.' He sat down again just as abruptly.

'Antigone.' I pointed over at Wozza. 'Wozza.' I didn't give our surnames. They were on our nameplates on our desks. They could read.

Riggs resumed his seat. 'What have you got?'

I gave them a quick overview of the case. Maddy. Missing baby. Josh McCreedy. The photos posted before the collision. Kasparas took notes in a notepad he pulled from his pocket. Riggs didn't.

'We've just come from the post-mortem examination and the doc thinks McCreedy might have been dead before the collision.'

'Why's that?' said Kasparas.

'Lack of bleeding,' said Wozza.

'So where did he leave the baby?' Riggs asked.

'If we knew that,' said Wozza, irritated, 'I'd be heading home to take my kids to the beach.'

The two grown men glared at each other like children.

'Moving right along,' I said, catching Kasparas's eye.

He stood to attention. 'What do you need us to do?'

Wozza and I palmed off our most tedious jobs to the newcomers, starting with checking people on the list Norma and Dawn had given us of pharmacy customers. Kasparas took a picture of the list with his phone, logged in to a computer and began searching for addresses to go with the names. We also had a list of people we'd identified from the CCTV who might have seen Josh in town yesterday.

While Kasparas was busy with the lists, Wozza made Riggs go through the CCTV footage from the supermarket's baby aisle and take screenshots of anyone who looked suspicious, and pretty much anyone who was buying baby formula but didn't look like they should be. Riggs identified several possibilities, and Wozza sent Riggs and Kasparas into town to talk to Rory, the supermarket manager.

By early evening, we finally got the new telephone data from the silos. I scanned it while Wozza watched. It turned out no other phones had pinged near the silos when Josh's did.

'But someone was with him,' said Wozza, poring over the photo with the shadow hand at the bottom.

'Whoever that someone was, they were not carrying a phone,' I said.

'Bugger,' said Wozza, chucking the photo back on the pile.

CHAPTER 13

THE POEM

Whenever things got too big, she wrote poetry in a secret notebook. She kept it in the laundry cupboard where her husband would never find it because laundry was a woman's job. So was cooking and cleaning. He usually did the shopping. Although she suspected that was not an effort to be helpful but an exercise of control.

The baby really was a dear little thing. And he gave her something to do in the long days when her husband was at work. When he slept, she read her favourite volumes of Emily Dickinson's poetry. She'd studied Dickinson years ago when she was a young student, before *him*. Back then, she read with wonder of Dickinson's shut-off life. Now, she mirrored it. She understood it. Her own poetry was an act of defiance, a chance to prove she still had a voice even if it was silenced.

I saw them in the street today,
The mother and the daughter—

Clinging together in their grief—
Over their missing boy.

We slowly drove past them—
And I ducked my head;
Their sorrow too profound
For mere mortals.

We passed the school, where children go
And Baby will go there—
When he is grown and happier;
After he forgets her.

In our back seat,
Tucked away—
Sleeps their hearts' desire
They can't have him so we can.

We drove past the gate
To the house where he won't live.
One loses so the other wins.
The victor thinks it's fair.

Love grows so quickly
For the baby boy
We will call him by a different name
And that will make him ours.

CHAPTER 14

MUM'S TALE

I was so glad to be home. Some days are just too full. Waffles didn't come when I pulled up to the gate. Not surprising since Mum was probably spoiling him rotten. I hadn't heard from her since her message this morning updating me on Amanda, but I knew she had planned to collect Nan from the nursing home and bring her back for the day. And then she was going to talk to us. Whatever it was that she needed to tell us momentarily took my mind off Maddy and her missing baby as I drove up the long winding driveway to the house. Mum's car was parked near the front door and I pulled up behind her. Once I was on the porch, I could hear the mad scrambling of paws and claws on the other side of the door. Waffles. My heart lifted at the thought of him.

When I opened the door, Waffles did his usual dance of delight. His tail wagged like a windscreen wiper, his nose nudging my hands as I bent to give him a pat.

'Who's a good boy?' If it was possible for a dog to smile, Waffles was smiling, mouth open, tongue hanging out. I lifted my head and called down the hallway. 'I'm home!' It was a nice feeling coming home to family. With a pang, I realised how much I missed it. Two voices called out 'hello'—Mum's voice strong, Nan's frail.

'Come on,' I said to Waffles, and we took off down the hall to greet my family.

Mum was in the kitchen and, from the smell, I guessed roast lamb was on the menu. Nan beamed from her armchair.

'Any news on the baby?' said Mum by way of greeting.

'Not yet.' I leaned down to give Nan a hug. When I straightened, I tried to stretch the day out of my back. 'We're doing line searches at all the locations where Josh photographed the baby. But our best hope is that someone took the little one and is looking after him. It's the only chance he has of survival.'

'That poor mother,' said Nan sadly.

I thought of Maddy. There was a torturous canyon between the missing and the dead. As a cop, I'd seen it plenty of times. You can't give up hope because hope is all you have, and you can't grieve because to grieve would be to admit loss. It's like living on a knife's edge. And each day it gets worse.

'Any more news on Amanda?' Mum put three plates on the bench.

I moved around to help her serve. 'I called the hospital for an update before I left. They've operated on her leg and there's some swelling on the brain so they're keeping her sedated for the time being.'

'She's in the best place,' said Mum, diplomatically non-committal. Doctor-speak. I knew it well.

We carried the plates to the table. If there's anything nicer than a roast that someone else has cooked for you, I don't know what it is. Crisp baked potatoes, roast pumpkin, cauliflower in cheese sauce, lamb, gravy, peas and corn—the favourite dinner of generations of Pollards.

Nan and I were silent as we settled at the dining table. It was like we both sensed that Mum would start telling us whatever she had to tell us in her own time. She raised a glass and made a toast to family. We clinked glasses and began the meal. Talk meandered through the weather, the investigation, the farm, Waffles and any other topic that wasn't the one she'd come to talk to us about. When we'd all finally finished eating, Mum took a deep breath then let it out slowly.

I glanced at Nan. She looked worried.

Mum began. 'I found out something recently that has'—she paused, looking uncharacteristically vulnerable—'quite frankly, knocked me for six.'

Nan patted her hand. 'It's okay, love. You can tell us anything.'

Mum nodded and her eyes welled with tears. 'Antigone, I've never told you this, but five years before I had you, I got pregnant. Mum knew at the time.'

Nan nodded sadly.

What! My mind raced. *Do I have a sibling?*

Mum continued. 'I was at uni, studying medicine, and got pregnant to . . .' She hesitated, then shrugged. 'It doesn't matter who. What matters is that I quickly found myself knocked up and having to make some hard decisions.'

I gave a small smile. Mum never minced words. I knew that she had found herself in a similar position when she got pregnant with me. She never kept it from me. Once the test came back positive, she decided that she wanted to be a mother and she would do it on her own. Who my father was remained a mystery, one that every now and again, I would like to have solved. Just for curiosity's sake, not for any need of a father. You can't miss what you never had.

'Just like with you, Antigone,' she continued, 'I decided I would keep the baby. There was a creche cooperative at uni and I knew I could manage. I saw a doctor a couple of times in Melbourne and everything was fine. When you're that age, you see yourself as this fertile goddess and never imagine anything could go wrong.' Mum shrugged. The years had clearly taught her otherwise. 'When my due date got closer, I had one last party with a bunch of friends, then I hopped in the car to drive back here.'

Nan nodded. 'We were very excited. Any baby in the family is a gift.'

Mum looked down at the table. 'On the drive home, I started having the worst pains imaginable. I got as far as Bellanook. They had a hospital there and I walked in the front doors and told them I was in labour. You know you've left the city when the nurses start calling you an "unwed mother" and ask if you're giving up the baby for adoption.'

'No way!' I said.

'Oh yes,' said Mum. 'The 1980s were just as judgy as the 60s and a young woman on her own was fair game.'

'Bloody hell,' I said before addressing the elephant in the room. 'So . . . you had a baby?'

Mum looked up and spoke in a low voice. 'The baby died at birth.'

I felt an unbelievable wave of sadness for my mum, and for the brother or sister I'd lost all those years ago.

Nan held Mum's hand. She was proud of her independent daughter. While Nan's life had been straight out of a 1950s good wife handbook, her daughter had been able to make very different choices.

'But here's the thing—I recently found out the hospital where I gave birth is about to be exposed for corrupt practices, including selling babies. It's become an open secret in medical circles because questions are being asked behind the scenes. That's how I found out.'

'*What?*' I said. 'So . . . you think . . .' I stopped, trying to get my head around what Mum was saying. Daughter mode stepped back and detective mode tag-teamed in. 'Did you see your baby at delivery?'

Mum shook her head. 'The baby was born. They said it died straight afterwards. I asked to see it then they gave me an injection that knocked me out. I just . . . I just believed them.'

I pictured my mum, a young uni student with very little life experience, surrounded by nurses and doctors, all alone in the hospital.

'When the rumours started to fly recently, I checked Public Records for a death certificate for my baby. There was nothing.'

Mum turned to me before continuing. 'I need your help.'

Mum had never asked for my help before. She was a veritable beacon of independence, never needing anything from anyone. And yet here we were.

'What have you discovered so far?' I asked, knowing she would have looked into it.

'It all came to light when a woman in Melbourne did one of those online DNA tests. She matched with a whole bunch of people she'd never heard of. Turns out, she had four siblings living in Bellanook. The woman's existence came as a surprise to her biological parents because they'd been told their firstborn had died. They were in their late teens when she'd been born. Unmarried. Too shocked and vulnerable to ask questions.'

'And I'm guessing other cases have come to light?'

'Four other cases.' Mum looked stricken. 'There's no death certificate for my baby so a reasonable conclusion is that the same thing happened to me.'

'What about a birth certificate?' Nan asked. 'Do babies that don't survive get birth certificates?'

Mum and I both said yes at the same time. Then Mum continued. 'Any baby born after twenty weeks' gestation gets a birth certificate. But the hospital doesn't apply for it. They give you the forms to fill out yourself. I remember filling them out for you, Antigone, and then the hospital sent them off. But the hospital at Bellanook didn't give me any forms.' Mum paused and I pictured her alone and distraught in the little country hospital. I imagine forms were the last thing on her mind.

Mum sat back a little. 'I suspect that the birth wasn't registered and therefore legally didn't occur.'

'Or,' I said, 'an alternative birth certificate could have been issued in the name of the parents receiving the baby. If you're in the business of stealing babies, you're not going to stop at applying for a fraudulent birth certificate.'

I was long overdue for a cup of tea and I suspected Mum and Nan were too. I got up from the table and put the kettle on. In the momentary quiet of the cool summer's night, the call of cicadas reached inside the house. I scooped spoons of tea into Nan's old aluminium teapot; her beautiful China one had been destroyed by a violent man in a home invasion a couple of months earlier. The kettle came to a boil and I poured the bubbling, steaming water over the tea leaves. 'How do you think they did it?'

Mum sighed. 'I've seen it hundreds of times in my career—you get one bad doctor who's entitled or self-righteous or charismatic and a couple of fawning medical staff who buy into whatever crap that doctor is selling.'

We drank tea and talked about stolen babies until the room cooled and Mum lit the fire. By the time we were on our second cup of tea, I had ordered an online DNA testing kit, just in case my sibling had survived to adulthood and had done a test as well. Mum offered to take the test, but I said I'd do it for us. I didn't tell her but I wondered if my father might have taken a test too.

Nan spoke, her voice soft and full of emotion. 'Was it a boy or a girl?'

Mum shook her head sadly. 'They never told me.'

Nan's eyes widened. 'You know what next week is? The twenty-first of January?'

Mum's nod was barely discernible. 'I always thought it was my baby's death-day . . . but now I can't help but think . . .' She stopped.

Nan finished the sentence. 'It could be their birthday.'

THE DREW NAYLE SHOW, THREE TRIPLE P

Wednesday, 15 January

Drew Nayle: *Yesterday morning we heard from Lincoln Steele reporting on the terrible situation playing out in the small coastal town of Deception Bay. On Monday, unemployed single mother Maddy Muir reported her baby missing. And then we all watched the tragedy unfold where the young father of the child—the non-custodial father kicked out by Maddy—died in a car crash that may or may not have been an accident. Police media are not commenting on that one, listeners. We have Lincoln Steele reporting from Deception Bay. What's the latest, Lincoln?*

Lincoln Steele: *Good morning, Drew. We've been speaking to locals and monitoring this story very closely.*

Drew Nayle: *Any sign of the baby?*

Lincoln Steele: *Nothing yet, Drew, but intense searches are taking place around town. Members of the SES are everywhere. Locals are out helping. And the ladies from the CWA are providing cups of tea and scones. It's all hands on deck out here.*

Drew Nayle: *Do police have any leads?*

Lincoln Steele: *I think we saw the calibre of the police at yesterday's press conference, Drew. Hostile and uncooperative. And Maddy Muir wasn't any better.*

Drew Nayle: *I watched that footage and, I've gotta say, Lincoln, I was unimpressed. I know I'll cop it from the bleeding-heart woke listeners, but that mother looked like she had something to hide.*

Lincoln Steele: *That's certainly what we're seeing here, Drew. Everyone we've spoken to has told us that Josh McCreedy, the deceased father, was a well-liked, active member of the community. He played footy and was often seen at the local church on a Sunday with his young friends.*

Drew Nayle: *Maddy Muir has accused him of taking the baby, and there were certainly pictures of him posted with the baby, but he was found tragically killed and the baby wasn't with him. Are we certain he took the baby, Lincoln? I mean, a baby of that age can't just get up and walk off, can it?*

Lincoln Steele: *You're absolutely right, Drew. As I said, I've spoken to many people who all agree Josh McCreedy was a great bloke. They're questioning whether he actually took the baby at all. Now, if he didn't, we have to look at where the baby was last—and that was with Maddy Muir.*

Drew Nayle: *Thanks, Lincoln. We are going to take some calls on this topic now because it's certainly a hot potato. We've got Lydia on the line. Go ahead, Lydia.*

Lydia: *Good morning, Drew. Long-time listener, first-time caller.*

Drew Nayle: *Good to have you on the program, Lydia. What did you want to say?*

Lydia: *Drew, I studied the mother on the television and I'm not convinced she's telling the truth. She looked* too *upset, if you get my drift. Overdone in my opinion. And did you see her eyebrows? I remember when I had my first baby, I never had time to get my eyebrows done. I mean, she claims to be a single mother. Does she take the baby to the eyebrow salon?*

Drew Nayle: *It's a good point, Lydia. Next caller is on the line. Go ahead, Tezza.*

Tezza: *She's pure evil. Standing with her parents, trying to get sympathy. For what! I taped the interview and then paused it and I swear, Drew, she was smirking. It's that bit where she raises her hand to her mouth. It's to hide a smirk. She's revolting. That baby is better off without her.*

Drew Nayle: *Thanks, Tezza. We're certainly getting a lot of women today who have taken an instant dislike to Maddy Muir. I'm a strong believer in women's intuition. Always have been. You women just know. You're up next, Jasmine.*

Jasmine: *I live in Deception Bay, Drew. Maddy's a neighbour of mine and she's a nice woman. She taught my son at the local school before she went on maternity leave. Her baby is missing, and I don't understand why everyone is pouncing on her. And why are you calling her 'unemployed' for God's sake? She's a teacher on maternity leave! It's like you're trying to put her down, make her sound like she's nothing and then kick her. All of you are the problem here. And bloody Josh is not the saint you're making him out to be.*

Drew Nayle: *I think you're getting a bit hysterical there, Jasmine. In my day, hysterical women would pop a Valium and have a strong cup of tea and a lie down. Time to hear from our sponsors.*

NEWS OF AUSTRALIA

The Truth About Baby Ethan

Lita Sumuštinis reporting from Deception Bay, Victoria

Wednesday, 15 January, 6.30 am

The search for missing seven-month-old baby Ethan Muir has entered its third day in the small coastal town of Deception Bay, a couple of hours east of Melbourne. The sleepy rural town was rocked when unemployed single mother Maddy Muir, 25, reported her infant son missing on Monday morning. Hours later, her estranged lover, Josh McCreedy, 25, was found deceased at the scene of a fatal car accident.

But according to locals, things are not as they seem.

This reporter spoke to a number of concerned citizens around Deception Bay. It would appear that Josh McCreedy was a popular young man and locals are finding it impossible to believe that he could have done what Maddy Muir is accusing him of.

In one online survey, nearly sixty per cent of voters said they did not believe Josh McCreedy took the baby.

'These virtue signallers live in a snowflake world,' posted one Deception Bay local man under the pseudonym 'Vote4Dutton'. 'How do they know she didn't kill her ex and is hiding the baby somewhere?'

The population of Deception Bay swells over the summer with holiday-makers, and locals and visitors all have opinions on the missing baby.

'Modern-day feminism teaches women to hate men,' said one holidaying professor who was lunching at the Commercial Hotel. 'There's a cult of outrage that seeks to disparage men. These militant feminists are no longer looking for equality. They bang on about the patriarchy, but I can cite several studies that show it does not exist. It's a construct built by angry women. This narrative of the missing baby taken by the evil man plays neatly into their hands.'

Things got a little heated when one local cafe owner tried to show her support for the single mother, but she was quickly shouted down by an esteemed local man who yelled, 'Are you one of those people who convict others based on allegations?' Police had to be called when the cafe owner then refused the man service and he in turn refused to leave the cafe. He claimed she had no right to discriminate against him under the law.

News of Australia will be following this case closely.

CHAPTER 15

THE TURNING

First thing I did on Wednesday morning was call around to Maddy's house on my way to work. The throng of journalists had diminished but a few still hung around the front gate, snapping pictures of Wozza and me as we arrived. Maddy's dad had already been out and bought the papers. The tabloid had headlines like *Missing Baby, Dad Tragedy*, and there was one particularly bad one: *The Truth About Baby Ethan*; the article was written by a Melbourne journalist called Lita Sumuštinis, who questioned whether Ethan was really taken at all.

'It's like we're on a reality TV program,' said Maddy's mum.

Maddy's dad was furious. 'These journalists are just writing whatever they want. There's no basis in fact! How can they do this? Especially when Ethan is missing.'

'It's an unwinnable fight,' I said. I'd seen this kind of thing so many times. Some members of the media created the narrative most likely to sell newspapers or get clicks online and then just ran with it. Josh was now the handsome young hero who died a tragic death trying to get his son back. Maddy was the villain for keeping Josh away from his son. None of it was true, but it made good headlines. And it diverted attention from the guilty to the innocent. People like Maddy and her family were just collateral damage as far as unscrupulous journalists were concerned.

'It's worse on social media,' said Maddy bleakly. 'Every time there's any mention of the story, I'm getting pummelled.' Her phone pinged with a notification and she flicked open the screen. 'Look at this one from some guy called Jeff: *Another woman playing the victim. She's not a victim till it's proven in a court of law*. Doesn't even make any sense.'

Maddy's phone buzzed again.

'There are messages as well?' I asked.

She nodded. 'Some are from friends, but most of them are from the media. People wanting interviews.'

Tilly reached across the table and gently took the phone from her daughter's hand. 'Maddy can't do that again,' she said. 'It's too distressing.'

I had to agree. With journalists like that guy yesterday ready to pounce, it wasn't worth it. The irony suddenly struck me: there were journalists out there who used their aggression to shut down the real story so they could create their own. The thought was a little scary.

Maddy burst into tears. Her sobs wracked her shoulders and made her gasp for breath. 'Oh god! I can't take this. I just want my baby back,' she managed to say between the heaving of her chest. 'I miss him so much.'

I felt utterly helpless in the wake of her loss.

Maddy wiped at her tears with a tissue offered by her stricken mother. She took a deep breath and composed herself. 'I think Josh must have left Ethan with a friend,' she said, a note of certainty growing in her voice. 'And as soon as they hear the news that Josh died in the accident, they'll come forward and give him back. That's what I think has happened.'

'I'm sure you're right, love,' said her dad, patting her on the back.

Maddy continued. 'Because Josh couldn't have left him by the side of the road or in a ditch. He would never do that.'

I exchanged glances with Paul and Tilly. Maddy's faith in Josh eclipsed ours, but we would never say it out loud.

Out of the back window I could see the January sun beginning its trek across the morning sky, colourful summer flowers lining a neat border in the yard. It was unthinkable that life could go on as normal outside, when inside this house the air was so thick with the trauma of a missing baby. Paul Muir, who had been busying himself in the kitchen, put a cup of tea in front of me. He hadn't asked if I wanted one, but I knew the restlessness of people waiting for news. The need to do, the need to control, the need to make tea.

Paul rubbed his daughter's back again. She wiped her tears with a tissue. Blew her nose. Then wrapped her arms around herself in a hug. 'Sorry,' she said in a quiet voice. 'I've been trying to keep it together, but sometimes . . .' Her voice trailed off.

'I can't believe that you ever fell for that monster,' said Tilly, putting the phone face down when it buzzed again. There was a note of mild recrimination in her voice, which I was sure

Maddy did not need right now. I was prepared to intervene if necessary, but Maddy got in first.

'Mum, you never saw it, but in the beginning, he was amazing. So thoughtful. Caring. He would bring me flowers. Finish work and come over here and cook dinner if I had a staff meeting at school, or arrive with fish and chips for a romantic sunset dinner on the beach.'

I took a sip of tea and listened to the way Maddy spoke about this part version of Josh. It was very different to the way she had described him on Monday when we spoke to her in the interview room. Almost as if she was talking about two different men.

'When did things change?' I asked her.

Maddy's gaze went beyond me to the sunlit backyard as she thought about the question. 'It was the first time I got morning sickness. Up until that moment, he'd been great. But that morning, I woke up and threw up. I expected him to be sympathetic and he just . . . he just lost it. He was ranting about how it wasn't his fault I was pregnant and how I was playing the sympathy card. He was a complete arse.'

'Did he apologise afterwards?' I was fascinated by these patterns of abuse and how they started.

Maddy nodded miserably. 'Flowers. Chocolates—not that I could eat them on account of the morning sickness, but it was the thought. He was beside himself. He didn't know what had come over him. He was so sorry.'

'Until it happened again,' I said.

Maddy looked down at the table. 'He moved in just before Ethan was born because he'd promised to be there for me, but he seemed to lose it when the attention went away from him. In just a couple of months, he went from this lovely guy to someone I didn't recognise. It was like walking on eggshells, living with him. One day a friend of mine saw us when Josh was in the middle of a tantrum. Later, she said, "What the hell are you doing with this guy?" and it was then I realised. I felt so stupid.'

'Don't,' I said in a firm voice. 'This kind of love-bombing is a pattern of behaviour we see a lot in cases of abuse. A guy meets a girl and he's literally the nicest guy in the world, can't do enough for her; he's sensitive, he's wonderful, and he becomes indispensable. Things move very quickly. Once the girl is absolutely invested in the relationship, things turn nasty. The girl is in love with the guy she knows he can be, the one he was in the beginning, but the beginning wasn't the real him.'

'Abuse?' said Paul, an indignant tone to his voice. 'Are you saying my daughter was abused?'

I kept my gaze on Maddy. 'It's not as simple as that, is it, Maddy?'

She shook her head. 'He was so nice in the beginning that when he turned mean, I thought *that* was the aberration.'

'But it wasn't, was it?' My heart ached for her and the high price she had paid.

'I came to realise that mean was his default setting. But I was lucky because this house,' she said, pausing as she looked around at the neat, cosy surroundings, 'belonged to my parents. He was a guest.'

'Did he know that when he moved in?'

Maddy's laugh was bitter. 'He thought it was *my* house and when things got really bad, just after I had Ethan, he threatened to take the house and the baby and kick me out. That was it. I told him the house wasn't mine and that he needed to leave.'

'We came up from town and supervised that,' said Paul, emphasising the word *supervised* to suggest Josh did not leave easily.

'And I rang his mother and got her over here,' Tilly said. 'It's amazing how Josh's behaviour improved when she arrived. I call it mum power.' She smiled at the victory.

Paul patted his wife's hand. 'Then we sat Tamara down and told her what had been going on. She was pretty mortified.'

I was curious. 'Did she bring her husband with her? Josh's dad.'

'Keith wouldn't come,' said Tilly. 'We found out later that he'd refused to be part of an "ambush" of his son.'

'How did you find that out?' I always try to trace information back to its source.

'Pub,' said Paul. 'Ralphy at the Royal. He's a mate. Reckons Keith had been in there having a rant on the day Josh moved back home.'

Ralph Murphy, proprietor of the Royal Hotel in town, was a decent man, and in my experience, a very good judge of character.

'It's not your fault,' I said, turning to Maddy. 'This pattern of abuse is unfortunately common. Women don't see it coming.'

Maddy's eyes widened with recognition. 'I remember after we broke up, one of my friends said I had bad taste in men, but that's not true. The guy I actually fell for was everything I could ever want. Until suddenly, he wasn't . . . and then he took Ethan.'

At that moment my phone pinged with a message from the journalist Tammy Millhouse. I liked Tammy; she had always been a fair reporter. Her podcast on a case last year had contributed to a just result in court. I flicked open the message.

Hey Antigone, reportage on Maddy is getting out of hand. I'd love to counter it with a fair story if she's interested. Tammy

I read the message out to Maddy. 'She's one of the good ones,' I said. 'But it's up to you.'

■●■

After tearing myself away from the Muir family, confident that Tammy Millhouse would champion Maddy rather than demonise her, I made my way back to the station. Riggs and Kasparas were sitting at the two spare desks, which made the office feel crowded.

Wozza sat primly at his desk. I saw no sign of our banana cake—he must've locked it in his drawer.

'How did you go yesterday?' I asked, sitting at my own desk to update my day-book.

Riggs reclined in his desk chair like he was about to take a nap, while Kasparas leaned forward. He flipped open his notebook and took us through what they had found out the previous afternoon.

'We checked everyone on Norma's list and none of them reported seeing anything amiss at the pharmacy. No one noticed the formula display or saw anyone remove a tin. We then showed, er'—Kasparas scanned his notes, found what he was looking for—'Rory, the guy at the supermarket, all the still shots from the CCTV of people in the baby aisle. He could identify about half as locals. This morning, we compiled a list of all their names and addresses, and we will door-knock them. The rest were tourists. We then attended at the Deception Bay Caravan Park and door-knocked all occupied caravans. We located five of the still images as holiday residents of the park. Four people in the photos are yet to be identified. Nil signs of the missing baby.'

Wozza listened open-mouthed. 'It's like watching an episode of *Young Sheldon*,' he said.

I gave him a look, then turned to Kasparas. 'Good work. That takes a lot off our to-do list. Today you can keep trying to track down the remaining people in the photos. And there's also a list of holiday rentals that needs to be checked.'

Wozza placed a protective hand over his locked cake drawer and suggested Riggs and Kasparas get a move on.

The banana cake appeared as soon as they'd left, and Wozza hurried off to the kitchen to make us both a cup of tea to have with it. Randall popped his head through the door and announced that a package had arrived for me. It was the DNA kit I'd ordered. I tore open the parcel, took out the small box and scanned the instructions. Seemed pretty simple. A couple of cheek-swab sticks, and the test resembled the Covid tests I'd done so often before visiting Nan in her aged care home. Before Wozza was back with the tea, I'd completed the test and sealed it in the express-post envelope.

An email pinged on my computer; it was the toxicology report on Josh McCreedy. I clicked it open, skimmed over the details of his demise and went straight to what was in his bloodstream.

'Whatcha looking at?' Wozza put a cup of tea next to my cake plate.

'It's the tox screen on Josh McCreedy.'

Wozza leaned forward.

'Says here, he'd consumed alcohol . . .' I kept scanning the document. 'And there was something else in his system . . . ever heard of *pregabalin*?'

'Prega—what?'

'Pregabalin.' I copied the word from the report into Google. Read out the results. '*Pregabalin is used to treat epilepsy and nerve pain*.'

'Was Josh McCreedy epileptic?' Wozza looked puzzled.

'No one mentioned it.' I remembered Doc Caldicott had asked the same thing at the autopsy. And then a thought occurred to me. 'Would he have had a driver's licence if he had seizures?'

Wozza pondered that question. 'I think you can drive with some forms of epilepsy, and with some, you can't.'

That was about the extent of our medical knowledge. Best call Doc Caldicott . . . or my mum, I thought suddenly. I wasn't used to her being home and available. I picked up my phone and dialled her mobile. She answered and I put her on speaker so Wozza could hear.

'Hi, Doc Pollard!' he called across the office.

'Woz, I've told you to call me Jilly.' My mum's voice was gently chiding. Wozza blushed.

'Sorry, Doc . . . Jilly.'

'Hey, Mum, are you familiar with pregabalin?'

She gave a short laugh and said, 'It can be a problem, that one.'

'Why, Doc Jilly?' Wozza sounded like a committed medical student.

'It's a Schedule 4 drug, which means that, while it's only available by prescription, it's not stored under lock and key like all the morphine-based drugs, which are Schedule 8. The Schedule 8 drugs are audited all the time so they're really hard to funnel out of the system, because someone will realise they're missing pretty quick.'

'So the supply chain for Schedule 4 drugs is easier?' I asked.

'They get knocked off from hospitals and they have a good street value. We had a couple of overdoses up north. Pregab comes in capsule form. I've known people to take it with alcohol—it apparently gives a better high. Problem is that the capsules come in all different dosages, from twenty-five milligrams to three hundred milligrams. So if your mate tells you that six pregab pills will give you a great high, well, it might in a lesser dose, but six three-hundred-milligram tablets would probably prove fatal.'

I scanned the report while Mum spoke. 'Stomach contents are consistent with his last known meal of hamburger and chips. Would this work slower or faster on a full stomach?'

'Give me a minute. I'll check.'

I heard the clicking of keys and guessed that Mum had set her laptop up on the dining room table like she always did when she visited. Her work was never far away.

'Here it is: *the rate of absorption is decreased when given with food . . .*'

Wozza said, 'Okay, so if he had a couple of drinks and a handful of the higher-strength prega-whatsits, then he's heading for grief but it might take longer?'

'Correct.' Mum's voice came through the phone firm and certain.

'So where did he get them from?' I wondered aloud.

'Sounds like that's your next line of inquiry,' said Mum. 'I'll leave you to it. I'm going to take Waffles for a walk, then spend the day with my mother.' And she was gone.

I leaned back in my chair, mind ticking over.

'If we find out where he got the drugs from,' Wozza said, 'maybe that will lead us to the baby.'

That meant the next step would be to talk to Josh McCreedy's parents. See if they could shed any light on the drugs in their son's system. Then we needed to make another trip to Filmore's Pharmacy. I could post my DNA kit while I was in town and potentially be one step closer to finding a sibling . . . or perhaps, even, a father.

CHAPTER 16

THE DEAD MAN'S FRIENDS

When we arrived at the McCreedys' house, a group of red-eyed people were leaving. Hugs were exchanged on the porch and Wozza and I stood respectfully to the side until the visitors left. It took Tamara and Keith several moments to register our presence after the group had made their way down the garden path.

'Oh,' said Tamara, then stopped as if she had no more words.

I understood the reaction. On our last visit, we'd told them their son was dead.

'We are so sorry to intrude but we have some questions if you're up to it. There's still no news on the whereabouts of the baby and every minute counts.' I kept stepping forward as I spoke, until I was standing at the bottom of the steps that led up to their porch. It looked like Keith was about to refuse us, but Tamara spoke first.

'Come on in,' she said, and turned to open the fly screen for us.

Minutes later, we were settled at their kitchen table with glasses of cold water. Wozza had his police diary open to take notes.

'Did Josh suffer from epilepsy?' I began, wanting to clear that up straight away.

Tamara looked puzzled. 'No. What makes you ask?'

'A drug called pregabalin was found in his system. It's prescribed to treat epilepsy, but it can be used, in larger doses, as a recreational drug.'

Tamara shook her head. 'I've never heard of it. It's not something that any of us are on. I'm the one who keeps track of all our prescriptions. I had to, with Pete's condition.'

So that made it almost certain Josh had taken the drug recreationally.

'Have any of Josh's friends come to you with any other information?' I asked.

'We've already spoken to everyone we can think of,' said Tamara. 'And nothing.'

Keith nodded and touched the screen of his iPhone, as if hoping he might find some answers there. 'None of them know anything about the baby,' he mumbled.

'What he means is,' cut in Tamara, 'they know about the baby, of course; they just don't know where he is.'

It was hard to read Keith's expression. There was grief there, but something else as well. The mystery was solved as soon as he spoke.

'Some of his friends can't speak to you,' he said, 'because it has become clear to me in my conversations with other parties that you were the one who locked a couple of them up last year.'

He looked directly at me. I noted the formal language, which some people used when they are trying to make a point. I also noted that he didn't look at Wozza, who had been my partner since I'd started working in Deception Bay; whoever I'd locked up, he had too. Long ago, I'd learned not to engage or defend myself in this sort of situation. I found a set of raised eyebrows worked better and saved words. I tried it on Keith. Worked like a charm.

'Lachie and Jimbo. Last year,' he blurted.

Ah, the rapists.

'Josh was friends with them?' Wozza asked.

Keith lifted his chin; he looked at Wozza. 'Josh and Pete grew up with them. They're good blokes,' he said. 'Known 'em since they were whippersnappers. Know their fathers. All good blokes.'

Wozza shook his head sadly. 'Well, Keith, as a copper, I know that good blokes can do bad things.'

I watched Tamara McCreedy carefully. She leaned ever so slightly away from her husband, a look of disbelief on her face. 'Just like Josh,' she said. 'He was a good boy but he took the baby and now the baby is lost.'

Logic was not what Keith needed in that moment, it seemed, and he stood abruptly, his chair scraping against the wooden floor. 'Yes, Tamara, blame all the men!' He glared at his wife and left the room.

The blood drained from her face. 'I'—she began—'I don't know what's come over him.' She plucked a tissue from a box on the table to wipe away her tears. 'Those people who were just leaving, they're Lachie's and Jimbo's parents. It's like we've all lost our sons. Theirs are in jail. Two of ours are gone. First Pete and now Josh. Our oldest, Ben, he's working in Canberra. He's got leave though . . . to come home for the funeral.' A sob caught in her throat.

A parent should never have to bury a child, and Tamara was about to bury her second one.

'Tell me about Pete,' I said quietly.

Tamara's face lit up. 'My baby,' she said. 'He was this fierce little boy, the youngest, but always scampering to follow after his brothers. He was trying to find his place in the world, and holding on for dear life. Take the camping trip, the one where he died. He hadn't been well but he was never one to miss an opportunity. He just wasn't as careful as he should have been with his allergy. I don't even know how he was exposed to peanuts. He was pretty careful and so were his friends. Josh was devastated. He and Pete were really close.' She nodded in the direction of the front door, invoking the departing parents from earlier. 'They all were.'

A feeling of dread came over me. If all those young men were so close, were Josh and Pete caught up in the sexual assaults last year? Wozza and I had uncovered a bunch of locals who'd been involved in the drugging and raping of young women. While we had caught some in the act and arrested them, we never thought we'd got them all. I decided to push a little, and find out what Tamara knew or believed about Lachie and Jimbo.

'How did Josh take the arrests?' I asked.

Tamara shook her head. 'He was devastated, of course. He could never believe Lachie and Jimbo would do that. And to be honest, neither could I. Those boys were lovely. We've known them since they were little kids. I'd never seen any sign of inappropriate behaviour.'

It wasn't the time to point out that until a rapist tries to rape you, he might seem like a perfectly nice person. And if they never try to rape you, they may forever seem nice from where you're standing.

Tamara hadn't finished. 'I mean, those boys' lives have been ruined.'

Beside me, Wozza tensed. I guessed he too was thinking about the actual victims, not the men who'd been made to pay the price for what they'd done. But I knew he wouldn't say anything. It was more important right now to let Tamara speak than to provide any counterpoint to her narrative.

'So Josh and Pete hung out with them?' I prompted.

'All the time. My boys were a bit younger, but all the families knew each other. You know how it is?'

We both nodded. We knew exactly how it was.

'What about your oldest boy?' Wozza asked.

'Ben,' said Tamara.

'Yes, Ben. Was he buddies with Lachie and the others?'

Tamara took a sip of water. 'Not so much. Ben is clever. He had his mind set on going to uni ever since he was little. As soon as he finished school, he was on a plane to Canberra to study law and politics.' She smiled sadly. 'Keith always says he was gone before the ink was dry on his Year Twelve results. He got a job in a law firm and is doing really well.'

She paused, and a sad expression came over her face. 'He doesn't come home much anymore.'

■●■

We left with a better understanding of the McCreedy family dynamic. Then it was time to visit Josh's three closest friends. Christos, Trev, Griffon.

We found Griffon and Trev together at Griffon's place. Or his mum's place, to be more accurate. The back room was dark and dank and set up as a games room, complete with a big TV, overflowing ashtrays and the smell of weed in the air. Both young men looked bleary eyed, like they hadn't slept. A little wired, maybe. We introduced ourselves when Griffon opened the door, then followed him inside after he agreed to answer a few questions. Trev didn't even bother getting up off the beanbag, where he lay clutching a gaming console and performing some sort of double-thumbed manoeuvre to the loud pinging of video machine-guns going off on the screen.

'Might need to pause it, mate,' Wozza said when Trev showed no signs of stopping his game. Wozza gave him about twenty seconds then moved to stand in front of the TV screen, blocking Trev's view. There was the sound of an explosion.

'Awww, man,' Trev whined.

Wozza grinned down at him. 'We're from the police. We need to ask you a couple of questions.'

Trev peeled himself out of the beanbag and brought a waft of stale body odour with him as he came over to the kitchen table and sat in a slouch on the chair closest to him.

whole thing and quit. It hadn't mattered because Maddy was on paid maternity leave so she paid the bills.

'How did he feel about becoming a father?' I asked.

Both young men shrugged. I got the impression that this had not been a topic of conversation among the three of them.

Wozza tried a different tack. 'So what do you think went wrong between them? 'Cos one minute he's there and the next minute, he's back with his mum and dad.'

'She kicked him out!' Trev's voice held outrage. 'Like just after he moves in—'

'Yeah,' cut in Griffon, 'and we helped him move boxes.'

'Anyway,' continued Trev, 'like the minute he moved in, she starts nagging at him. *Oh, Josh, you should be more helpful and you should do housework*'—more of the high-pitched whining voice—'like he didn't do it at home, so why would she expect him to do it at her place?'

'Because that's what adults do,' said Wozza. Sometimes he couldn't help himself.

Trev wasn't fazed. 'Then, like after about two months, she kicks him out. Like out of the blue.'

'Yep, out of the blue,' said Griffon, reaching for a pack of smokes.

Wozza reached over and took the pack from him. 'After we've gone, mate. After we've gone.'

Griffon nodded, looking annoyed but not willing to challenge a cop.

Trev snickered. 'For Christmas, we got him a T-shirt with "Bitches Get Stitches" on the front of it.'

Griffon snorted a laugh. 'He even wore it a couple of weeks ago when he went around to Maddy's. That's when she said he couldn't see the baby anymore.'

'How'd he feel about that?' asked Wozza, frowning at their complete absence of insight.

'He was pissed off,' said Trev.

Wozza tried his best to clarify. 'So he wears a T-shirt to provoke her, then he gets pissed off when she's provoked.'

'You're not getting it, man,' said Griffon. 'The T-shirt was a *joke*.'

Wozza looked like he was about to argue, but it wouldn't help.

'Where do you think the baby might be?' I asked.

Both men looked blank.

'Dunno,' said Trev.

'Me neither.' Griffon shrugged.

I tried again. 'Not sure if you saw the pictures he posted the day he took the baby, but in the last one, there was the shadow of someone's hand. The picture was not a selfie. Do you have any idea who Josh could have been with?'

Both men shrugged.

'How about a new partner? Did Josh find someone else?' I asked.

'Nah,' said Trev. 'He swore off girls for good. They're only looking for one thing.'

My mind boggled. 'And what is that thing?'

'A man to support them.' Trev spoke with such authority.

I remembered how Maddy had said Josh moved into her parents' home rent free, didn't have a job, and played video games for two months until she told him to leave.

'In what ways did he support her?' Wozza asked. He seemed as interested as I was in hearing their answer.

Griffon spoke. ''Cos he was there.'

'And he thought just being there would be enough for her?'

'Of course,' said Trev.

Changing the subject, I asked if Josh had ever taken pregabalin. I watched their faces closely for signs of recognition.

Trev reddened slightly and squirmed a bit in his seat. 'Nah.'

'Ever heard of it?' said Wozza.

Griffon this time. 'Nup.'

Final question: 'Where were you both on Monday between ten and two thirty?

Trev got in first. 'We were here. Monday was the big Summer Tournament.' He nodded towards the enormous screen in the games room. 'It's on all week.'

Griffon frowned. 'Josh was supposed to be here too. He was going to join our team but he never showed.'

'He registered and everything,' said Trev.

My interest was piqued. 'And he didn't show up? Did you try to call him?' I flicked back to my notes about the recent calls to Josh's phone. Trev, Shags.

'Of course we did. He didn't answer.'

'There was a missed call from you on his phone.' I looked at Trev. Then at Griffon. 'And a missed call from someone called Shags . . .'

Both young men snickered.

'Is that the name you're under on Josh's phone?'

Griffon straightened his face and nodded with a slight blush.

'That's 'cos he's good with the ladies,' said Trev.

'And after you tried to call him?' said Wozza, nipping any talk of ladies in the bud.

'Just played without him,' said Griffon. 'You snooze, you lose.'

I slid the CCTV photo out of the folder. 'Do either of you recognise this guy? Josh was talking to him on the street after he took the baby.'

Both answered at once. Trev said, 'Hey, looks a bit like—' at the same time as Griffon said, 'Nah, never seen him before.'

Then Trev fell silent. Picked at a thumbnail.

'Do you recognise him?' I asked pointedly.

Trev didn't look me in the eye. 'Nah,' he mumbled.

■●■

Back in the police car, ready to track down Christos, Wozza was aghast. 'Those guys were . . .' he searched for a word. 'Morons! Oh god, if any of my daughters ever brings home a dude like that, I'm going to have to shoot him.' He tapped his firearm.

'They just don't get it, do they?' I said, ignoring Wozza's death threats and checking my notebook for Christos's address. I typed it into my phone. Read out the directions to Wozza.

'Lying like cut snakes when you showed them that photo,' said Wozza. 'And lying about the pregabalin too, if I'm not mistaken.'

'I agree. I wonder what this next guy will be like.'

■●■

Christos was very different to the other two. For starters, he was clean-cut and neatly attired, and his home smelled of scented candles and fresh laundry. He invited us in straight away and made us both a cup of tea. Set out a plate of homemade Anzac biscuits.

'I could see it all playing out so clearly,' Christos said when he finally sat down at the table with us. 'He was always going on about Maddy and how she treated him, but you know, I could see her point. Josh behaved like an immature slob. I visited them a couple of times and I could see her frustration, even if he couldn't.'

'Ever broach the subject with him?' Wozza asked, checking to see if Christos was an advocate or a bystander.

'All the time,' Christos said earnestly. 'I told him it wouldn't last, but he had this sense of entitlement.'

'Did you ever see Josh take any drugs?' I asked.

'No way.' Christos sounded adamant. 'Not in front of me. I don't even drink.'

It was hard to see how these men were friends. I said as much. 'You seem really different from them.'

Christos smiled. 'We all met in kindergarten. Friendships like that are . . .' His voice trailed off and he smiled nostalgically. Then his eyes glistened. 'But now he's gone . . .'

Wozza gave him a moment, then gently pressed on. 'Any idea where he could have left baby Ethan?'

Christos composed himself. 'I've thought about it, but I don't know. I can't see him leaving the baby with any of our friends.' He blushed slightly. 'If he did, I guess it would have been me.'

'I can see why, mate.' Wozza looked around the neat home. 'For elimination purposes, where were you between ten and two thirty on Monday?'

'At the supermarket. I'm working there over the summer,' he said. 'I recently went back to do Honours and so I take every job I can over the uni break.'

'You didn't see your mate in the baby aisle, by any chance?' said Wozza.

Christos shook his head. 'I work in the deli. All I see is the fruit and vegie section from where I'm standing.'

'Worth a shot.' Wozza made a note of this.

Christos looked thoughtful. 'He did try to ring my mum though.'

'What's your mum's name?' Wozza got his pen ready to write it down.

'Lesley.'

'Lesley Gillis?' I said, flicking back through my notes. 'Was she his teacher in high school? Runs the clothing stall at the church?'

'That's my mum.' Christos looked proud. 'She said she got a voice message from him that morning, asking about baby clothes, but when she tried to ring back, he didn't answer.' He paused. 'It was probably too late by then.'

'Yep,' said Wozza.

'But she definitely would have helped him,' Christos said quickly. 'She helps everyone.' Then he looked sad. 'I just can't believe Josh is gone. Mum always says that life teaches you lessons and that you learn as you go along. Deep down, Josh was a nice guy with a good heart. I reckon he would have learned over time. But as it turns out, he didn't have time, did he?'

'Nah, he didn't,' agreed Wozza sadly.

'When is your mum due home?' I looked at my watch. It was getting late.

'She's got evening choir,' said Christos. 'So it's my night to cook dinner.'

Wozza nodded. 'Wouldn't want to keep you from that, mate.'

'One last question,' I said. 'The pictures Josh posted on Monday of himself with the baby—one of them wasn't a selfie. There's the shadow of a hand taking the picture of Josh and the baby. Can you think of anyone he might have been with, out at the silos?'

Christos's eyes widened. 'Someone was with him?' He scratched his head. 'I can't think of anyone. He'd lost touch with a lot of the guys we went to school with. I dunno . . . could he have just bumped into someone random?'

'Sure,' I said, watching him closely. 'The reason we're interested is that the crash happened not long after that photo, and Josh has the baby in the photo, but at the crash, he didn't. Whoever that hand belongs to is the person we hope has baby Ethan and is looking after him.'

'I'm sorry I can't help you,' he said, looking down.

'How about this?' I pulled the CCTV photo out and slid it across the table towards Christos, at the same time realising that *he* bore a resemblance to the image.

Christos glanced at the photo and looked away. 'I don't know anything about where the baby went.'

Wozza stood up and folded his notebook shut. 'The baby didn't *go* anywhere,' he said. 'Someone took him.'

Just then, there was a high-pitched wail from somewhere deep in the house.

'What's that?' said Wozza.

Christos reddened. 'It's my cat.' He paused awkwardly. 'He's in the laundry. I'll let him out after you go. He's a scratcher.'

'Good idea,' said Wozza. 'I'm not a cat person.'

'Mind if I use the bathroom?' I said quickly.

Wozza pointed to a painting he could see in the lounge room and asked about it as I went off to have a look around the house to see if there really was a cat.

■●■

As we drove off, I checked with Wozza about the difference between the noise a baby makes and the noise a cat makes.

'No sign of a baby and there *was* a cat in the laundry. It was sleeping on one of those cat beds.'

'Sounded like a cat to me rather than a baby,' said Wozza. 'But to be fair, I have repressed the babyhoods of all my three daughters. It's a coping mechanism.'

I laughed. 'I'll take your word for it. I haven't had cats or babies, but ask me the difference between Waffles's greeting bark and his alert bark and I can tell you.'

We headed straight for Filmore's Pharmacy to follow up the pregabalin lead. Norma was serving a customer up the front of the store but she caught my eye and raised an eyebrow in a question. I shook my head. *No sign of the baby.* We headed up the back towards the dispensary. Dawn was barely visible behind the high counter where all the medicines were.

'Hey, Dawn,' I called out.

She looked up and smiled broadly. 'Hey, Antigone. Any news on the baby yet?'

'Not yet,' I said because saying *yet* meant that, in the future, there might be news. 'Could we have a quick chat to you about Josh McCreedy and any prescriptions he might have had?'

'Sure.' She stepped down from the raised dispensary and stood behind the computer on the counter below it. Clicked a few keys. Frowned. Clicked a few more. Then smiled. 'There it is,' she said. 'He filled a prescription for antibiotics last October.'

'Does it say what they were for?' Wozza asked.

'It was penicillin, so maybe something like tonsillitis, at a guess.' Her forehead creased as she remembered. 'In fact, I think I do remember him coming in with tonsillitis . . . but you'd need to take a look at his medical records.'

'That was after his brother died?' I said. 'Pete McCreedy.'

Dawn's face tightened. 'Yes. So tragic. Pete McCreedy. Last year.'

I lowered my voice as a holidaying couple in sunhats came into the store to browse the sunscreens. 'Did Pete get his EpiPens here?'

'The whole family comes in here for everything,' Dawn said without checking the computer.

'The family's now half the size it was,' Wozza said to no one in particular.

Dawn reddened but said nothing.

'Do you stock pregabalin?'

Dawn nodded.

'How easy is it to get?' said Wozza.

'Very easy if you have a script.'

'Did Josh have a script for it?' I asked.

She clicked a couple of keys on her computer. 'Nope.'

'See much abuse of it?' Wozza leaned on the counter.

Dawn blew out a breath. 'Last year there were some guys who had scripts from some online telehealth site that I reckon was dodgy. We had a bit of a rush on pregabalin. Apparently, it gives you high if you take enough of it, especially with a couple of drinks.' She shrugged. 'Not that I'd know. I don't do that kind of thing.'

I smiled at her. 'I'm with you,' I said. 'I try not to do anything that interferes with the clarity of my thinking, even alcohol.' I tapped the side of my forehead for emphasis.

Dawn's eyes widened in solidarity. 'Same,' she said. 'It makes a girl vulnerable.'

Looking closely at Dawn in her white chemist's-assistant dress and neatly brushed hair, I saw a vulnerability that didn't need alcohol to make it worse. Last year, we had reason to believe that she might have been one of the local women targeted in a drink-spiking spree, but she'd never come forward. I didn't blame her. The way the system treated victims was appalling. And sadly, with every victim who was spat out by the system, the message snaked its way out into the world, whispering to all victims: *It's not worth it*.

'Do you remember which guys last year had scripts for pregabalin?'

Dawn looked thoughtful. 'It was more the scripts themselves that I remember. Mr Filmore said they looked odd, but at the end of the day, if someone has a script, we fill it.'

I changed tack. 'You and Norma left just as Josh was walking past on Monday. Did you see him later in your lunchbreak?'

Dawn shook her head. 'Even if I did, he wouldn't have said much more than what he usually does.'

'What does he usually say?' said Wozza.

Dawn rolled her eyes. 'He usually says, "Hey, Chemist Girl, got any drugs?" just like they all do.'

Wozza grinned. 'You should offer them laxatives.'

Dawn smiled. 'I'll remember that one,' she said.

■●■

On the footpath outside the pharmacy, Wozza and I exchanged a quick summary of what we'd learned so far. Josh didn't have a script for pregabalin but he'd had it in his system. His friends had no idea where he might have left Ethan, and we were no closer to finding him.

'Hold on a sec,' said Wozza. 'Didn't Doc Caldicott say there was a faint odour of beer at the autopsy?'

'Yes,' I said, remembering our conversation in the examination room.

Woz became animated. 'And the tox screen said he had alcohol in his system. Well, where did he get it from?'

'Could he have had it with him?' My voice was uncertain. I didn't transport beer around with me on account of never drinking it so I couldn't be sure.

'Think about it,' said Wozza with a growing excitement in his voice. 'The only thing we found in the car was the baby bottle. There was no esky or cooler. Warm summer's day so you need to drink it cold.'

I looked at him wondering where he was going with this.

'Trust me, it's a thing,' he said. 'So just say, sometime during the day, he meets up with some dude who gives him pregabalin, then he palms off the baby and decides to indulge in the pills, so he has to get takeaway cold beer.'

'The drive-through!' I said.

'My thoughts exactly.' Wozza was already heading for the car.

■●■

The odds were strong that the man at the drive-through bottle shop would be a mate of Wozza's, so I wasn't surprised that when we got there, he clapped a bald guy in a black T-shirt on the back and greeted him like a long-lost pal.

'Knuckles! How ya been, matey?' Wozza beamed.

'Woz, howzit hanging?' the bald man said.

'Just fine, thanks,' said Wozza. 'We're here on official police business. This is my partner, Senior Detective Pollard.'

The man shook hands with me. 'What do you need? Coupla bottles for the police picnic?' He laughed.

'Nah, nothing like that, mate.' Wozza moved a little closer to Knuckles and lowered his voice. 'We're investigating the missing baby . . .' He let that sink in and the jovial man turned serious.

I pulled a photo of Josh from my folder. 'Did you see this guy on Monday afternoon?'

'Yep. He drove through here.' He nodded towards the driveway. 'Bought a half-dozen cold Great Northerns.'

'That's a beer, right?' I said.

Wozza and Knuckles looked at me indulgently. Both nodded.

'So he bought six beers. Did he have a baby with him?'

'Didn't see one.'

I wanted to clarify how the drive-through worked. 'So he drives in, and then you go to the driver's-side car window?'

'Yep.'

'Then you go get the beer and bring it out. Where do you put it?'

'Most of the time, if it's a case, they pop the boot and I stick it in there, but this was just a half-dozen. He wanted them on the front seat.'

'So you put them on the front seat and there was no baby there?'

He looked confused. 'Why would anyone have a baby on the front seat of their car?'

'Didn't you see him all over the news?' said Wozza.

A shrug. 'Nah, mate. Who has time for watching the news? I finish here, I hit the surf.'

'Fair enough,' said Wozza.

'Do you remember the exact time he came through?'

Knuckles offered to check the transaction records. He came back with the exact time: 1.37 pm.

As soon as we were back in the car, I flipped through the file notes. There it was. Josh posted the final picture from out at the silos at 1.35 pm, which meant he was sitting in the car at the drive-through bottle shop when he posted it. It was taken by someone else at 1.09, and in it, he was holding the baby. Fast forward twenty-five minutes and he's ordering beer and doesn't have the baby.

Wozza followed my logic. 'The odds are getting stronger that whoever gave him the pills also took that photo, and took the baby.'

I shook my head. 'We don't know that. Maybe you're right about the photographer having the baby, but Josh could have had a stash of those pills in his pocket. Or the photographer could have given him the pills, then Josh dropped the baby somewhere before he took them.'

Even with all these unanswered questions, it felt like we were getting a bit closer to the truth.

CHAPTER 17

THE EARTH-MOTHER VIBE

Riggs and Kasparas looked tired when we got back to the office. They'd spent most of the day tracking down people who'd purchased baby products and then canvassing around town. The sun was dipping in the sky and the sea breeze was coming in through our office window. We exchanged progress reports. It all added up to little. And even though investigation was just as much about elimination as fact-finding, the eliminating parts felt like failure when a baby's life was at stake.

Wozza grabbed his jacket from the hook in our office. 'I'm off,' he said.

I looked at the two city cops. Normally, when colleagues visit from out of town, you roll out the red carpet and take them out for dinner. Clearly Wozza wasn't in the mood, and I had Mum and Nan waiting for me at home.

'I'm off too,' I said, reaching for my phone and keys. I left the visitors with a couple of recommendations for local eateries and then I was gone.

As I put my seatbelt on, my phone pinged with a message from Daniel.

How's the investigation going? Any leads?

I was just about to reply but then pressed 'call' instead. I told myself it was so that I could drive and talk rather than waste time with a long text. I wanted to get home. He answered straight away.

'Hello.'

His deep voice always sent an involuntary shiver through me. I did my best to ignore it. 'We've got nothing,' I said, starting the engine and switching Daniel's voice from my phone to the car speaker as I pulled away from the station.

'Take me through it.'

'Our best lead is a shadow in the final picture he posted near the silo. It's not a selfie. Someone was with him.'

'Any other phones pinging at the same location?'

'Nope. Just his.'

'Time?'

'He posted the silo pic at one thirty-five but it was taken twenty-six minutes before that. That's what he did; he took the photos then posted them after he left each scene. We now know that he was sitting in a drive-through bottle shop minus the baby when he posted that one.'

'Any leads coming in from the public?'

'We've had our city slickers following up,' I said.

There was a deep laugh on the other end of the line. 'Not long ago, you were a city slicker too, Miss Brunswick.'

I laughed too. Pictures flooded my memory of coffee in Brunswick. Patrolling the streets and alleyways. But then, like malevolent flickers, other images seared through my brain—images of cases that went wrong. Violence. Fleeing. Daniel. Our final fight. Me leaving the city with a carload of my belongings and my new dog beside me on the front seat. I took a deep breath. 'Not anymore.'

A pause on his end, then his voice resumed. More formal this time. 'Have you seen the headlines?'

I was momentarily thrown by his change of direction. 'I've seen some. They're pretty brutal.'

He continued. 'Some of your grimier news establishments are having a field day. Headlines like'—newspapers rustled—'*Fathers Fight Back*, and another one . . . *Father Pushed to the Limit*. It's the usual media sabotage.'

'Bloody hell,' I muttered.

'While we're talking . . .' Daniel paused.

My mind pulled away from the media and Maddy and came back into the present as I watched the golden late-afternoon landscape of Deception Bay fly past my windscreen: trees, cows and sheep, and the smell of the bay coming through my window.

'Yes?' My heartbeat quickened.

'I've got the weekend off and I want to come up and see you.'

I felt the catch in my voice. 'When were you thinking of coming?'

'Saturday morning.'

I thought of Mum and Nan and Maddy and baby Ethan, and could hardly believe my own ears when I heard myself say, 'Okay.'

■●■

Waffles was waiting for me at the door when I got home. So was a swing-dance tune from one of Nan's old records, filling the house with memories of my childhood. My mother and grandmother were at the bench—Nan sitting on the visitor side and Mum standing at the business side—serving up steaks and salad on the good plates. It was a sight for sore eyes.

I stood next to Nan and took in the scene. Nan reached an arm around me and squeezed.

'I hope you don't mind, but I'm going to stay a while longer,' she said.

'Of course I don't mind! It's your house!'

'Your mother is going to look after me while she's here. She can do my medications for me.'

Mum beamed at the two of us as she sprinkled some fresh-cut basil across the plates.

Over dinner, Mum and Nan told me about the day they'd had. A short walk along the coast and then fish and chips on the beach. Waffles had kept them company and had a swim in the sea. I looked at him lying on his cushion in front of the fireplace. He looked fluffy enough to suggest a post-beach bath. He met my gaze and wagged his tale.

'We met a friend of Waffles's down there,' said Nan. 'A teenager. She was on her lunchbreak and Waffles ran up to her and sat by her side.'

I laughed and turned to my dog. 'Did you see Crystal?' His tail thumped his big cushion. 'He tracks Crystal when we go for a run.'

Nan's eyes widened.

'It's part of his original police-dog training. He was trained to follow the most recent scent and we practise on Crystal. She hides and then gives him a treat when he finds her.' Speaking of Crystal reminded me that I'd promised to help her with her maths over the summer. I glanced at my mum and realised that she would make an excellent maths tutor too. I sent Crystal a text to see if she had any free time between her shifts at the pharmacy.

The dancing dots appeared under my text. Then my phone buzzed.

Gotta work tomorrow and Saturday. Gotta go out tomorrow night for Andy's birthday. Russell said do you wanna come coz Andy's got no friends.

Andy? Then I remembered meeting Russell's buddy Andy at the cafe, the one who'd left town and was now back. I laughed and interpreted that Russell had meant Andy had no friends *in town*.

I texted back. *I've got my mum and nan here.*

Dancing dots.

Russell says they can come too. Azzurro's. 6 o'clock.

Surprisingly, Mum and Nan were keen, probably because I kept raving on about how good the pizza at Azzurro's was and they wanted to try it, so I texted Crystal to say that we'd all be there. I got a thumbs-up in reply.

Dessert was Nan's apple sponge, made by Mum under Nan's watchful eyes. Apples stewed with sugar and fragrant cloves, under a layer of sponge, served hot from the oven with whipped cream on top. I wasn't sure if there was a biblical heaven, but if there was, it would have apple sponge on the menu.

■●■

After dinner, Nan retired to her old bedroom, which Mum had made up with fresh sheets and decorated with a bunch of wildflowers from the garden. Her walking stick clunked rhythmically as she made her way up the hallway. Dishes done, lights off, and the room lit only by a standard lamp and a row of candles on the mantlepiece, Mum and I settled into the comfy chairs with cups of tea.

'So, how's Daniel?' Mum never danced around a topic when she could waltz right in.

I considered her question. How *was* Daniel? To be honest, I had no idea.

'He's coming for a visit on Saturday morning,' I said, then smiled because I realised he'd be arriving at the farm expecting to see just me and he would get my whole family instead.

Mum did not subscribe to the school of romance or the I-need-to-find-a-man-to-complete-me narrative. Her advice, ever since I was a small child, usually centred around finding things to do that you loved, and building yourself into an independent person. Thinking about Maddy and Josh made me think about my mum. She always said she never needed a man, but for the first time, I wondered if there had been a man and he had fallen short, like Josh had.

In the candlelight, I told Mum about Maddy and Josh and Maddy's independence and how even some of his friends blamed her for the breakup.

Mum nodded, looking a little tired. 'It's an old story, Antigone. Women feeling they have to have everything under control because they can't rely on their partners. Some men weaponise incompetence. The biggest thing that's changed since your nan's time is that women can earn their own living now.' She smiled at me. 'I loved raising you on my own, and when I had to step away with work, your nan was there to help. You were our greatest joy.'

'You seemed pretty determined to have a child,' I said. This wasn't a subject me and Mum usually discussed, but now that I knew about the pregnancy before me, either Mum was really bad at contraception or she'd really wanted a baby.

Mum laughed at the memory. 'My fiercely independent vibe was mixed in with a ferocious earth-mother vibe. Both were strong.'

I looked at my mum and told her that, while I had inherited her independence, I had no earth-mother inclinations towards children. I almost flinched wondering what she would say in response.

'Each woman is on her own journey,' she said. 'The pressure to reproduce is a social construct as well. If you don't feel it, don't do it. And don't ever let yourself be persuaded otherwise.

I've seen too many women pressured into having a child by a man who desperately wants one, then he goes back to work and she spends years fitting her life around the child. There's no guarantee he'll stick around, and if he does stick around, there's no guarantee things will be rosy.'

I had seen it too. Back when I was in uniform, it was a rare shift that didn't include a family violence call. Women with children could get stuck in terrible situations. So much family violence was about one partner trying to control the other partner, disguising the control as love. But it wasn't love, it was power. You can't love someone when you make them tremble with fear. You can't love someone and hurt them at the same time. That's not love; it's abuse. Talking about it with Mum made me wonder if maybe it was those cases that contributed to my almost pathological need not to let anyone in. When I'd left Daniel and the home we'd shared, all my stuff had fitted into a suitcase and four boxes. Anything precious was here on the farm. Perhaps, unless I was here, I would always be ready to run.

In the flickering candlelight, I chanced a question I'd never asked Mum before.

'Did my father stick around, even for a little while?'

Mum sighed but looked like she was going to respond. Just then, though, my phone buzzed with a text. It was from the hospital. *Amanda's awake. Call for an update.*

'Work?' said Mum, looking at her watch.

'It's the hospital. Amanda's awake. I've got to call and find out how she is.'

Mum offered to interpret the medical-speak if I made the call on speakerphone. The surgery had gone well, we learned, and Amanda was conscious. It was all good news.

It wasn't till I lay in bed late in the evening that I realised I'd missed a chance to talk with Mum about the father I'd never known.

NEWS UNLIMITED ONLINE

The Real Truth About Baby Ethan

Tammy Millhouse reporting from Deception Bay, Victoria

Thursday, 16 January, 6.15 am

The search for missing seven-month-old baby Ethan Muir has entered its third day in the small coastal town of Deception Bay. But instead of focusing on the man responsible and what he may have done with the baby, some in the media and the community have turned on the mother, 25-year-old teacher Maddy Muir.

Yesterday I spent some time with the young mum and her parents. People have been posting the most awful things about her online and it's making an impossible situation even worse.

'I don't understand,' said Ms Muir. 'The worst thing has happened and so many people want to shift the blame from Josh to me. It doesn't make any sense.'

One of the biggest accusations online and in the media is that Maddy had kept Josh McCreedy from his baby son.

'It's simply not true,' said Maddy. 'If he visited and was polite, he could spend all the time he wanted with Ethan. He just wasn't that interested.'

Ms Muir is a well-respected teacher at the local primary school and is very involved in community activities and fundraisers. Before the baby was born, she was a popular member of the Deception Bay netball association and part of the winning team that took the grand final cup two years ago.

Deb Jackson, principal of St Mary's Primary School, spoke on behalf of the school community when she expressed sorrow at the abduction of Ethan Muir. 'Maddy is one of our favourite teachers. We are all very fond of her. She's brought little Ethan in to visit several times.'

Mrs Jackson has been instrumental in organising a parish roster of searchers to cover several areas on the outskirts of town. The group has worked closely with the SES and Police Search and Rescue to cover as much ground as possible, near the sites where the baby's father Josh McCreedy posted cruel, taunting images on social media on the day he took Ethan.

While rumours are circulating that McCreedy didn't take Ethan, this reporter saw footage that proves he did. In a haunting baby-monitor video, McCreedy is seen lowering the side of the cot and removing Ethan. Minutes later, he took a photo of the baby lying on the front seat of his car, unrestrained.

'At a time of such horror for the Muir family,' said Senior Detective Antigone Pollard from the Deception Bay police, 'we urge the public to stand with Maddy and help us find her baby.'

Members of the public can join searches by checking the Deception Bay police website for locations.

CHAPTER 18

WHEELS OF JUSTICE

Wozza loved getting phone calls really early in the morning. You could tell he was excited because he could hardly do more than grunt. However, when I told him that Amanda had regained consciousness and we could speak to her, he spluttered into actual words.

'That's good news,' he said, voice full of both sleep and excitement.

'Hope I didn't wake you,' I said, trying to keep the hint of amusement out of my voice.

'Nah,' said Wozza. 'I had to get up anyway to answer the phone.'

We made arrangements to meet at the hospital at eight. That gave me time for a quick shower after my run with Waffles. Then I got myself ready and, twenty-five minutes later, I dashed out the door as Mum and Nan emerged from their rooms in dressing-gowns in time to say goodbye.

'Let me know how Amanda is,' Mum called as I closed the door.

■●■

The hospital ward was dim as Wozza and I entered. Amanda had a room to herself and the blinds were shut, the lights turned down. Wozza winced when he saw her. Her face was bruised and her head bandaged. A box shape under the blanket suggested her leg needed to be protected.

'Hey, Amanda,' I said in a soft voice, trying to gauge whether or not she was awake. The nurse we'd spoken to at the nursing station outside her room told us that she had been awake earlier and had seemed fairly alert.

Amanda let out a soft groan that made both of us rethink the wisdom of disturbing her. I took the seat at the side of her bed. It was an armchair the colour of a slug. The peace of the room was shattered when one of the machines by Amanda's bed started shrieking.

'Is she dying?' said Wozza in a panic.

A nurse wandered in and pressed a button on the machine and the beeping stopped. She lifted Amanda's arm and I could see that a tube connecting her to a bag of liquid hooked onto the machine was kinked. The nurse straightened out the tube, and calm was restored. My racing heart took a little longer. When Amanda began to curl her arm back up, I placed my hand on it, careful to avoid the bandaged part that held the cannula in place.

'Amanda, it's Antigone and Wozza,' I tried again.

Her eyelids fluttered as if she was trying to open them. And then, slowly, she awoke. It took several moments for her to focus her gaze, first on me, then on Wozza, who was hovering nervously behind me.

'G'day, boss,' he said with false cheer.

'G'day, Wozza,' she croaked back, then looked at me and smiled.

I let out a relieved breath. She recognised us and she could talk. Two very good signs.

'We are so glad you're okay,' I said.

'Not so okay.' She looked ruefully in the direction of her leg. I was glad there were no mirrors so she couldn't see her face.

'I brought you this,' I said, reaching into my pocket and pulling out her phone. 'I charged it for you. Thought you'd need it to stay in touch with everyone.' From another pocket, I pulled out the charger I'd taken from her office.

Amanda reached for the phone with her good arm, then placed it on the tray stand next to her bed. I plugged the charger into a nearby socket and positioned the charging cord in easy reach. She didn't click on the screen, which was good because when I'd tapped it earlier, there were thirty-seven messages. She could do without that level of stress for the time being.

'Everyone at the station sends their love,' said Wozza, who seemed to have edged even further back from the bed.

'Do you remember what happened?' I waved my hand in the vague direction of her box-covered leg.

Amanda looked pensive. 'Not really,' she rasped.

'Do you remember why you were on your way to my farm?'

Her eyes widened with memory. She cleared her throat but no words came out. Wozza moved around the bed and handed her the glass of water with a straw in it from her tray. She took a sip. Tried again. 'You texted me,' she said in a slightly less croaky voice.

I shook my head. 'No, I didn't.'

Her forehead creased in confusion.

'We looked at your phone. The text didn't come from my number. We think someone lured you out there.'

Amanda looked overwhelmed. We didn't have much longer.

'Do you remember anything before the crash?' I pressed.

Amanda's gaze wandered to the ceiling and her forehead creased in thought. It looked like she was trying to chase down a memory. And failing.

'Maybe the man made me swerve . . . I'm not sure.' With that, her eyes closed and we lost her to sleep, which seemed like the best place for her to be right now.

'*What*?' I kept my voice low and looked at Wozza.

'A man? Bloody hell,' he muttered.

I suddenly remembered Waffles, nose down, walking over to the side of the road. Did he pick up a scent? Did someone force Amanda off the road? And leave her alone in a smashed car with life-threatening injuries?

We crept quietly out of the room so as not to disturb her further. On the drive to the station, we both agreed that it would be a while before she would be able to talk to us properly, and that hopefully her memory of that night might return in the meantime.

■•■

When Senior Sergeant Bill Wheeler went on sick leave, no one had expected him to come back. The months without him had brought hope to us all. The vibe had changed around the station. A pall had lifted, and so had the prevailing on-edge feeling. Sometimes, the absence of something brings the problem into sharp relief. When Wheeler's absence was first announced, one thought danced into my mind: *Ding, dong, the witch is dead.*

But of course, he wasn't dead. And now he was back. Striding into the muster room as if he hadn't walked out in disgrace months ago . . . which I suppose, in his mind, he hadn't. The room fell silent when he entered. He was in uniform, chest puffed out.

Wheels held up his hands as if we had met him with applause rather than silence. His expression was magnanimous. His accent, Schwarzenegger. 'I'll be back.' Then he laughed. A moment later, his voice turned serious. 'I don't know Senior Sergeant Amanda Filipovic but join me in wishing her a speedy recovery.' Wheels paused and cast his eyes downwards. Seconds later, he resumed speaking. 'Anyway, Amanda did a fine job of keeping my seat warm, but Force Command wanted me back at this crucial time.'

Force Command? Wheels was such a tosser. He made it sound like the Chief Commissioner herself personally rang and invited him back. I knew that was absolutely not the case. Probably the harried local inspector, desperate to fill the position at short notice, had asked.

Randall, ever the diplomat, said, 'Welcome back, sir.'

Wheels beamed at him. 'And it's good to be back, Randall.' Then he turned to Wozza. 'Update us on the Muir baby investigation.'

Wozza jumped to attention. 'We have the family staying at the Muir home. Crime Scene techs cleared it Monday night. Found nothing of evidentiary value. We have SES teams working with our Search and Rescue team in clusters fanning out from the three known photo stops: near the cliff, out by the old roadhouse and near the silos on the edge of town. Antigone noticed the shadow of a hand holding the phone in the final photo, the one at the silos. We believe it wasn't a selfie and that someone was with McCreedy at that time, someone who could have the baby. McCreedy was seen at the bottle shop not long after, buying beer, and he didn't have the baby at that stage so we've narrowed down the window. Searchers are also checking around the car wreckage. Riggs and Kasparas have been examining CCTV and electronic records from the supermarket for anyone purchasing baby formula, bottles, dummies or nappies since the baby was taken. We've had reports of one missing tin of baby formula from the local chemist so that's a possible lead too. A seven-month-old baby needs baby formula. Best-case scenario, we are hoping that baby Ethan has been taken by, or left with, someone who knows that. Traces of a drug were found in Josh McCreedy's tox screen so we are going to track down possible sources for that.'

Wheels nodded. Didn't look at me. 'Now that I'm back, I'll be doing all the press conferences, especially considering Tuesday's disaster.' He glared at me, then continued. 'All right, you've all got your jobs. Get on with it.' He flicked his wrist at us by way of dismissal.

Wozza and I weren't quick enough to escape, even though we tried. Wheels snapped his fingers at us.

Yep. Actually snapped.

'You two. My office.' With that, he swept out and, I guess, he expected us to follow him.

'That wasn't his happy snap,' whispered Wozza.

I rolled my eyes. My tolerance for this kind of arrogance was low.

By the time we got to Wheels's office, he was already sitting in the power position behind his desk. He gestured to two chairs opposite, which were slightly lower than his. So he could look down on us, I guessed.

'What are the two city guys like?' he asked Wozza.

Wozza shrugged. 'Okay for city guys.'

Wheels nodded. 'Major Collision are investigating Amanda's accident . . .' He let that hang. Left a silence. We didn't fill it. He saw what we were doing and started talking again. 'I went out there today. Looks like an accident to me. I don't know why you called them in.'

I looked him in the eye. Didn't say anything for a couple of beats because my mind was racing ahead. What should we tell him? It wasn't his investigation. But he'd cast his eyes over the scene and already drawn his own conclusions. And Wheels was the kind of guy to set his quickly drawn conclusions in concrete.

Luckily Wozza spoke. 'Boss, we wanted to play by the rules since it was our senior officer. Just being cautious.'

I jumped in. 'Major Collision were in town; we thought we might as well get them to take a look.'

'Yeah,' Wozza said. 'Dot i's and cross t's and all that.'

'You've both wasted valuable resources.' He set his mouth in a grim line. 'Storm in a teacup if you ask me.'

I took a deep breath. 'The Major Collision investigation is already in motion, sir. There's nothing we can do about it now.'

Wheels gave us his trademark smirk. The Smirk of Superiority, Wozza called it.

'I disagree,' he said. 'You can call the lead investigator and tell him there's nothing to investigate.'

I pictured Amanda lying badly injured in hospital and tried to slow my breathing. Wheels was the master at making people feel on the back foot. It usually took all my strength not to rise to the bait. Sometimes I failed. Today, I decided to employ a strategy where, instead of arguing our side, I would get Wheels to argue his. 'On what do you base that, sir?'

I'd kept my voice calm and it did what I thought it would.

Wheels turned on the angry-man faucet. 'I've been a police officer for thirty-seven years, Pollard. You think I can't tell a crime scene from an accident scene?'

The anger and the raised voice were both designed to get me to apologise and bend to his will. Wasn't going to happen. I repeated my question in the same even tone. 'On what *evidence* do you base your conclusions, sir?'

He stood up and banged the desk. Wozza and I both flinched but I held my nerve. There are times when you can walk away but there are other times when you just can't. This was one of them.

I stood too. 'Banging your desk, no matter how dramatic, is not evidence. It's just a temper, which, in your position, you need to manage a lot better.' I cast an eye down to his hands, clenching into fists. 'If you have actual evidence or a cohesive argument as to why we should call off the Major Collision investigators, please come to our office and let us know.' I turned quickly, my heart beating way faster than it should. Then I walked out.

Wozza was hot on my heels. 'Pollard,' he said as soon as we had put some distance between ourselves and Wheels's office, 'you're either super smart or the biggest dumbarse in the world. But either way, you're a legend.'

'Thanks . . . I think.' I continued walking to our office as my heartbeat returned to normal.

It took a cup of tea and a piece of banana cake before both Wozza and I were ready to get back on the job. I tried Lesley Gillis's number again. Left another message when she didn't pick up.

Wozza was just about to say something when the city slickers invaded the office. Riggs came in noisily, in the middle of telling Kasparas a story about some case he'd solved. 'And the way I figured it out was . . .' He stopped when he saw we were there. 'I see your old boss is back,' he said.

'You certainly are a master of observation,' said Wozza.

'I worked with him in Melbourne a couple of years back when he got seconded there on promotion. Good bloke.' Riggs sat down at the desk he'd claimed and leaned back on the office chair, making himself comfortable.

Wozza spoke to Kasparas, who'd remained quiet. 'You ever met Wheels before?'

He shook his head. 'No, but I sensed tension when he addressed the room before. He's not well liked?'

'You're a good judge of rooms,' said Wozza.

Kasparas looked pleased. 'What have you got for us today?'

By now Wozza was expert in dispatching the city slickers. In minutes, he had them packed off with a list of things that still needed to be done. Things that Wozza didn't like doing.

An email pinged on my computer. The mortuary had sent through a set of Josh McCreedy's fingerprints to our Fingerprint Branch. We'd sent Josh's phone straight into town for examination in the hope that whoever had met him at the silos had left prints behind on it too. According to the report, our experts had found only Josh's fingerprints on the phone and a few smudges that weren't clear enough to be analysed. Another dead end.

After touching base with Maddy, Wozza and I agreed to meet her at a gathering of volunteers who had come from all over the state to join the search. We needed to connect with her every day, to interact with her and her family. It wasn't just to show a police presence, it was to show human decency, to let them know we cared. Since Tammy Millhouse's article had come out and gathered support, the tone of some of the reporting seemed to have changed.

'The default setting of public discourse seems to be negative until someone points it out, then everyone scrambles to self-correct,' I said to Wozza as he turned the car into the driveway of the local school oval where people were gathering.

''Cept for those radio muppets.'

I guessed he was talking about Drew Nayle. He and his ilk would never change. Our only hope was that the voice of their opposition rose up and grew stronger than them.

'Speak of the devil!' Wozza exclaimed, pointing to the throng of media at the edge of the gathering.

'Dang it,' I said, immediately spying Lincoln Steele, the reporter from hell.

Crossing the oval, Wozza and I skirted around the members of the press to Maddy and her parents, who were talking to a tall, dark-haired woman.

'Any news?' Maddy said as soon as she spotted me.

I shook my head and watched her hope deflate. 'But this is a great turnout.' I gestured at the growing crowd of volunteers.

'Deb organised it.' Maddy introduced the tall woman next to her as Deb Jackson, principal of St Mary's Primary. 'She's my boss,' said Maddy with a weak smile. 'And she's been awesome.'

'Team effort,' said Deb, stepping forward to shake my hand. 'If there's one thing a primary school is good at it is mobilising the masses. You should see our cake drives.'

'Did someone say cake?' Wozza looked around.

I ignored him and asked Deb what the plan was. She explained that they'd organised some more search locations with the SES and our Search and Rescue teams, and the CWA were making sure all the searchers had water, sunscreen and a map. 'And,' she added, looking at Wozza, 'there is plenty of cake.'

While Wozza followed Deb in the direction of the CWA food table, I took the chance to catch up with Maddy and her parents.

'How are you all holding up?' I could feel my phone vibrate in my pocket, but I ignored it.

Paul Muir put a protective arm around his daughter, who seemed to sink into him. 'We're holding up.' He paused for the longest moment. 'But we are missing that little guy.'

Maddy let out a sob. 'My arms feel so empty.'

Despite the crowds and the media, it all boiled down to the little baby with the curl of blond hair and the aching empty arms he left in his wake.

I put a hand on Maddy's shoulder. She was almost at breaking point and I could see that her parents were too. We looked out over the throngs of people. Josh could have left the baby with any one of them.

There was a flash of a camera with the accompanying automatic whirl and clack like the press use. Then Lincoln Steele stepped right up to us.

'Very cosy,' he said.

Paul Muir spluttered. 'What are you talking about?'

Lincoln Steele was holding a recorder up in our direction and I tried to signal for Paul to stop talking. The photographer behind Lincoln held his camera still and I guessed he'd switched to video mode, which meant whatever he filmed had a good chance of ending up on the evening news.

I braced myself, wondering what Lincoln's angle would be today, knowing that it was his job to provoke us. I turned to Paul and moved him a couple of steps away, so both of us had our backs to the camera. 'It's really important not to let him rattle you. They're filming and he'll try to get a rise out of you, then plaster you all over the news. As difficult as it is, try to stay calm.'

Paul's anger turned quickly to gratitude. 'Thanks, Antigone,' he said in a low voice, and both of us turned back to face Lincoln Steele.

'The baby went missing Monday morning and here we are, Thursday morning, with no sign of it.'

Steele hadn't asked a question so I didn't answer him.

Paul whispered in Maddy's ear and she didn't fight back against Steele, even though she'd flinched when he referred to her baby as 'it'.

Steele paused arrogantly, then faltered when no one was provoked by what he'd said.

'Did you have a question, Mr Steele?' I asked evenly.

'Any updates on the missing baby? Why haven't you found it?' His tone lacked the strength it'd had a moment ago.

I gestured out to the crowds of police, SES and locals. The camera guy followed, sweeping the camera along the horizon of colour as people fanned out in the search. 'As you can see, we have everyone joining in to help with the search for baby Ethan Muir,' I said. 'The local police, with reinforcements from Melbourne, are exploring all avenues in the investigation. It has been a tireless effort.' I stopped.

Maddy took a step forward. 'And we are very grateful.'

Lincoln Steele gave a gruff thank you and then stalked off.

'Bet that won't make the evening news,' said Wozza, who'd wandered back from the cake table holding half a big slice of Victoria sponge on a plate.

When I checked my messages, I saw that Lesley Gillis had finally called back. She said she had her hands full helping Josh's parents with the funeral arrangements and would try to come in to the police station soon.

We were just about to leave when a yell sounded from some bushes that two searchers had just disappeared into. Wozza and I hurried over. A hundred metres into the bush, we came to a clearing.

'What is it?' said Maddy, who was right behind us. She sounded panicked.

I searched the faces of the two SES volunteers who'd clearly called the alert. They were not looking horrified so I deduced with relief that it wasn't Ethan they'd found. I hurried over and saw six empty bottles of Great Northern beer lying scattered on the ground near a fallen log that was worn smooth enough to have been used as a seat. This was where Josh McCreedy must have come to drink his beer and take his pills. I took in the bush setting. It was a beautiful spot, with remnants of a campfire near the log.

'What did they find?' Maddy sounded relieved because she couldn't see anything connected to Ethan.

I pointed to the beer bottles. 'They're the same brand that Josh bought at the drive-through. We'll test them for his prints, and if they're his, we can assume he came here to consume them.'

Maddy looked around the area. 'This looks like where he and Pete used to come to smoke dope,' she said. 'He always talked about a spot next to the oval.'

A careful search of the area revealed the discarded pill packet with six empty blisters of pregabalin. They were the three-hundred-milligram tablets. The fatal dose.

CHAPTER 19

THE BIRTHDAY PARTY

Mum and Nan hadn't been to Azzurro's before. It was a new business in town that had quickly become a favourite of mine. Their ham and pineapple pizza with lashings of cheese was a melt-in-your-mouth experience of rich Italian flavours.

To add an extra layer of excitement to our night out, I told Mum and Nan that I'd got a notification that my DNA kit had arrived and was 'in process', which I hoped meant we'd get a result soon. Nan looked pleased. Mum looked nervous.

When we arrived at the restaurant Andy was already seated with Russell and Crystal at a table for eight. I wondered who else they had roped in to help him celebrate. Like him, I was light on friends, but at least I had Mum and Nan. Andy stood up to greet them and I made the introductions.

Nan leaned over and extracted a gift from the pouch of her walker. It had a red ribbon wrapped around it. 'I made you an apple cake for your birthday,' she said, handing Andy one of her beautifully illustrated vintage cake tins.

'And I got you this.' Mum put a bottle-shaped gift on the table. 'A little birdie at the Royal told me it was your favourite.'

Andy blushed with pleasure. 'This is so thoughtful,' he said. 'I can't remember when I've felt so spoilt on my birthday.'

'Who else is coming?' I nudged Crystal and nodded towards the two empty seats.

'Here they are!' Crystal was looking at the front door, clapping her hands together gleefully.

Norma and Dawn from the pharmacy. Of course. Crystal had done a good job of making Andy's birthday table seem full.

'So how old are you, Andy?' Crystal was looking quite dressed up, with her multicoloured hair in some kind of up-do and her make-up more painstakingly applied than usual.

'Crystal!' Russell interrupted. 'It's rude to ask people their age.'

'Why?' Crystal was an out and proud fifteen-year-old.

'I'm eighty-three,' said Nan. 'Pleased to meet you.'

Crystal laughed, and I could tell her and Nan were going to be friends.

The rest of us settled at the table. Norma sat on Nan's other side. The two were old friends. Dawn sat opposite me and smiled shyly.

'How's your visit to Deception Bay going?' I asked Andy.

'It's going well. For the next month, I am a man of complete leisure. I'll read a few books. Take walks along the coast, and head back to that wonderful cafe that serves the awesome coffee.'

'And pastries,' I said, thinking of Wozza's addiction.

Andy patted his stomach. 'Already found those.' He had warm eyes and an easy smile, and he seemed genuinely interested in all of us. He positioned his presents in a neat pile. 'I feel overwhelmed,' he said, emotion cracking his voice. 'I was an only child and parties weren't really a thing at my house.'

Mum leaned over and patted Andy's hand. 'You're making up for it tonight,' she said.

'What do you do, Jilly?' said Andy after the dinner orders were taken.

'Jilly's a renowned doctor.' Nan answered before Mum could get a word in edgewise.

Mum laughed. 'Not sure about the *renowned* bit.'

'Always top of her class, even at secondary school.' Nan turned towards Crystal. 'It's never too early to put in your best effort.'

Crystal groaned. 'But . . . maths.' She made a noise like she was being strangled, which got an indulgent laugh from all the adults at the table.

'What about you, Andy?' asked Nan.

'I'm about as far away from medicine as you can get,' Andy said with a grin. 'My dad's a doctor, though, so our family's filled its quota of medical experts. I do safety audits for women fleeing violent relationships.'

I looked at him with fresh interest. Our professional paths may well cross if he decided to move back to Deception Bay. I had a bunch of questions I wanted to ask, but given the festive nature of the evening, I parked them for another time. I turned to Dawn instead.

'How's your summer been? You're on a break from uni?'

She nodded and blushed. Her awkwardness made me want to try extra hard to put her at ease. She seemed like a really nice young woman, especially after we'd seen her giving those icy poles to the hot kids outside the pharmacy.

'I've got two years to go.' She looked down at her hands.

'Are you enjoying studying to be a pharmacist?'

She met my gaze. 'It's really interesting. I mean, you'd think it wouldn't be, but it is.' Her words came out in a rush.

Nan gave Dawn a warm smile. 'What's the most interesting subject?' she asked.

Dawn brightened. 'Toxicology by far. We've learned so many fascinating things. Just before the break, we looked at the toxicology of mushrooms.'

The topic led to some robust discussion on several recent cases involving mushroom poisonings. As everyone flung theories around the table, a mantra repeated in my head: *What can you prove? What can you prove?* Because a theory was only half the battle.

'How's your brother?' I asked Dawn when everyone had exhausted themselves with talk of mushrooms. Last year, we had crossed paths with Dawn's teenage brother when we had caught him graffitiing a local solicitor's office.

'He's doing really well. He's been coming into the shop a bit.' She grinned at Crystal. 'I think he's got a crush on someone.'

Crystal shrieked in horrified delight. 'No way!'

Dawn laughed and raised an eyebrow. 'I can tell him to stop coming if you don't like it.'

Crystal backpedalled like a champion. 'He can come in if he wants. It's a free country.' She blushed and turned back to continue her conversation with Nan about learning to sew so she could make her own clothes.

'So you still live at home?' I asked Dawn.

'Yeah. Our mum has MS and finds it a little hard to get around. Mum got pregnant really young and my dad didn't stick around. Then she met another no-hoper who also didn't stick around when Xavier was born. So, it's just the three of us.'

'You take care of your mum?'

Dawn smiled. 'She's not quite at that stage yet. Good days and not so good days but she's fairly independent. It's unpredictable. That's why I'm taking double the subjects during the semester at uni, so I can finish my course early and be home with them both. Xavier fills in the gaps when I'm away. We don't mind because Mum is awesome and she's always been there for us, no matter what.'

I looked across at my own mother, who was laughing at something Andy had said. Anyone lucky enough to win the cosmic lottery and end up with a good mother was very lucky indeed.

Before I could slide back into question mode, which is a detective's default setting, Dawn got in first.

'Do you feel settled in Deception Bay yet? What's it been? Six months?'

'Feels like so much longer,' I said, more to myself than to her. So much had happened in those months since I had fled from the city and come to this seemingly idyllic seaside town.

Dawn nodded. 'Well, you've had a lot on your plate, haven't you?'

I took a sip of Coke Zero. 'It's been a challenge workwise, but I love the slower pace. In the city, everything felt rushed all the time. Here, it's busy, but we take the time to sit and have a cuppa, or go to Angie's Cafe for a pastry.' I stopped talking. I didn't usually share stuff like this. Dawn gave me a look of encouragement, though, so I kept going. 'And I reckon this is what life should be like.'

'Me too,' she said quietly.

'Like when you gave those kids icy poles. That really made their day. You'll forever be the lady from the chemist who noticed them enough to bring them an icy pole.'

'The unnoticed always notice,' she said.

'What do you mean?'

'I don't take up a lot of space in the world,' she said. 'I just get on with my business and, I guess, no one really notices me.'

I was about to interrupt, to assure her that people did notice her, but she continued.

'It's not a bad thing,' she said. 'When people aren't looking at you, you can look at them.'

'You'd make a good detective if the pharmacy thing doesn't work out.' I laughed.

Dawn blushed and shook her head. 'I'm just observant, that's all. It's a useful skill for a pharmacist too. People come in all the time with aches and pains and want our advice. Sometimes, they tell us things they'd never tell anyone else. It's an honour really.'

Our conversation was interrupted by the arrival of plates of pasta and pizza. Nan was trying gnocchi for the first time and looked impressed, especially after the young Italian waiter grated parmesan over her meal then went to work with an oversized pepper grinder.

Just as we were eating, another group arrived. The woman at the front of the dozen or so people held a big cake box.

'Hey, Angie!' Crystal cried.

Angie came over to our table. 'Hello, everyone! What are you all celebrating?' Her smile was wide and she looked different without her usual black apron and white T-shirt.

'It's Andy's birthday,' said Crystal.

'Oh! It's my birthday too,' said Angie.

Our guest of honour stood up and shook her hand. 'Andy Gilbert,' he said, 'your birthday twin.'

She took his hand and winked at him. 'I won't ask your age. Gets to a point where it just seems a little mean.'

'Too right,' said Andy, raising his beer in her direction. 'Happy birthday!'

And then Angie was gone to a chorus of popping champagne corks and laughter.

As I watched her go, three men sitting on the other side of the restaurant caught my eye. It was Riggs and Kasparas having dinner with another guy who I couldn't quite see because their table was half hidden behind a corner. I felt a slight pang of guilt. Wozza and I hadn't taken them out for dinner yet. It hadn't been the week for it, but I'd also had no desire to spend a minute more in Riggs's company than I absolutely had to. Kasparas was okay. He couldn't help who his partner was. But they were a package.

Dawn interrupted my thoughts, leaning in to speak in a low voice. 'Did he say his name is Andy *Gilbert*?'

'Yes,' I said, 'do you know him?'

Dawn shook her head. 'No. He said earlier that he left town ages ago, before I was born.' Dawn began eating her pizza and she was soon making the same noises of appreciation that Nan was making over her gnocchi.

At the end of the dinner, Andy rose and made an impromptu speech. 'I am so grateful to you all for coming tonight,' he said.

'I'll drink to that!' said Russell, taking a sip of beer.

Everyone laughed.

Andy waited for the noise to die down and continued. 'This is my first birthday without my mum. Every birthday, she would drive all the way to Melbourne and take me out for dinner. She'd order my favourite cake and she would always get me a thoughtful gift. When she died a couple of months back, I thought all my future birthdays would be bleak. But you all'—he raised a glass to the table, then pointed to his present pile—'and these gifts . . . it's like Mum is still here.'

I saw Nan pull a tissue from her sleeve and dab at her cheeks.

Andy's eyes glistened as he sat back down.

'Is this your first time back here since she died?' Mum said to Andy in a quiet voice when the conversations around the table started up again.

'Yes,' he said. 'The funeral was in Melbourne, where Mum's family come from. I'm housesitting while Dad's overseas. I'm going through my mum's things. So much to sort, so many memories.'

'I'm sorry for your loss,' Mum said, taking his hand just like a mother would.

THE DREW NAYLE SHOW, THREE TRIPLE P

Friday, 17 January

Drew Nayle: *Welcome to our Friday-morning program. We are going to start the show on a sombre note. Today marks the fourth day since Baby Ethan Muir went missing from the home of his single mother, and the fourth day that the family of his poor father, Josh McCreedy, have had to mourn the loss of their beloved son.*

Josh McCreedy has become a martyr for the cause of fathers everywhere who are fighting for the right to have their children in their lives. But I think it goes deeper than that, listeners. I think we now live in a culture where young women throw men away for almost no reason. I've been watching some feminist videos online, listeners, and I tell you, it's bloody disturbing. Some woman without a lick of make-up is telling ladies to leave at the first sign of—and I'm going to read you a list because this shows how horrific this is—she says leave the first time they: lash out at you, lie, they're evasive, they make a racist, homophobic or misogynistic comment, they behave badly and blame you or somebody else for why they had to behave that way.

Now, listeners, I gotta say that a lot of Boomer marriages wouldn't have lasted five minutes with that list. Where's the forgiveness? Where's the understanding? I tell you, men are under attack.

We've got our reporter Lincoln Steele on the line with an update from Deception Bay. Good morning, Lincoln. What is the latest?

Lincoln Steele: *Good morning, Drew. It's an absolutely heart-breaking scene in Deception Bay for some. We've been talking to friends of Josh McCreedy and, I gotta tell you, they're angry.*

Drew Nayle: *Not surprising, Lincoln. A young man, a young dad, cut down in his prime.*

Lincoln Steele: *It's certainly a town of grief here in Deception Bay. We've been told there will be a memorial service for Josh McCreedy next Monday.*

Drew Nayle: *I have no doubt the church will be packed. I heard he was a church-going man.*

Lincoln Steele: *That's correct, Drew. In fact one of the last people he reached out to was a respected member of the local church, Lesley Gillis.*

Drew Nayle: *Now I heard that the message he left for Lesley Gillis was to ask for help with baby things.*

Lincoln Steele: *It was his last message, Drew. The last message left by a father who just wanted to be with his son.*

Drew Nayle: *What have the police got to say about the investigation? They seem to have gone quiet on the subject. Are they doing anything?*

Lincoln Steele: *After the atrocious rudeness on Tuesday by Senior Constable Antigone Pollard when we asked her a question, the media have been left hanging. And you'll never guess what the hard-working Senior Constable was doing last night, Drew.*

Drew Nayle: *What?*

Lincoln Steele: *She was at the local pizza parlour for a birthday dinner. Not a care in the world. Having a lovely time.*

Drew Nayle: *When there's a baby missing! I'm speechless.*

Lincoln Steele: *Saw her there with my own eyes, Drew.*

Drew Nayle: *Have no fear, listeners, we'll be putting in a call to the police minister about this. The people of Victoria deserve better.*

Lincoln Steele: *Good on you, Drew! You're the most popular radio host in Melbourne. If anyone can get something done, it's you.*

Drew Nayle: *It's our reason for being here, Lincoln. Keep us updated, mate. Anita, love, get the minister on the line.*

CHAPTER 20

THE PRESSER

Sometimes fury pulsates with tentacles that reach out and spread through spaces. That's what it felt like when I parked my car at the police station early Friday morning. I'd driven past a couple of journalists waiting outside in the same position they'd been in the morning after Ethan was taken. The feeling in the station was sparking as I entered, and it took all of my will not to reach for my gun.

What the hell is going on?

There was ranting coming from the muster room. It had to be Wheels. No one else carried on like he did. I pushed open the door leading into the room and it was like opening the door to a raging fire. Randall was leaning up against a cupboard, trying to make himself smaller. Jane's face was ashen. Even Stu looked nervous.

Wheels rounded on me. 'Ah, here she is,' he spat. 'The queen of the radio!'

'What?' I made sure my voice was loud enough to sound annoyed rather than intimidated because Wheels was like a rabid animal when he smelled fear.

'Oh, she hasn't heard it!' He whirled around and addressed everyone else. 'Hasn't heard how she is dragging down the reputation of everyone here.' Then he turned back to me, his face in a sneer. 'Enjoy your pizza last night?'

His rage emboldened me. I took a deep breath. Someone had to stop him. 'What the hell are you talking about?' My voice was loud enough to compete against his. I saw him jolt a little. He was always surprised when anyone pushed back against him. 'And why are you scaring the locals?' I looked around at Jane and Randall and Stu, then took a step towards him. I was pleased to see him take a step back.

'The radio this morning,' he snarled. Even though he lowered his volume, his voice was still oozing aggression.

I held up a hand in a stop gesture. 'I'm not going to engage in any kind of conversation with you until you're able to manage your emotions. When you've calmed yourself down, feel free to come by for a chat.' And with that, I walked out of thc room and headed to my office.

Wozza looked up as I entered. 'He seems to have stopped yelling,' he said.

I sat down at my desk. 'Do you know what he was talking about? Something about the radio and me eating pizza?'

'Drew Nayle and that dodgy reporter Lincoln Steele mentioned you on their program this morning.'

'Don't tell me you listen to Drew Nayle!' In no universe could I imagine Wozza listening to the claptrap that man sprouted.

'Nah, mate, not me.' Wozza cut a bit of banana cake and handed it to me as a peace offering. 'Wheels had the radio on in the muster room earlier. Apparently, he's a big fan of Nayle's.'

Now, that I could believe. 'Do I even want to know what he said?' Suddenly, I felt tired. This week had been exhausting and frustrating. We were no closer to finding the baby than we had been on Monday, and not only that, now we had a raving lunatic for a boss. Four days had changed everything.

There was a knock at our door and Jane poked her head around. 'Turn on your TV,' she said urgently. 'Wheels just went outside to do a press conference.' She shut the door behind her as if she needed to take respite in the safety of our office. Wozza cut her a piece of banana cake and handed her a plate. He pressed the remote on the TV in our office, then flicked through some channels until he came to one with the news playing. Sure enough, a minute later, the anchor announced a live cross to the Deception Bay police station for an update on the baby-kidnapping case. And there was Wheels. Just ten minutes ago he'd been acting like a child having a tantrum and now his face was set and his tone was even. His public persona was full of professional concern.

'He gives me the creeps.' Jane turned to me and grinned. 'Love how you stand up to him though. Makes him turn a funny shade of purple.'

'Good life lesson, Jane,' I said. 'When your self-worth is based on dominating others, the moment they stand up to you, you're toast.'

'He's talking!' Wozza scrambled to increase the volume with the remote.

'Senior Sergeant, can you give us an update on the missing baby, Ethan Muir?' a journalist in the front of the pack asked.

We watched the screen as Wheels puffed out his chest and answered. 'We have had teams searching all of the locations the baby's father posted photos from on social media. We have checked out all available CCTV and followed up every lead. I can't say too much because, as I'm sure you'll appreciate, it's an ongoing investigation.'

'Sir, how do you respond to the allegations this morning that one of your lead detectives was out socialising last night? The public are outraged.' It was Lincoln Steele, looking slick and polished for his appearance on camera.

Wozza spluttered over his banana cake. 'Bloody hell! He's the one who was on the radio trash-talking you! Are we allowed to shoot him?' He put his hand on his sidearm.

'No!' Jane and I both said in unison.

I looked at him sternly. 'Woz, I've talked to you before about people you're allowed to shoot and people you aren't. He's not one of them . . . even if he does deserve it.'

Jane laughed. It broke the tension as we tuned back in to hear Wheels's response.

'The member in question has been reprimanded,' Wheels said smugly.

'No shooting!' I reminded Wozza.

'But there's been no progress?' said Lincoln Steele, determined to lay the boot in again. 'Have you considered a door-to-door search? If someone has the baby, that would be one way of finding it.'

'How do you get a search warrant for every house in town?' spluttered Jane.

But Wheels was happy to sail right in. 'We've certainly been considering that possibility,' he said. 'I mean, what law-abiding citizen would refuse to let police search their house? We are talking about a baby here.'

'We have *not* been considering that possibility.' Wozza was furious. 'Geez, the last thing we need is an outraged local population thinking we'll be going through their cupboards.'

On the TV screen, Lincoln Steele looked smug. I guess he had his headline.

THREE TRIPLE P ONLINE

Senior Police Promise Door-to-door Search in Baby Kidnapping

Lincoln Steele reporting from Deception Bay, Victoria

Friday, 17 January, 10.30 am

Senior Sergeant Bill Wheeler, the officer in charge of the Deception Bay police, today promised a door-to-door search as the hunt for missing seven-month-old Ethan Muir reaches its fifth day. Senior Sergeant Wheeler claimed that people would understand there was a missing baby at stake and throw their doors open to the police.

In a case that has captivated people around the state, local police are facing mounting criticism for their handling of the investigation into the disappearance of baby Ethan.

The case began on Monday, when Ethan's mother, Maddy Muir, reported him missing from her home in the sleepy seaside town of Deception Bay. It has been alleged that the baby was taken by his father, Josh McCreedy, who subsequently died in a car accident. Despite an extensive search effort and widespread media coverage, there has been little progress in locating the baby, leading to growing frustration among local residents.

This reporter saw Senior Constable Antigone Pollard, the lead investigator, out eating pizza at a party last night.

'It's outrageous!' said one local. 'Just look at her and there's a baby missing and all.'

Senior Sergeant Wheeler said the officer in question had been chastised over the inappropriate behaviour.

As the search for baby Ethan continues and the pressure on the police intensifies, the community remains hopeful that the dedicated efforts of local SES personnel and the public will lead to the safe return of the missing infant.

CHAPTER 21

THE TRACKER

Wozza called it PizzaGate all morning, until I told him to stop. Offering a moment of respite, my friend Pip—the Chief Commissioner of Police—called to tell me she was on her way to Deception Bay for a private visit with Amanda. Pip had been my mentor when I first joined Victoria Police in Melbourne, before she was promoted. She wanted a quick meeting with me away from the station to discuss what I had found at the scene of Amanda's car wreck. Pip didn't want to alert the media to her presence. She hated using injured cops as photo ops.

'Let's meet at that wonderful cafe in town,' she said. 'I'll be incognito.'

'It's called Angie's Cafe,' I said, smiling at the thought of the Chief Commissioner in disguise. She used to do it all the time when we'd go out in the city. People rarely recognised her away from her public persona—always in uniform, hair tied in a bun and no make-up. In her downtime, she looked very different.

'I'm going to pop around to Angie's,' I said to Wozza. 'Won't be long.' I didn't tell him who I was meeting. I didn't want to advertise Pip's presence to Kasparas and Riggs, who were also in the office.

'Bring me back a pastry,' Wozza said as I grabbed the car keys and headed out the door.

■●■

Pip was already seated with a cappuccino and a vanilla slice when I arrived. On my side of the table was a latte with chocolate on top and a lamington.

'I ordered for you,' she said, taking a sip of her coffee.

'Thanks!' I took a load off and sat opposite her.

'Saw Wheels's press conference this morning,' she said. Her face was grim. 'What was he thinking? Searching all the houses in town. Bloody idiot.'

I shrugged and spooned some chocolate foam off my latte. 'Afterwards, our phones rang hot with locals complaining.'

'So how did you spin it to the townsfolk?' Pip took a bite of her slice and savoured it. 'Best vanilla slice I've ever tasted.'

'That's because you're in the country. It adds flavour,' I said. 'As for the spin, we told the locals that Wheels meant a door-knock, not a search. Now we have to organise a bigger one of those than what we've already done. On the bright side, old Mrs Wilkinson rang to see what time we'd be coming so she could have some fresh scones ready for us.'

'Swings and roundabouts,' said Pip. 'And how long will the media be reporting on you eating pizza?' There was a trace of amusement in her voice. She knew as well as anyone what the media did in a beat-up.

'Wozza reckons the story will explode even more when they find out I like pineapple on my pizza.'

'A sensible choice,' said Pip.

Our conversation segued to the kidnapping case and I gave Pip the short version. Baby still missing. Mother distraught. Searches finding nothing, and the only glimmer of hope was a tin of formula that had gone missing from the chemist.

Pip nodded. 'Now, I want to hear all about Amanda's wreck.' Her tone was grave. An attack on one of us was an attack on all of us.

This time I gave the long version.

'The Major Collision blokes took casts of some tyre marks that weren't Amanda's, so that may or may not lead anywhere. They also found some shoe impressions which they photographed. They reckon it looks like someone walked over to Amanda's car and back.'

'None of your lot?' Pip said.

'No. The shoe impressions originated from where Amanda's car swerved. I kept everyone away from there. Got Jane and Randall to set up cones.'

Pip's brow furrowed. 'Who would lure her out to your farm?'

I shook my head. 'I don't know . . .'

She gave a small smile. 'I thought you'd locked up most of your enemies. Did you make new ones?'

Before I could answer, a hand touched my shoulder and made me jump. I turned to see Marina Christopoulos, one of the women from the self-defence class I teach.

'Hey, Antigone!' she said cheerfully.

'Oh hey, Marina.' I scanned her for injuries, but I couldn't see any. Last year when she had started classes with me, Wozza and I intervened after her husband Dimitri had assaulted her and she had laid him flat with a well-practised knee to the groin. She had been voted class champion. There had been cake. I gestured at Pip. 'This is a friend of mine from Melbourne, Pip.'

'Nice to meet you, Pip,' said Marina, showing no signs of recognition. Not surprising, I thought. Today, Pip was in a flowing floral dress with her hair out and sunglasses perched on the top of her head. She'd placed her sunhat on the table and the whole look was more relaxed middle-aged woman on a summer break than Chief Commissioner of Police.

Pip smiled at Marina, then glanced at me. I could tell she was hoping that Marina wouldn't join us; our conversation was not one to be shared.

'Oh bloody hell!' spluttered Marina, looking in the direction of the cafe entrance. 'Everywhere I go, he's there!' Her voice had grown fearful.

I followed her glance and saw Dimitri coming through the door. The last time I'd seen him was after Marina had kneed him in the groin when he'd assaulted her. He'd been lying on the kitchen floor clutching his private parts. He looked taller this time.

Marina scooted around the table and sat down next to me. She put a hand on my arm and I could feel her shaking. 'I thought when I told him to leave that would be the end of it.' Her voice was low.

Dimitri headed straight for our table. He was glaring at Marina and didn't seem to register Pip's or my presence. Pip raised her eyebrows at me.

Marina held up her hands in a placating way. 'Please, Dimitri, leave me alone. Our marriage is over.'

His eyes narrowed. 'It's over when I say it's over.' He banged his fist on the table, rattling our coffee cups.

That was all Pip needed. She stood up. 'I'm afraid you're going to have to leave,' she said in a voice that normally invited no criticism.

But Dimitri was full of rage and entitlement. 'Shut up, bitch,' he snarled.

'I'm so sorry,' Marina whispered to Pip.

It was my turn to stand up. I reached for my badge and held it in front of him. He went to slap my hand away, but I used the momentum of his arm swing to grab his wrist and twist it in such a way that his whole body had to follow. As he swung around, I wrenched his arm up his back until he cried out in pain. I pulled a pair of handcuffs out of the case on my belt and snapped one on the wrist I held, then grabbed the other wrist and completed the set.

'Oh god, oh god!' Marina was crying now.

Pip moved in and put an arm around her. 'It's okay. Antigone has him.'

Marina leaned into Pip.

Dimitri let out a growl, which I ignored. 'Do you have a restraining order against him? An AVO?' I asked.

'Yes,' said Marina. 'But he's always where I am.' She stared at him contemptuously, something she could only afford to do now that he was restrained. 'He says it's just an accident; he blames living in a small town.'

'Might be good to check her car for a tracking device,' I murmured to Pip.

She nodded. She would look after Marina while I took Dimitri down to the station to charge him with breaching the AVO.

■●■

The anger of Dimitri Christopoulos filled the interview room with huffs and muttered curses and body language a puffer fish might envy. The posturing didn't work on me though. I turned on the recording equipment and read him his rights. Even though he had the option to remain silent, it quickly became obvious that Dimitri was not going to use it.

'I have every right to be in Angie's Cafe!' he roared before we'd even started the interview.

'We'll get to that in a moment,' I said calmly. 'I've checked our records and Marina has an AVO out on you. Do you understand what that means?'

I could almost feel Dimitri's blood pressure rising from across the table.

'I did everything for that bitch and this is how she repays me!' He thumped the table.

The posturing was all part of it and I refused to give it oxygen. 'Why do you think she took out an Apprehended Violence Order against you?'

'To ruin my good name!' Dimitri spluttered.

'A court wouldn't grant an AVO to ruin your good name,' I said. 'The judge granted it because you're violent.'

Dimitri went to stand and I put up a hand and told him to stay seated.

'I've never laid a hand on her.'

I shook my head. 'Sorry, that won't cut it. Remember last year when my partner and I arrived at your house just after you punched Marina in the face?'

Dimitri settled back into his chair; he looked sullen and didn't respond.

I prodded. 'Remember when we got there, you were lying on the floor because Marina fought back and kicked you in the privates?'

Silence. Glaring.

'And remember she had to call an ambulance because you were sure that she had . . .' I paused for effect and said, 'broken your balls.'

If looks could kill, I'd be dead. Turned out, Dimitri did not enjoy being the target.

'I need you to understand the consequences of breaking an AVO. Judges do not look kindly on men who don't respect the court's orders.'

'You can't prove I didn't run into her by accident.' His tone was defiant.

My phone buzzed with a message from Pip. *Tracking device found in Marina's car.*

I looked up at Dimitri. 'That was a message from a police colleague. Seems a tracking device has been found in Marina's car.'

Dimitri's smug certainty wavered a little. 'You can't prove I put it there.'

'See, that's where you're mistaken,' I said, reaching for the evidence bag with Dimitri's phone, wallet and watch in it. 'If you've checked Marina's whereabouts on your phone, then we will find the app you used. All the data will be right here. And of course, there's fingerprints. If you didn't wear gloves when you put it in her car, then your prints will be on it.' I placed the bag down in front of me. 'So if you put it there, we'll find the evidence.'

Dimitri's eyes flicked between me and the bag. 'I will never give you the passcode to my phone,' he growled.

'Does Marina know it?' I said.

He paled. Most people don't bother to change their passcodes unless they have to. It was probably his birthday or 1234.

He filled with anger again, which I guessed was his default response to any kind of challenge.

'I gave that woman everything! She owes me.'

'Exactly what does she *owe* you?' I said. I was so tired of this line. 'Tell me so I understand.'

'Everything we own, I paid for!' He was about to bang his fist on the table again but caught my eye and changed his mind. He clenched his hands together, white-knuckled.

'And what was Marina doing while you were paying for everything?'

'Her job! She cooked and cleaned and raised our two daughters.'

'Her job?'

'Yes! Her bloody job!'

'So, how much did you pay her for doing her bloody job?' I asked, keeping my voice even.

He looked confused. 'I paid for everything.'

'Yes, but if you got paid for the work you did, then why didn't you pay her for the work she did? I mean, if that's your logic. Or did you expect her to work for free?'

It looked like his mind was racing for an answer that would enable him to reassert his authority. He came up blank.

I continued. 'She provides free labour to you seven days a week and, while she's trying to look after you, you feel entitled to use violence on her, and then she leaves. So what is it you think she owes you?'

'I'm her husband.'

'Not anymore.'

'But I gave her everything.' Dimitri's voice was quieter now.

'But you didn't give her everything. You put a roof over her head so she could do everything for you, but you hit her. You wanted to keep her scared so you had control over her. And now that's she left you, you won't let her go. And you think you can come into Angie's Cafe when Marina is sitting at my table and threaten her, as well as me and my friend? Well, you picked on the wrong women.'

Dimitri's eyes glinted, calculating. 'Who would believe you women over me?' he said, patting a palm on his chest.

'Oh, Dimitri,' I said, shaking my head. 'The other woman at the table was the Chief Commissioner of Police. So, who would people believe? Not you.'

I stood and left the room.

CHAPTER 22

THE CHIEF COMMISSIONER

I was just finishing the paperwork for Dimitri's arrest when Riggs and Kasparas returned to the office. Kasparas held up a bag with a tracking device, looking at it with wonder.

'We just attended a job in the main street. Check out what we just took out of a car,' said Kasparas. 'Looks like stalking to me. It was connected to the car's on-board diagnostics port. One of the women at the scene told me that's the port that mechanics use. If a tracker is connected to the OBD port, then it runs off the car battery and will continue to run until it's removed. And look.' He flipped the clear plastic evidence bag over and pointed to something on the back of the small device. 'It's got an ID number here so you can trace it back to the buyer.'

Riggs didn't look as enthusiastic. 'Wife reckons her ex put it there, but I wouldn't put it past her and her mate to cause a little havoc for the poor bloke.'

'Her and her mate?' I said, wondering what the hell this idiot might have said to Marina and the Chief Commissioner.

'Yeah. She had a mate with her who knew way too much about tracking devices, if you know what I mean.' He touched the side of his nose.

Kasparas had started googling the device.

'Wow,' he said, swinging his laptop around. 'Look at this. Those women were right.' He read some more. 'And we can track it on his phone . . . unless he deletes the app.'

'He didn't delete the app,' I said, picking up my own evidence bag.

'Legend!' Kasparas came over to my desk. 'Can I have a look?'

I pulled on a pair of gloves and took the phone out of the bag. 'I messaged Marina. Passcode is his date of birth.' I tapped the buttons and the screen came to life. 'Here's the app.'

I scrolled through maps showing the movement of Marina's car and a list of alerts that showed when the car moved. 'Proves those women were right,' Kasparas said to Riggs. 'The ex-husband *was* tracking her.'

Riggs huffed out a breath.

Kasparas continued with a slight shake to his voice. 'So considering they were right, the way you spoke to them was'—he searched for the words—'kind of rude.'

Riggs rolled his eyes. 'All I said was if they know so much about trackers, how do we know they didn't put it there? Blame it on the ex, bit of revenge? Looks good in court too. It's our job as detectives to ask these questions. Anyhow, what does it matter?'

I smiled. 'You really have no idea who the woman with Marina was, do you?'

'Just some old chick,' said Riggs.

'Who's an old chick?' The voice came from the doorway.

Riggs looked uncomfortable as Pip came into our office. She was still wearing the hat and glasses.

I did the introductions. 'Senior Constable Riggs, I don't believe you've formally met the Chief Commissioner.'

Pip took off the hat and glasses and Riggs's smug look faded. The colour drained from his face.

'Ah, Senior Constable,' said Pip, reaching out to shake his hand. 'I'm so glad I caught you. I have some feedback on the way you handled the situation with Marina. Do take a seat.'

Kasparas and I scrambled out of the office to leave Riggs to his fate. We bumped into Wozza in the muster room and told him not to go back into our office for the time being. Wozza chuckled when we explained why.

'Just desserts is a dish best served cold,' he said.

'You're getting your desserts mixed up,' I said. 'I think you mean revenge.'

'Whatevs.'

Kasparas weighed in. 'The deserts in *just deserts* aren't actually desserts like pavlova. The word is a derivative of *deserve*.'

'Righto, Einstein,' said Wozza. 'What's next on the agenda?'

Kasparas did not register Wozza's sarcasm and continued undaunted. 'I had an idea about Wheels's door-knock for baby Ethan. In Melbourne, we had one of the psychs prepare a questionnaire for a door-knock we did. Helped hone the responses. In this one, we could ask if people have heard a baby crying in the houses on either side of them when they know a baby doesn't live there. That way, we're not just trying to gauge whether the house we're checking has a baby in it, we're trying to gauge if they've noticed anything unusual in the neighbourhood. Another question could be whether they've noticed anyone buying baby things if they don't have a baby.'

'Great idea,' I said. 'Any chance you could ring that psych and get them to suggest the best questions for our uniforms to ask?'

Kasparas looked pleased and pulled out his phone. 'On it.' He moved towards a desk, taking a notebook out of his pocket.

'He really is Einstein,' muttered Wozza.

Jane came up with a Post-it note in her hand. 'Mrs Gillis called in when you were in the interview room,' she said, then blushed. 'I mean *Lesley* Gillis. She was my English teacher in Year Twelve. It's almost impossible to call a teacher by her first name.'

'What did she say?' I said.

'She said she knew you were looking for her and she stopped by on the chance you were here. And that she'll try again next time she's passing.'

■●■

Half an hour later, Kasparas had a list of questions for the door-knock that Wozza and I judged to be really good. Wozza had laid out the local map on the muster room table and had started allocating street grids to our uniforms, and teams who'd been sent in from neighbouring towns. Randall handed out clipboards and pens and Kasparas gave each team a bunch of photocopied questionnaires.

Wozza smothered himself in sunscreen and swiped white zinc across his nose. When Jane and Randall looked at him funny, he said huffily, 'I burn.'

In town, Kasparas and I walked together because our allocated streets joined at an intersection.

'So how long have you and Riggs been partners?' I asked.

Kasparas let out a low moan. 'Three long months.'

'How'd you get stuck with him?'

'Just lucky, I guess.' He didn't sound lucky.

I turned to face him and he stopped walking. 'I really like the way you called him out on how he treated Marina today. You have no idea how vulnerable she is and how much she has put up with. So, thank you.'

'I used to work in a family violence unit.' The pain in his eyes clearly echoed his memories of that time.

I patted his arm. He didn't need to say any more. I could imagine the things he had seen.

He pulled himself together. 'So, we take stalking very seriously where I come from.'

'What puzzles me,' I said, continuing walking, 'is why Riggs doesn't.'

'Look, Antigone, I've got a confession to make. When you were at the pizza restaurant, we were there too . . .'

I remembered I'd seen them there. 'You were sitting with . . .' And I suddenly realised.

'We were sitting with that reporter Lincoln Steele.'

'But why?' I couldn't fathom a connection.

Kasparas looked miserable. 'We went in there to get dinner. When Lincoln came in they were full so Riggs offered him a seat at our table.'

'But you knew who he was?'

'Of course! I tried to object but Riggs had already offered, and Steele had accepted. Over dinner, he was trying to pump us for information.'

I pictured Riggs holding court.

'I couldn't believe he made a story out of you having dinner there. You were there for less time than we were and he didn't mention us at all.'

I looked him in the eye. 'You didn't do anything wrong.' I meant it. Riggs, on the other hand, was a bloody menace.

■•■

What followed was an exhausting four hours of knocking on doors, asking about the baby, then answering the many questions about where the baby was, and have we found any clues, and can we make their parking ticket go away. My feet were aching by the time I got back to the car in the centre of town. A couple of uniforms finished at the same time as me. One had been lucky enough to hit Mrs Wilkinson's street and carried a bag of fresh scones that she'd insisted were to be taken back to the police station. I gave them a ride. The uniforms hadn't had any more luck than I had. Lots of concerned citizens, most were as helpful as they could be, but still no sign of baby Ethan. Someone near the Holy Trinity church had heard a baby crying two nights ago, but they figured it was a family stopping by on one of the many vigils that had taken place in the lead-up to Josh McCreedy's funeral. I made a mental note to drive by there on the way home.

It wasn't until the end of the day that I realised I hadn't seen Senior Constable Riggs since his visit with Pip. I checked the staff car park. His car was gone.

I called Pip, curious to find out how she'd gone with Riggs and about her visit to the hospital to see Amanda.

'We need to talk,' she said as soon as she answered.

It was getting late so I offered her an overnight stay at the farm instead of the drive back to Melbourne in the dark. 'Mum and Nan are there,' I said to sweeten the deal.

There was a pause and I imagined Pip reorganising her schedule in her head. 'Done!' she said. 'I could use a break after the day I've had. I hope we're going to eat at your place, though, because neither of us will survive a second pizza scandal.'

'Mum's cooking a roast.'

'I'm on my way.'

■●■

By the time I arrived at the farm gates, Pip was pulling up behind me. I drove forward and let her through then shut the gates again.

'Where's the beast?' Pip said out of her window.

'Waffles will be sitting in the kitchen waiting for scraps, I imagine.'

She followed me up the winding drive and parked behind me. 'Lucky I always carry an overnight bag in my car.' She hoisted it out and followed me up the steps to the porch.

'How did you go with Riggs today?'

Pip laughed. 'The boy got quite a shock, didn't he?'

'Yeah,' I said. 'Looked like he was going to pass out.'

'Well, it's nothing a long sensitivity training course won't fix.'

Waffles was on the other side of the door when I opened it. I was pleased when he sat politely to greet Pip. 'Good boy,' I said. 'She would have been your boss if you didn't fail your Dog Squad test.'

Pip patted Waffles. 'Living on a farm is not a bad consolation prize for him.'

The smell of a lamb roast drew us down the passageway to the back room. Nan was sitting in her favourite chair. Pip leaned over to give her a hug then repeated the gesture with Mum, careful to avoid the carving knife Mum held.

'Pip! So wonderful you could join us,' said Mum. 'Can I get you a wine?'

Pip extracted a four-pack of soft-drink cans from her carry-all and put the pack into the fridge for later. 'Better not. No telling what might happen in this crazy one-horse town.'

'As a matter of fact,' said Nan primly, 'I heard we have two horses now.'

Pip laughed and plonked herself down on the couch. 'I stand corrected.'

'How's Amanda?' I asked.

Pip's brow furrowed. 'She was more coherent than when you saw her. But she said something quite worrying.'

I sensed Mum and Nan listening; glanced at them then at Pip to make sure what she was about to say could be shared with my family.

Pip got my message. 'This is to go no further than this room.'

Mum and Nan nodded.

'Amanda said she remembered seeing a car pulled over and a man stepping out onto the road right in front of her. It was when she swerved to avoid him that she hit the tree. Before she passed out, she saw him come over to her car then leave again. She assumed he left to get help but . . .'

We all knew that hadn't happened. I shivered as I remembered feeling the cold bonnet that morning.

'The Major Collision guys found footprints. Did she recognise him?' I said.

Pip's mouth was set in a grim line. 'That's the problem. She thinks it might have been Wheels.'

'What?' I spluttered. 'But why would . . .' I didn't finish because I knew exactly why he would. 'He's back at the station. Reckons Force Command tapped him on the shoulder to come back. I did wonder about that.'

'More likely one of his buddies gave him the nod,' said Pip. 'He's been around long enough to have a coterie.'

Nan shook her head in disbelief. 'So you mean he forced Amanda off the road so he could get his job back? That sounds quite unhinged if you ask me.'

'We've all seen him fly off the handle. It's not so hard to believe.' I scratched Waffles's soft velvet ears and he leaned into me and let out a few contented little grunts.

'Men like him can find it hard to let go of a police career,' said Pip. 'I've seen it so many times. Their whole identity is being a copper. They don't know who they are when they're not in the job and they won't do the work it takes to find out.'

I could understand what she meant, and when I thought about it, I realised that I might be like that too. Being a cop was such a big part of who I was. But then I stopped myself. I was also a daughter and a friend and someone who cared about the community. Still . . .

'Dinner's ready,' said Mum brightly, perhaps hoping to change the tone of the gathering.

I made a concerted effort to change the subject for Mum and Nan's sake. Mum soon had us laughing at stories of the mischief she used to get up to on the farm, while Nan smiled in a way that made me suspect Mum hadn't gotten away with most of the things she thought she had.

We talked long into the evening, which grew cool enough for a log fire, then we all watched, mesmerised, as the embers burned down to glowing orbs like dragon eyes that were watching us watching them.

THREE TRIPLE P ONLINE

Family Braces for Funeral

Lincoln Steele reporting from Deception Bay, Victoria

Saturday, 18 January, 8 am

As searchers continue combing the countryside around the picturesque coastal town of Deception Bay, police have failed to find any trace of missing seven-month-old baby, Ethan Muir. The unsuccessful searches are a slap in the face to the McCreedy family as they prepare to bury their second son in as many years.

Josh McCreedy's brother Peter died last year after suffering an anaphylactic shock on a camping trip.

A funeral service will be held for Josh McCreedy at Holy Trinity Church on Monday morning and organisers expect a packed church service to honour the devoted father.

'We would have held the service sooner,' Keith McCreedy told the media, 'but the bloody coroner took this long to release Josh's body. As if this wasn't hard enough already. We didn't even want an autopsy.'

Baby Ethan is still missing and Josh McCreedy's family want answers.

Police refused to comment on the ongoing investigation. The closest the public came to answers was Senior Sergeant Bill Wheeler from the Deception Bay police promising door-to-door searches of homes around town. This began yesterday while the ground searches for the missing baby are being scaled down.

It is not known if the mother of the missing baby will attend the funeral service. The feeling around town is that she would not be welcome.

CHAPTER 23

DANIEL AND THE LION'S DEN

After talking deep into the night with Pip, I woke up early on Saturday morning and took Waffles for an extra-long run. All the way, my mind was racing with ideas about the next steps in the hunt for baby Ethan. I swept my eyes across the paddocks and gullies on my run, wondering if he lay out of reach somewhere out there. I tried not to think about the possibility he might never be found. All week, I had let Waffles off the lead and sent him to sweep the areas we ran through. I'd even varied our route so he could search other roads. But he'd found nothing. When we got home, Pip, Nan and Mum were sitting around the kitchen table in their dressing-gowns. Waffles and I burst through the door, panting with exertion, and I stopped at the sight: my favourite people all in the one space.

Mum pushed her chair back. 'You take a shower and I'll get breakfast started. We waited for you.'

Waffles, sensing there would be breakfast for him too, hurried over and sat by Mum.

In the shower, alone with my thoughts, a blinding realisation popped into my head. *Daniel!* He was visiting today. In all the drama of the week, I'd forgotten. I whipped some shampoo into my hair, followed by conditioner, then rinsed and stepped out of the shower. My phone was on the bathroom counter and I checked my messages. There was one from Daniel, sent about two hours earlier. He was on his way from Melbourne.

Ten minutes later, as I was sitting down at the table to a generous plate of bacon and eggs, I let everyone in on the news. 'Daniel's on his way to visit,' I said, conscious of a girlish smile on my lips that was highly embarrassing.

Pip laughed. 'How is our favourite detective inspector?'

Nan answered before I could. 'We're not sure he *is* still our favourite, are we, Antigone?'

'Correct,' I said. 'We have no idea.'

'Poor thing,' said Nan, reaching over to pat my hand. 'I'm thankful that desire dims with old age and common sense returns.'

We all laughed, and I offered to do the dishes while the others got dressed. Not sure Daniel could have handled seeing the Chief Commissioner in the fluffy dressing-gown from our guest bedroom.

The doorbell rang as we were taking our second cup of tea of the morning out on the side verandah near the kitchen. Waffles barked and scuttled back inside and ran down the corridor. I followed him, my heart beating faster, cursing the fact that it did.

Daniel's outline was visible through the stained-glass side panel on the door. Why did the thought of seeing him almost bring tears to my eyes? I needed to control my emotions. Deep breath. I opened the door, pretending that the man on the other side hadn't tilted my world out of alignment.

'Morning,' he said in his deep voice, a smile playing on his lips.

'Morning,' I said, stepping back so he could come inside.

Daniel hesitated, looking down at the space I'd created for him to enter. Waffles was blocking it.

'Is your pooch going to let me in?'

'Waffles is definitely undecided,' I said, before putting my hand on his collar and nudging him out of the way. 'Oh, and I have visitors.' I moved down the hallway and Daniel followed. By the time we got to the kitchen, Mum, Pip and Nan had all come inside and formed a wall of women to greet Daniel. I could have sworn he shrunk a little.

'Daniel,' said Pip, holding out a hand, 'fancy seeing you in this neck of the woods.'

'Chief.' Daniel nodded and shook her hand. 'Jilly, Annie, good to see you both again.' If he was surprised at my entourage, he didn't show it, but then again, he had the cop poker face that most of us perfect.

Nan manoeuvred her walker to the table and pulled out a chair. She patted the back of it. 'Sit,' she said to Daniel.

I put the kettle on while Daniel found himself seated at a table full of women.

'So, Daniel,' said Pip, 'what brings you to town?'

Daniel glanced over at me. I tried to keep a straight face. *You're on your own, buddy.*

He cleared his throat. 'I had hoped to talk to Antigone.' The poker face had gone and he looked uncomfortable.

'What about?' said Nan sweetly.

Daniel turned in my direction, and although he was answering Nan's question, he was speaking straight to me. 'I wanted to see if there was a chance of repairing our relationship. You see, I can't stop thinking about Antigone.' He broke eye contact and turned back to Nan. 'And I sense it's the same for her.'

My heart was in my throat. I did not like being so vulnerable where a man was concerned. My whole life was about closing the gaps of vulnerability. The martial arts classes I'd taken since I was a child, my cop's badge, my gun, even Waffles. Daniel was the chink in my suit of armour and I didn't like it.

'Sounds like an important conversation,' said Mum. 'Last night Antigone was telling us that she wanted to check in with the searchers on the foreshore this morning. You should go with her.'

I put a cup of tea in front of Daniel and joined him at the table.

'Before you two head off,' Pip said, putting down her newspaper, 'we need to talk about Wheels.' She filled Daniel in on Amanda's suspicion that it had been Wheels who'd stepped in front of her car, causing her to swerve off the road, then failed to call for assistance.

'What's the next move?' Daniel looked like he had his own thoughts about the answer.

'Whatever we do, it's a shitshow for Victoria Police,' said Pip. 'One senior sergeant runs another senior sergeant off the road.'

'He nearly killed her,' said Mum in a soft voice. 'If Antigone hadn't found her when she did . . .'

We all took a moment to consider this.

I broke the silence. 'What he did was awful, but we need corroborating evidence. Amanda suffered a blow to the head in the collision, so a good lawyer would make mincemeat out of her testimony. And Wheels told Wozza and me that he went out to inspect the scene, which means any evidence on his shoes or his car can be explained away. The only hope is the Major Collision Squad's evidence.'

'The Major Collision Squad that he wanted you to call off?' said Daniel.

'Makes sense now,' I said, marvelling at Wheels's audacity.

'What about phone data?' said Pip. 'Could it place him at the scene of the accident?'

'We can try, but if he set Amanda up with that level of cunning, it's my bet he would have left his phone at home.'

Daniel took a thoughtful sip of tea. 'Can we get him to admit it?'

'Yes!' said Nan. 'On the crime shows, they always secretly record the confession.'

We all looked at Nan.

'Or that CCTV that you see on television,' Nan continued, buoyed by our interest. There was not an episode of *Midsomer Murders* she hadn't watched.

I was about to tell Nan there were no CCTV cameras on the dirt road near our farm where Amanda had collided with the tree, but stopped myself. We had an approximate time for Amanda's collision based on the timing of the text she'd received. If Wheels had travelled out that way by car, he could have been caught on CCTV en route. We had just spent a week chasing down CCTV to trace Josh McCreedy's movements and I was now a veritable expert on the placement of every camera in Deception Bay. I knew Wheels lived in a little street off the town centre because he hosted a station barbecue there not long after I moved to town. I could think of at least four cameras that would have captured his car on the way to my farm—if it was him. I said as much, and Pip reached for her phone.

'We need to keep this off-grid,' she said. 'I don't want Wheels getting wind we suspect him of anything. I'll brief Professional Standards and get our traffic team in town to check cameras and see if we can pick up his car making that trip late Monday night.'

'Sounds like a plan,' I said, getting up from the table and giving Daniel a meaningful look. We needed to get moving.

'I still think you should record him,' said Nan, 'like on TV.'

■●■

Half an hour later, Daniel and I were climbing down the steps from the cliffs of the Devil's Corner and stepping onto the sheltered beach below. It was the most glorious of summer mornings in Deception Bay.

'You've chosen a beautiful part of the world to run to,' said Daniel, gazing out over the sparkling water.

The sound of the waves crashing and rolling to the shore drowned out the noise of the beachgoers as we wandered towards the SES tent at the north end of the beach. Seagulls circled in the air and cried *arrkk*, looking for generous patrons to feed them, or at least little kids with a careless grip on their mid-morning snacks.

In the shade of the SES tent, two volunteers, Kerrie and Margaret, were bent over a map. They'd been in the SES for as long as I could remember and I knew they'd have the latest updates.

'Hi, Antigone,' said Kerrie, looking up and shading her eyes against the glare of the day.

'Hey, Kerrie, how's it going?' I looked out at the line of people in orange jumpsuits, combing the dunes.

Kerrie shook her head. 'Nothing yet . . .' she paused, 'which is a good thing I suppose.'

I agreed. This beautiful cove of beach was the last place we would want to find any traces of little Ethan Muir because if Josh McCreedy had left him here alone, he wouldn't have survived.

'Who's your friend?' Margaret asked, looking at Daniel.

'Where are my manners?' I smiled. 'This is Daniel. He's an inspector from the city come to check out the search.' Not technically true, but the truth was a much longer story.

Margaret looked him up and down, and said dryly, 'Well, we won't hold that against you.'

Daniel laughed. 'Appreciate it.' He looked around the beach. 'How long will it take to finish here?'

'Nearly done,' said Kerrie, her hand resting on the map. 'We've also got a team at the state forest behind Maddy's house, and yesterday we finished the fields behind the silos where he took those photos.'

Kerrie had avoided saying Josh McCreedy's name and I didn't blame her.

Daniel nodded.

'We're running out of places to look,' said Margaret. 'The whole town's been out searching.'

'It's pretty bleak when you think that the only hope for the bub is that someone took him,' said Kerrie. 'But there it is. I hope someone took him.'

'Me too,' said Margaret.

Both women knew from experience what the elements did to the vulnerable.

We left them to their maps and moved on up the beach, trying to avoid kids throwing beachballs, and the odd stray frisbee. As we walked side by side in an easy rhythm across the sand, I wondered what Daniel would say. Was I ready to reconnect? Thoughts tumbled through my mind like waves. If he wanted to get back together, would he expect me to move back to Melbourne? Did I want to leave Deception Bay? Waffles was happy on the farm. I loved being near Nan. Wozza. Crystal. All my new friends.

'Antigone—'

We had ended up at the water's edge, both staring out at the sea.

'I can't move back,' I blurted.

'Wait, what?'

I turned to him, standing closer than I should. 'I'm just pre-empting what you're about to say.' Then I felt a little silly since he hadn't said anything.

Daniel put his hands on my shoulders and I felt his warmth. He looked deep into my eyes. 'Let's take this back to basics and talk logistics later. Okay?'

I nodded.

'Ever since you've been gone, I've missed you. I've missed *us*.' The pain of missing was echoed in his eyes. 'I miss waking up next to you. I miss our morning coffees at our favourite cafe. I miss talking cases with you. I miss disagreeing over books. I miss binge-watching crime shows with you. And I miss . . .' his voice trailed off as he moved his hands from my shoulders to cup my face.

I shivered. I knew exactly what he was missing because I missed it too. He leaned in and kissed me. Holy moly. It started out gentle and tentative and then grew more urgent. I could feel all of our history firing in the space between us. It would be so easy to fall back into what we had.

Then the kiss ended, as all kisses must.

The waves rolled in, petering out just shy of my shoes. White froth and bubbles dissolved like promises into the sand.

'You feel it too, don't you?' Daniel's voice was quiet as he turned back to the sea.

'Yes. I—'

A yell of 'Hold the line!' came from one of the SES searchers. The line of people in orange uniforms stopped. It looked like they'd found something.

I tore my thinking away from Daniel and we both hurried back towards the tent. On the short journey across the sand, I hoped against hope that they hadn't found a body.

'What is it?' I said to Kerrie when we got close enough to the tent.

'Glad you're here,' she said, breaking away from a couple of her SES colleagues. 'They radioed through that they found a baby's dummy. Might not be related, but you never know. They say it looks new.'

'Did anyone touch it?' My voice sounded more urgent than I intended.

'Of course not.' Kerrie looked a little insulted.

'I didn't mean—' I stumbled.

'We know you didn't, love,' said Margaret. 'Come on. It's over this way.' She walked towards the line of SES searchers across the dunes at the bottom of the cliff stairway.

The dunes were covered in grass and then bushes and then, closer to the cliff face, trees. We followed her up a steady incline to a spot several metres from the stairs. The line of searchers parted to let us through.

Daniel stood by my side as I stared down at the little dummy. It was one of those novelty ones, shaped like a cartoon lion.

'That's a Simba dummy,' Kerrie said. 'My granddaughter has one. They sell them at the supermarket.'

Daniel shaded his eyes against the sun and looked over at the staircase. 'Someone could have thrown it from the stairs.' He looked up further. 'Or tossed it over the cliff.'

I followed his gaze while I took my phone out of my pocket. I was no expert on dummies but this looked like the one in the photos I had of Ethan. A couple of taps on the screen and I was looking at the pictures Maddy had sent me of the baby on the day he went missing. In one, he was smiling for the camera, and in another, his mouth was hidden behind a big orange dummy. Same as the one lying at my feet.

'Did he have it in the photos the father posted?' Daniel was now in cop mode.

I swiped to them. Picture one, on the front seat of Josh McCreedy's car, Ethan had the orange dummy in his mouth. Picture two, at the Devil's Corner cliff tops above us, Josh was holding Ethan and he was crying. No dummy. Picture three, roadhouse, dummy. Picture four, silos, dummy.

Kerrie was leaning in to look at the photos. She pointed to Josh's hand when I flicked back to the Devil's Corner photo. 'He's holding the dummy there.'

I made the photo bigger and, sure enough, in the hand that held the baby, there was a flash of orange between his knuckles.

'When they start wailing, the dummy falls out,' said Margaret. 'Easier to hold it than to keep brushing sand off it whenever it hits the ground.'

Daniel and I glanced at each other. We were both oblivious to the mechanics of dummy maintenance.

'If this does belong to Ethan, then someone has come back to the cliff and . . .' I looked around, scanning the area.

'Thrown it down here?' finished Daniel. 'But why?'

'They'd know we'd find it,' said Kerrie. 'Everyone in town knows how thorough the SES is.'

She had a point. The SES volunteers knew Deception Bay like the backs of their hands. And we all knew it. So was this a sign that the baby was still alive? Was the person who had the baby trying to send a message? If this dummy did belong to Ethan, then the person must have come back later and thrown it over the cliff.

I photographed the dummy and bagged and tagged it, then climbed the steep staircase back up the cliffs with Daniel at my heels. We were back in the car and on the move before he broached the conversation we'd started by the waves.

'I don't want you to make any decisions yet,' he said, his voice tentative. 'Just don't close the door on this.'

Not trusting myself to speak, I simply nodded.

CHAPTER 24

THE BABY AISLE

After logging the dummy into evidence at the station, I asked Daniel if he'd like to come with me to the supermarket, to see if it stocked the Simba dummy. It was possible the one at the bottom of the cliff didn't belong to Ethan. I wanted to see how commonly available they were. For all I knew the local landscape could be full of lost Simba dummies.

'Happy to help out while I'm here,' Daniel said, 'unless you think it will put your partner's nose out of joint.'

I laughed. 'Normally it would, but not on a Saturday. He has a bunch of wild little daughters at home and I'm sure he will be grateful not to be called in. Especially when we don't even know if the dummy is related to our case.'

It felt weird to be out and about on policing business with Daniel. It required switching from personal to professional, like changing stations on a radio. I sensed he was enjoying it too, not just because he was with me, but because he was back on the street. With every promotion up the chain came a greater distance from coalface policing.

The store manager, Rory, was at the front service counter and greeted me like a long-lost friend.

'Antigone! Hi! Any news?' His volume attracted attention, which I immediately tried to dampen.

Daniel and I moved up to the counter so we were close to him. 'Nothing yet,' I said in a low voice. 'We just have a couple of questions.'

'Of course.' Rory motioned for us to follow him through the supermarket until we came to a door at the back marked 'Staff Only'. The boppy music faded as we stopped at another door marked 'Manager'. We went in and Rory gestured to a couple of chairs. 'What can I do for you?' he said as we sat.

I pulled out my phone and opened the picture of the Simba dummy I'd taken at the beach. 'I need to see if you stock these dummies.'

Rory looked concerned. I could see why. There was something sinister about a dummy lying discarded on the ground when there was a baby missing. He nodded. 'We stock it.' He clicked on a keyboard at his desk, which was connected to a large upright screen. Frowned in concentration. Clicked some more. 'Sales average is eighteen per week. Popular item.' He looked at me sadly. 'Look, it's none of my business, but I saw the pictures Josh McCreedy posted on Instagram. The baby has that dummy . . .'

I felt a sudden affection for Rory. We were all just townsfolk worrying about a lost baby and hoping he would be found. I nodded but didn't say anything.

'And I heard that one of our employees actually met with Josh and the baby that day!' Rory sounded scandalised that any part of this could land on his doorstep.

'Who?' I asked, puzzled.

'Christos Gillis.'

My brain scrambled to remember Christos's story. He'd told us he was working on Monday. He didn't say anything about meeting Josh that day. 'Christos met Josh?'

Rory nodded. 'Someone else from the deli saw them together. I thought you knew.'

'No, we didn't know.' My mind raced. Why hadn't Christos told us he saw Josh on the day he took the baby? I remembered the similarities I'd noticed between Christos and the picture of the man Josh met near the fish and chip shop. We'd shown him that photo and he'd said nothing. *What the hell!* 'Did he see Josh on his lunchbreak?'

'Lunchbreak?' Rory looked puzzled. 'He doesn't have a lunchbreak on Monday. He only works a morning shift.'

What the actual hell! 'Are you able to confirm that on the roster?' I nodded towards his screen, trying to keep my voice calm.

Rory tapped a few keys. 'Yep, there it is. Christos worked a six am till midday in the deli.'

Daniel and I left as soon as we could, walking out via the baby aisle and spotting a neat row of Simba dummies. On impulse, I took one and paid for it on the way out. I didn't say it out loud but I bought it as an act of faith. I was hoping I could give it to Maddy when we found Ethan, just in case his was the one at the bottom of the cliff.

As soon as we were clear of the supermarket, I felt enraged. Christos had lied to us! What was he hiding? We hurried back to the police car and, en route, I explained to Daniel how we'd asked Christos what his movements had been between ten and two thirty on Monday and how he'd said he'd been at work.

'Did you ask what time he left work?' Daniel asked.

I flicked though my notes. 'Not specifically.' I described our visit to Christos in his neat home with Anzac biscuits and scented candles. 'He seemed like a nice young man. Especially after the other two unwashed gamers we had just visited.'

'So he was the one in the CCTV image?'

I nodded. 'It does look a bit like him, but he didn't admit it when we showed it to him. What was he trying to hide?' Something else came to mind. 'He did say that if Josh was going to give the baby to one of his friends, it would have been him, but he was working that day.' I told Daniel about how we'd heard a wailing sound which Christos had told us was his cat in the laundry, and how there really *was* a cat in the laundry.

'How thorough was your search?'

I pictured myself disappearing up the corridor while Wozza distracted Christos, quickly opening doors and glancing into rooms, finding the cat, then coming back to Wozza. 'Not very,' I said.

■●■

I rang Wozza. It wasn't fair to keep this latest piece of information from him. He picked up on the second ring and sounded distracted. There were squeals and loud music in the background.

'Where are you?' I raised my voice a little.

'At the arcade.' His voice was raised too. 'I promised to bring the kids here today. I'm already regretting it.'

'Wozza, I—'

'Hold on. I'll find somewhere quieter.' I could hear the sound of footfalls, fading music and the heavy breathing of exertion. 'That's better,' he said. 'What's up?'

I gave him the short version of what Rory had told us about Christos Gillis leaving work at lunchtime and my suspicion that it was him in the CCTV footage.

'Bloody hell,' said Wozza. 'We need to get over to his place to check him out again. But I've got the kids . . .'

I could almost hear the mental calculations Wozza was making about how quickly he could offload his offspring.

'Is Jess . . . ?'

'She's away for the weekend with her girlfriends. For her mental health.'

'How about your parents?'

'Nah, their mental health is fine because they never answer my calls on the weekend. They think I only ring to offload my kids.'

'Very astute of them,' I said dryly. 'Look, if you can't get away, there's an inspector up from Melbourne . . . I could take him with me.'

'Wait, what?' Wozza's voice dripped with suspicion.

'He's the one who helped us last year.' I looked over at Daniel. 'He's up from the city to check out the investigation.' Small lie.

'He wasn't a bad bloke,' conceded Wozza begrudgingly.

'He's okay.'

Before Wozza could say anything else, I heard a scream in the background—'Dad! Lily fell over!'—and Wozza quickly excused himself and ended the call.

'Looks like it's you and me, kid,' Daniel said, aiming for Bogart and sounding nothing like him.

That's what I'm afraid of, I thought.

■●■

Pulling up outside the house where Christos and his mother Lesley lived, I paid more attention this time. Everything about the little weatherboard was neat. The lawns were freshly mowed; there was no sign of peeling paint or cobwebs around the ornate timber fretwork lining the porch. Some houses just felt loved and this was one of them.

Daniel said, 'Nice digs.' I could tell from the way he said it that he was looking through a cop's eyes. For us, *nice digs* spoke to something much deeper than real estate prices. It spoke of priorities and care, but it could also speak to a fastidious control that could be unyielding.

I rang the bell and listened for sounds of footsteps from inside the house. My heart beat a little quicker. If baby Ethan was here, then the odds were that he was being looked after. Christos seemed like a nice young man when we'd spoken to him. Even Wozza had been impressed. And his mother, Lesley, by all accounts, was a beloved pillar of the community.

There was no answer. There were a million places a young man and his mother could be on a Saturday. I just hoped one of them wasn't behind this door, hiding with a baby. Daniel knocked again, a little louder this time. Then a voice sounded from the other side of a hedge lining the driveway. 'Are you looking for Lesley and Christos?'

I followed the voice, which seemed to be walking down the driveway next door.

'Mrs Wilkinson!' I said when I saw her appear from behind the hedge. 'I didn't realise you were Lesley's next-door neighbour.'

'I've lived here for sixty-two years,' she said proudly.

'Thanks for the scones yesterday. They were a big hit at the station.'

She nodded, pleased.

'We were hoping to catch Christos. Have you seen him today?'

Mrs Wilkinson looked thoughtful. 'I don't think so. I saw Lesley head off earlier. She said she was on her way to church'—she lowered her voice—'to set up for that young man's funeral on Monday. Lesley is a very active member of Holy Trinity.'

Mrs Wilkinson looked sharp as a tack and I didn't want to set off her suspicions so I made my voice sound as casual as I could. 'We were here the other day talking to Christos. He was a friend of Josh's and he was helping us with ideas about where Josh could have left the baby.'

'Such a sad thing to have happened,' said Mrs Wilkinson in the murmur the elderly perfect to keep the flow of conversation going.

'Christos was great. We were hoping to pick his brains again but he doesn't seem to be home.'

'Like I said, I didn't see him leave, but you know what these young people are like.'

I nodded. 'And I was hoping to see their gorgeous cat again. I love cats.'

'It's a funny one, that one. Some nights it yowls so loud it sounds like a baby crying.'

'Look at the time,' I said, glancing at my watch. 'We've really got to run. Thanks again for the scones you gave the door-knockers.'

As soon as we were safely back in the car, I turned to Daniel. 'At the door-knock, someone reported hearing a baby crying in the vicinity of Holy Trinity the other night. And now Mrs Wilkinson is telling us that it sounds like there's a baby crying here.' I nodded towards the neat house and the retreating figure of Mrs Wilkinson.

'Take me to the church,' said Daniel as he strapped on his seatbelt.

■●■

The church was a red-brick affair with big stained-glass windows on either side of a central set of stairs leading up to the entrance. We climbed up and entered a foyer area with another set of doors into the main church. There were several women in the foyer setting up a photo display board with pictures of Josh McCreedy. Several more were arranging a memorial signing book and funeral booklets, which featured a picture of Josh holding a much younger version of baby Ethan. I flinched at the sight. Bit tactless considering Ethan was missing because Josh took him.

One of the women recognised me and said hi. She seemed familiar and I guessed we'd met at the CWA or at one of the many town functions I'd attended.

After we exchanged greetings, I addressed my questions to her. 'Someone reported hearing a baby crying close to here a couple of nights back. We're following up every lead in the search for baby Ethan.' I nodded at the picture of Josh holding the baby.

'Oh goodness, yes,' she said.

'We are not sure if the crying baby was actually in the church or just nearby.'

The woman looked thoughtful. 'People come here with babies all the time. There could have been one crying here. Haven't seen anyone with a baby today though. Feel free to take a look around.'

'Is Lesley Gillis here?' I asked her.

'You just missed her,' she said. 'Is there anything we can do for you?'

'No, I just need to touch base with Lesley about something. Is she coming back?'

The woman shook her head. 'She started early today so she could finish early. I think she had something else on. I can't remember . . .' Her voice trailed off as she selected another photo of Josh McCreedy and stuck a small ball of Blu Tack on each corner of it.

'Her son Christos isn't here by any chance, is he?' I made my question sound like an afterthought.

'Nope. Haven't seen him for a while. Probably too upset

to help. He and Josh were best friends since they were tiny. Christos would've done anything for Josh.'

'Thanks,' I said cheerfully, and walked over to where Daniel was standing discreetly by the door. 'She's not here and neither is he,' I said in a low voice. 'And that woman just said Christos would do anything for Josh. Now I'm wondering if that could mean hiding his baby.'

Daniel and I returned to the police car. 'What's Lesley Gillis like?' he asked.

'She runs the charity stall here. Josh called her on the day he died, asking for baby clothes.' I explained to Daniel how we had tried a couple of times to speak to her since the baby went missing but hadn't been able to connect. 'Josh's message to Lesley made us wonder if he had planned to keep baby Ethan somehow.'

'Not such a good planner if he had to get formula from Nick at the fish and chip shop,' said Daniel. 'And from what you told me, his parents weren't expecting him to bring the baby home.'

'None of it is consistent,' I said. 'Asking for baby clothes, not having formula but having a bottle in his pocket, treating the baby tenderly in front of witnesses but posting taunting messages to Maddy as if he intended to hurt him, and not having him in a proper car seat.'

Daniel looked thoughtful. 'Even the most community-minded people can do strange things if they think they're helping someone. Could Josh have convinced Christos and his mum that the baby needed protecting from Maddy?'

I thought back to our interview with Christos. 'It's hard to imagine. If anything, Christos seemed to side with Maddy, not Josh.'

'But he did try to mislead you by not mentioning that he had lunch with Josh . . .'

I turned on the engine. Time to go back to the home of Lesley and Christos Gillis and see if the community-minded mother and son had turned into kidnappers.

■●■

Daniel knocked loudly on the door, and this time I heard footsteps inside the house. The door opened a crack and one side of Christos's face appeared.

'Yes?' he asked in a voice croaky enough to suggest he'd just woken up.

'Police,' said Daniel, using his best cop voice. 'May we come in?'

'What?' Christos rubbed his face and blinked against the glare. He looked hungover—or sleep deprived.

Stepping into his line of vision, I used a gentler voice, like cops did in Deception Bay. 'Hey, Christos, it's me, Detective Pollard. We spoke to you the other day about helping us find baby Ethan.'

That worked. Christos pulled open the door and stood aside to let us in. I gave Daniel a look that hopefully conveyed something about catching more flies with honey. He looked abashed and followed me through the door. Unlike the other day, this time the house was in darkness and smelled a little closed up. It was a very different vibe. Christos looked different too. On Wednesday, he'd been neatly dressed and clean. Now, he wore a robe that needed washing, over grey sweatpants and a stained T-shirt. He led us to the same place we'd sat on our last visit, but he stopped short at the state of the table. It was covered in baby clothes, great big piles of them.

He didn't say anything, but I did.

'Has anyone here had a baby since my last visit?'

Christos jolted forward and, with a sweep of his arm, he moved the piles to the other end of the table, then sent them over the edge into a laundry basket similar to those I'd seen in the church.

'It's just donation stuff Mum is sorting,' he said, gesturing for us to sit at the table.

No tea and Anzac biscuits this time, just a frazzled young man who looked like he had something to hide.

I let him sweat for a moment before beginning. 'When we first spoke to you, you told us that if Josh was going to give the baby to anyone, it would have been you.'

He nodded.

I continued. 'But you said he couldn't have given the baby to you because you were working.'

He nodded again, but now he looked miserable.

'What hours do you work on a Monday?'

His eyes widened. 'I-I'd have to check my roster,' he said, looking mighty uncomfortable.

'We already did.'

'All right!' he blurted. 'I ran into Josh on my lunchbreak. I guess in all the shock of losing him and then the baby going missing . . . I swear I only just said hi and that was it.'

'The CCTV footage shows you both speaking for over two minutes, then walking off together in the same direction.' I kept my voice even but relentless.

Christos squirmed in his chair. 'Sure, I mean, yeah, we spoke, like I asked how the baby was and about Maddy and all that.'

'And what did he say?' I said.

'Nothing really. He said the baby was fine . . .' Christos paused, embarrassed. 'And he said a couple of things about Maddy that weren't very nice, like he always did.'

'Did he ask you to take the baby?'

He shook his head.

'Did you eat lunch with him?' I asked. 'He'd just bought a boatload of burgers and chips.'

Christos started to hyperventilate. I stood up and went into the kitchen to fetch him a water. 'All right, I did eat lunch with him, but I didn't know that he'd taken the baby without Maddy's permission. I swear. Ethan fell asleep pretty much straight away. Josh said he'd just given him a bottle.'

'Why didn't you tell us all this from the get-go?' I said, stupefied at his revelation. 'When you don't tell us important information, it can make you look like you've got something to hide.'

Christos seemed miserable.

'Have you got anything to hide?' I asked.

He shook his head. 'I know what it looks like, right? I was the last person to speak to him and I didn't pick what he was about to do.'

'And how do you think it looks now that we've found out?'

'It makes me look guilty,' he muttered.

'You were Josh's best friend. You're the last person we know of to see him and the baby.' I let my eyes wander to the laundry basket. 'And now you've got a bunch of baby clothes and you look like something's been keeping you up late. And one of your neighbours thinks your cat sounds like a crying baby.

'Do you have baby Ethan here?'

He clapped his hands over his mouth, then gasped. 'It *was* a crying baby.' A look of realisation dawned on his face. 'We've had my sister's baby here, Mum and I, for the last two days. His name is Simon but we call him the Lord of Darkness. Four months old and screams blue murder all day and all night. I haven't slept since he got here. Mum's driving him back to Melbourne as we speak. I'm completely shattered.'

A sudden thought. 'We came round earlier. I know your mum was helping at the church this morning, setting up for the funeral, but were you and the baby home?'

He rubbed his forehead like he had a headache. 'Simon finally settled around six this morning. So yeah, I imagine we were both dead to the world.'

'Mind if I take a look around,' Daniel said, getting up from the table and giving Christos no real chance to object.

'So you've been babysitting?' I said, watching him closely.

He nodded, looking too tired to speak.

Moments later, Daniel returned with a large nappy bag. 'Looks like the Lord of Darkness left his stuff behind.'

Christos shrugged. 'Too late now. Mum's long gone.'

■●■

The first thing I did when I got into the police car was ring Norma. I was certain she'd know Lesley Gillis.

'Antigone,' Norma said when the call connected, 'what can I do for you? Has Wozza eaten all the banana cake?'

'Of course he has,' I said, trying to keep my voice calm. 'I just have a really quick question for you which I would appreciate discretion around.'

'Okay,' said Norma, sounding cautious. 'Anything I can do to help.'

'Does Lesley Gillis have a baby grandson? Simon?'

I heard a laugh echo through the phone. 'She calls him the Lord of Darkness. Right little blighter, that one. She called into the pharmacy with him in the pram yesterday. Dawn tried a game of peek-a-boo and he screamed the place down.'

My breathing calmed. 'So she's been minding him?'

'Much to her horror.'

I thanked Norma for her help and disconnected the call. 'The Lord of Darkness exists,' I told Daniel.

CHAPTER 25

SUNDAY, SUNDAY

On the promise of the best Sunday market in the world, Pip had extended her stay at the farm, which meant Daniel had retreated to a roadside motel on Saturday night. He checked out early to come to the farm and join the clan of women reading the Sunday papers and lounging around in dressing-gowns on what turned out to be a golden summer morning.

'It's so nice when someone cooks for you,' I said as Mum brought plates laden with bacon and eggs to the table.

'What's on the agenda for today, Antigone?' said Pip, who was equally enjoying Mum's cooking skills. 'Don't suppose you'll have time to come out to the market with us.' She patted Waffles on the head. He'd spent a lot of time sitting by her side. I think it was because she was slipping him bacon.

Daniel looked at me. 'Are you heading out to see Maddy and her family?' He knew we would be maintaining daily contact with them.

I looked at my watch. 'I'll see if they're home.' Picking up my phone, I sent Maddy a message and got an instant reply. A thumbs-up emoji next to a sad-face emoji. Home and sad. Maddy's new normal.

■●■

Pulling into Maddy's driveway with Daniel, I was pleased to see that the press were leaving her alone today. Maybe they were all in town having breakfast.

The door opened before we had a chance to ring the bell and Maddy greeted me like she always did. 'Any news?' A question laden with both hope and dread.

'We haven't found Ethan yet,' I said, although almost a week into the search, the 'yet' was getting stuck in my throat. 'But the SES searchers found a dummy on the beach yesterday.' I had collected the evidence bag from the station on the way to Maddy's and I pulled out the Simba dummy now to show her. 'We have to keep it bagged because it's evidence, but is there any way you can tell if it's Ethan's?' I passed the clear plastic bag to her as we sat down at her table and her dad made us a cuppa.

Maddy held the dummy close and squinted in concentration. 'It's Ethan's,' she said, pointing to a black dot on the handle. 'See this? One of the other babies in my mothers' group had the same dummy and I was worried they'd get mixed up at playdates, you know how babies are.'

I nodded, though I didn't.

'I marked Ethan's dummy with a permanent marker so we wouldn't get them confused. This is his. Where exactly did you find it?' She closed her hands like a prayer around the dummy in its plastic evidence bag.

'On the beach at the bottom of the Devil's Corner. We think someone threw it off the cliffs, near the staircase.'

Maddy looked puzzled. 'But the dummy was in all the photos. Why would someone throw it . . .' And then she stopped, no doubt because she was flooded with possible scenarios, not all of which ended well for Ethan.

'There was no sign of anything else,' I assured her. 'If someone went to the trouble to put it there, it might be to throw us off the trail.'

'But why?' Maddy's voice was close to breaking.

I gave her the only reason I could come up with. 'Because if you put something over there'—I held up one hand and gestured to the left—'then people won't look over here.' I held up the other hand and gestured to the right. 'If I'm right, it's a classic misdirection.'

Maddy's dad stood behind her, hand on her shoulder. 'When are they starting those house searches that cop on TV promised?'

Bloody Wheels, I thought. *He speaks and we clean up the mess.* 'Paul, they aren't actual searches of people's houses. That'd be illegal unless we had a search warrant for every house in Deception Bay. Senior Sergeant Wheeler was talking about door-to-door canvassing, which we've been doing since Ethan went missing and ramped up on Friday.'

Daniel cleared his throat; he looked uncomfortable. 'We apologise if Senior Sergeant Wheeler gave the wrong impression.'

Paul looked indignant. 'Well, I think it's a bloody good idea,' he said. 'Search everyone's houses until you find the baby.' Then indignation turned to hopelessness and his eyes welled with tears.

Maddy reached for a tissue. 'I don't know how much more of this I can take. I just want to go to the hospital and get a doctor to put me to sleep and then you can wake me when you find Ethan.'

Tilly Muir spoke for the first time since we'd arrived. 'The not knowing is killing us.' Her voice was small and had lost the forthright tone it'd had a couple of days ago.

It felt like the air was going out of the whole family.

Maddy seemed to have a sudden thought. 'What if the door-knockers knock on a door and hear Ethan crying but they don't know that the family shouldn't have a baby and they just ignore it?'

Things were getting out of hand. I needed to calm everyone down because panic would help no one. 'Maddy, we just have to have hope that Ethan is safe and that we will find him.' Even as I spoke, I knew my words were hollow. This little family were so tightly strung with grief, I worried they might snap.

■●■

We spent the best part of the afternoon with Maddy and her parents. It was good to see friends calling by and giving them moments of relief from the tension of their impossible situation. On the way back to get Daniel's car from the farm, we stopped off at the cliffs.

Parking at the top of the Devil's Corner with a view of the beach was like meditating. I'm not sure what it is about looking out over the sea that calms people, but it does. Add a sunset and I was in heaven. Add a Daniel and I was in agony.

Luckily the cliffs and the smell of the salty breeze and the dying summer's day made conversation optional. For a while at least.

'Have you thought about what you want to do?' Daniel said, breaking the silence.

'Do?' I looked at him.

He reached over and took my hand in his, our fingers intertwining, his warmth radiating into me. I shivered.

'I'm not going back,' I said finally.

'To the city? Or to me?' His voice was desolate.

Thoughts and memories tumbled through my mind. His love, his inflexibility, his laugh, his irritating habits, his company, his strength. It was such a coin toss, such a gamble—there were no guarantees. But maybe guarantees were overrated, or perhaps they didn't exist at all, even when we thought they did.

I turned to face the man who had occupied my mind and my life for so long. 'I'm not going back to the city . . . but I think you still hold a place in my heart.' There, I'd said it. I waited, not knowing how he'd react.

He leaned over and enveloped me in a hug. And soon we were clinging to each other like we were on a life raft. Perhaps we were.

'We will find a way to make it work,' he whispered.

I almost believed him.

CHAPTER 26

THE FUNERAL

Wozza was already at his desk when I arrived at the office. He looked up from his computer and sniffed.

'Have you been watching inspirational videos on Instagram again?'

He nodded. 'These guys just rescued a goat from a mineshaft. They're heroes.'

'Remember we talked about this . . .'

Wozza nodded and clicked out of the screen. His expression hardened. 'So, how did you go with your big-city inspector? Was he here to offer you a job back in Melbourne?'

I searched Wozza's face for irony. Found none. He didn't suspect Daniel was here because we had history. He suspected Daniel had come to lure me back to the city. It took my mind a couple of seconds to reset. 'I love it here, Wozza. I have no plans to go back to the city.'

'You didn't answer my question, Detective.'

'You're not as silly as you look, Detective.'

'So he *does* want you to go back to Melbourne?'

The devil was in the phrasing and that was a very different question. 'It doesn't matter what *he* wants,' I said, 'it matters what *I* want, and I'm definitely staying.' And in speaking it out loud, I saw the truth.

Wozza sat back and smiled. 'That's a relief,' he said, opening his cake drawer and bringing out an impressive-looking chocolate cake. 'Norma dropped this off this morning.'

'You did ask her for a chocolate one.'

'I feel heard.' Wozza cut a generous slice for both of us.

Sitting at my desk, eating chocolate cake for breakfast with a partner I really liked—this was my version of heaven. Why would I ever leave?

'What time's the funeral?' Wozza asked.

I checked my watch. 'Starts at ten thirty but we'd better aim to get there half an hour early. See if anyone is acting weirdly.'

'Or see if anyone is holding a seven-month-old baby with a curl on the top of his head.' Wozza sighed, stood, stretched, and grabbed his keys. 'We've got time for a coffee first.'

Ten minutes later, we were walking into Angie's Cafe. I breathed in the smell of coffee beans and muffins still warm from the oven. It was early enough to sit a spell and watch the world go by. Even Wozza was knocked out of his regular pastry trajectory by the smell of the muffins. He ordered a chocolate one and I ordered a blueberry one. Chocolate cake for breakfast and muffins for morning tea. The detective's diet.

When Angie brought over our muffin plates, she said, 'Sorry your visit to Azzurro's made the papers.'

'PizzaGate,' said Wozza, taking his plate from her and tucking into his muffin.

'Crazy, right,' I said. 'Bloody journalist was there at the restaurant.' Then I remembered. 'How was your birthday?'

'The party was good. It was the only night everyone was free. My actual birthday is today,' she said, grinning. 'So far, I've been up since six, and been hard at work ever since.'

'Bummer,' Wozza said through a mouthful of chocolate muffin. 'But happy birthday!'

'Thanks.' Angie collected our coffees from the counter and set them on the table, mine a latte with drizzled chocolate and Wozza's an iced coffee. 'So who was the guy whose birthday you were celebrating?' She raised an eyebrow.

There was a definite twinkle in her eye, which I ignored. As a feminist, I loathed the way you couldn't be seen with a man without there being some kind of suggestion of intimacy. I thought of Andy and his kind face and his sense of humour and how lovely he was with Mum and Nan. My life was complicated enough without adding the attraction of another man. 'That was Andy Gilbert,' I said. 'He's in town minding his dad's place. He said he recently lost his mum.'

'Are they local?' Angie said, leaning in.

I thought about this. Andy hadn't talked about his parents much. 'I think he said his dad was a doctor.' I knew Angie had a finger on the pulse of everyone in town because, sooner or later, they were drawn into her cosy cafe to eat pastries or muffins and tell her their life story.

She looked thoughtful, then frowned. 'He's not Wonky George Gilbert's son?'

'Wonky George!' said Wozza, dropping a clump of muffin on the front of his shirt. 'We know him!'

'He's one of the pathologists at the morgue,' I said thoughtfully, trying to picture thin old Wonky George against the image of his strapping son and failing. I didn't say it to Angie, but Wonky George was not well-respected and several of his findings had actually been called into question.

'Between you and me,' said Angie leaning in closer, 'Wonky George is not a very nice man. Cranky.'

'Not even after one of your fabulous muffins?' said Wozza in shock.

'He's gluten free.'

'That would make me cranky too,' Wozza reached for his iced coffee and slurped a gulp.

The bell above the door tinkled as a group of tourists entered the shop in a wave of towels, suntan lotion and thongs. Angie bid us goodbye and disappeared behind the counter, ready to take their orders.

I turned to Wozza. 'That is so weird about Andy being Wonky George's son. You'd never pick it. But I guess it does explain why he left town as soon as he could. His father is not a pleasant man.'

Wozza nodded.

I checked my watch. We had fifteen minutes before we had to go. Wozza and I discussed ways we could be as unobtrusive as possible at the funeral.

'The media will be there,' he said, brushing crumbs off his tie.

'Maddy will be there too, with her parents.' I checked my texts for an update.

'Do you think that's wise?'

'She'll be damned if she does and damned if she doesn't,' I said.

Turned out, I was right.

■●■

From the moment the Muirs arrived at the church, there was a shift in the vibe of the crowd outside. They seemed to move in waves, coming slowly and deliberately towards Maddy and her parents. Not surprisingly, it was Trev who fired the first salvo. He rushed up to Maddy and, in a raised voice, told her that Josh hated her and that he was dead because of her. Maddy flinched like she'd been hit. Paul Muir tried to step between the two of them, and Trev did a classic shirt-front manoeuvre.

'I'm tagging in,' said Woz, leaving the shade of an old oak tree outside the church and hurrying over to the growing throng moving closer to Maddy. Thankfully Tamara and Keith McCreedy had already gone inside the church and missed the skirmish.

I followed Wozza at a bit of a distance so I could get the measure of anyone else who might be threatening to the Muirs. I saw a tall, good-looking young man, notable because he stood back, arms crossed in front of him, looking dismayed at what was happening.

Wozza grabbed Trev by the arm and pulled him away from a sobbing Maddy, who was flanked by her distressed parents.

'You should never have come!' yelled Trev.

'Calm down, mate,' said Wozza. 'Off you go now.' He pushed him in the direction of the church steps and thankfully Trev complied.

Most of the others followed him inside the church as the sounds of organ music wafted from the doorway.

The tall young man I'd observed followed the crowd at first but then stopped and turned back. He strode over to Maddy. I stepped forward just in case he was going to have a go at her too. But he didn't. He stopped in front of her and held out a hand.

'I'm Ben McCreedy,' he said. 'We haven't met, but I'm Josh's brother.'

Maddy looked up and her eyes widened, first in fear that he was going to confront her, then in gratitude when he didn't.

Ben continued. 'I'm so sorry for what he did to you.' He held out his arms and Maddy stepped forward and the two embraced.

'Thank you,' she said in a barely audible voice when the hug ended. 'That means a lot.'

'I hope they find Ethan.'

'Me too,' she whispered, tears rolling down her cheeks.

The church music got louder and Ben glanced at the doorway.

'Go,' Maddy said to him. 'We won't follow.'

THREE TRIPLE P ONLINE

Mother of Lost Baby Provokes Anger at Funeral

Lincoln Steele reporting from Deception Bay, Victoria

Monday, 20 January, 3 pm

The crowd erupted into violence today at the Deception Bay funeral of fallen father Josh McCreedy. It is thought the affray began with the arrival of Maddy Muir and her parents.

Several male friends and relatives of Josh McCreedy surrounded Maddy Muir and her parents and expressed unhappiness at their presence. The funeral resumed without the Muirs but with attendees still visibly angry at their attempt to join the mourners. In a string of tragic events, the beloved local man's demise has been linked to the denial of his parental rights, which forced him to take extreme measures to see his baby son.

One young man, introduced only as 'Trev', spoke at the service in memory of his best friend.

'He was a bloody good mate,' Trev said, wiping a tear from his eye. 'Give you the shirt off his back, he would.'

Another friend, Griffon, struggled to control his emotions as he praised Josh's skills at computer games and called him the 'God of Fortnite'.

But perhaps the most heartbreaking speech of all came when McCreedy's parents both stood before the church gathering to farewell their son, the second they'd lost in tragic circumstances. Josh's father, Keith McCreedy, spoke about the father he knew his son would have been to baby Ethan if things had worked out differently.

'He was a young man with some growing up to do but we were confident that he would have risen to the challenge, like he's done with everything else in his life, and been a great father. Now, he will never get the chance.'

Mr McCreedy had to be helped from the altar by his wife.

What followed was a timely warning by the minister about the evils of broken relationships and the effect on children. 'Women,' he said, 'need to be more tolerant and generous towards men.' This sentiment was met with applause from the congregation.

Despite extensive searches by police and SES, there have been no signs of the missing baby. It has now been a week since little Ethan was taken from his crib at the Deception Bay home of his mother. With each passing day, hopes for his safe return fade.

At a press conference following the funeral service, Senior Sergeant Bill Wheeler promised door-to-door searches would continue this afternoon, but it's hard to imagine anyone will be at home to answer their door. It seems like the entire town turned out for the funeral.

The Muir family were unavailable for comment.

CHAPTER 27

THE PUB TEST

The music was pumping from the private room behind the bar, which spilled out into a beer garden. If the hundreds who'd packed the church had all made their way to the Royal Hotel, the space out the back would be full to overflowing. I wondered if the anger from the service had also migrated to the pub.

Ralph Murphy, publican, father of many, purveyor of wisdom, was behind the bar pulling a beer when I entered. I climbed onto a bar stool and waited till he had a free moment.

'How's my favourite detective?' he said, his voice jovial.

Exhaustion dragged at my return smile. 'How many detectives do you actually know?'

'Well, Wozza of course, but you smell better. And those two new ones'—Ralph paused—'the one with dimples is a complete tosser. The other one is all right, but that still leaves you as my favourite.'

'Fair enough,' I said. 'As long as you've given it some thought.'

'Your usual?'

I nodded. 'Ta.'

With the sweeping motions only managed by bartenders, Ralph magically produced a coaster, a can of Coke Zero, a glass of ice and a straw in the blink of an eye.

'You're a legend,' I said, taking a sip straight from the can. I reached out and tapped my card to the machine.

Ralph gave a kind, fatherly smile. 'You look exhausted, love,' he said. 'Any closer to finding that baby?'

My gaze shifted in the direction of the back room and its pumping music. I shook my head. 'That's why I'm here. I wanted to talk to you about the McCreedys.'

Ralph nodded but looked troubled. 'I'm not one to talk out of school,' he said.

My eyes were pleading. 'There's a baby missing, Ralph.'

He raised his hands in surrender. 'I know.' He looked around to make sure no one was within earshot.

I scanned the room too and saw only a smattering of locals; everyone else was attending the wake.

'Look, Antigone, you stand behind a bar for long enough and you start to pick types. And before you say anything, I get that blokes often blame a gutful of grog when they act out of character, but maybe a gutful of grog also shows you who they really are. One thing I listen out for is the way blokes talk about women when they're alone. I have to protect my staff and my lady customers.' He paused. Tilted his head to the left. 'Like that bloke over there, for example. Timothy Wainwright. Big wig at the Deception Bay Bank, but gotta keep a close watch on him. Good customer. Bad human.'

I glanced at Timothy Wainwright. Guy in a suit, drinking alone in the afternoon and staring at some horse race on the pub's big-screen TV. I needed to keep Ralph on track. 'So, the McCreedys?'

'Tamara's a sweetheart but Keith . . . they come in for dinner sometimes and he's rude to the waitstaff. You can tell a lot about people by how they treat waitstaff, in my humble opinion.'

'Rude, how?'

'Made one of my waitresses cry a couple of weeks ago. Tamara always rushes in to apologise, but the damage is done. After their son died—the first one, Pete—we kind of let it go. Grief and all that. And now with Josh . . .' Ralph wiped a hanky across his brow. 'But you can't indulge that kind of behaviour. It only ever gets worse, not better. And the rights of my staff to be treated respectfully don't change because Keith's going through a rough time, you know?'

I nodded. I did know.

Ralph crossed his arms in front of him. 'We had young Maddy and her folks in last night for a meal. You can only imagine what that lass and her family are going through, but you don't see them treating the waitstaff badly. They're the opposite. Grateful. Gracious. They're good people.'

'Two sons,' I said, getting back to the McCreedys. 'That's a lot for any parent to bear.'

'To be sure,' said Ralph. 'But you know the saying: if you lie down with dogs, you get up with fleas.'

'What do you mean?'

Ralph looked resigned. 'Those guys last year with the drink spiking—well, let's just say the McCreedy boys were . . .' Ralph paused to find the right word. He settled on one. 'They were *lucky*.'

I sat up a little straighter on my bar stool and pressed the cold can against my hot cheek. 'Lucky?'

'You know as well as I do that those blokes you arrested weren't the only ones. That kind of behaviour, it's like bees to honey.' Ralph grabbed a glass from a rack in front of him and poured himself a lemonade. Took a gulp. 'But they've all paid, haven't they?'

I gave him a quizzical look.

'Dropping like flies, they are. Four dead. Three in jail. It's like someone's picking 'em off.' He paused. 'Present company excluded.'

I shrugged. The three in jail were my doing, but I hadn't really thought about the deaths in this context. Two men had died last year during the investigation into drink spiking. And now, the two McCreedy brothers. The information rocked me. Four dead. Three in jail. I knew it, of course; I'd just never said it out loud.

I picked up my Coke and thanked Ralph for his time. *Four dead . . . It's like someone's picking 'em off.* The words echoed in my head.

Timothy Wainwright blocked my path to the door as I tried to leave.

'So, what do you say? You and me?' He gave a wink that he obviously felt was subtle and suggestive but just came off as sleazy.

'No,' I said.

His eyes narrowed and he waited a beat. He looked taken aback at my directness. I stayed silent and braced myself. His anger didn't take long, and I wasn't in an ignore-it kind of mood.

'Whore,' he snarled in a low voice.

These moments of change from charm to offensive were always jarring.

'What's a whore?' I asked in my most innocent voice.

Timothy's snarl faltered when he saw the insult hadn't landed. It was a typical response. He stumbled over his answer. 'Well, it's a slut who sleeps with anyone.'

I considered that. Put a finger on my chin. 'So you're accusing me of being a woman who'll sleep with anyone, *except you*. Gee, that's awkward.'

'Bitch!'

I pulled my badge out. 'That's enough of that.' He flinched and I turned and walked away.

■●■

All the way home, Ralph's words echoed in my head. *Four dead . . . It's like someone's picking 'em off.*

It was late when I got home. Mum had gone to bed and Nan was reading under the lamplight in the living room.

I made a cup of tea for the both of us and then curled up in an armchair.

'How did you go with Daniel?' she asked.

I took a sip of tea before answering. 'Did you ever love anyone so much you felt they could consume you?'

Nan smiled up a memory. 'Oh yes,' she said. 'When I was young, before I met your grandfather, there was a boy.' She got a faraway look in her eyes, and I imagined time slipping away until he was standing in front of her again.

'Tell me the story,' I said.

She laughed. 'Not much to tell. He lived on a farm like we did. But he was further out than we were. I'd catch the bus to school each day and he'd save me a seat. Such a gentle boy.' Nan's eyes glistened and I wasn't sure whether it was due to tears or the magic of memory. 'There's nothing nicer than resting your head on the shoulder of a boy in a flannelette shirt,' she said.

I breathed in deeply and could almost smell Daniel, feel my head on his shoulder. I came back to the present moment. 'What became of your boy in the flannelette shirt?'

'Ah,' said Nan, 'sometimes the passion that draws two young people together is the same passion that drives them apart.'

I looked at her closely and saw shadows of loss in her expression.

She smiled sadly. 'Sometimes love burns too brightly and the flames consume everyone.'

'So,' I said, 'the age-old question: is it better to have loved and lost?'

Nan's smile was wistful. 'If you're strong enough to step away, absolutely. And I say this from the vantage point of age. Even when you lose a great love, you'll always have the memories. No one can ever take them away.'

'So the feeling of flannelette never leaves you?'

'Never.' Her eyes shone. 'I'm old and done with desire, but the life I look back on is filled with the most wonderful memories. My dad always told me it was better to regret the things I did than regret the things I didn't do. I honestly have no regrets.'

'Do you miss it?'

'Desire? Goodness me, no! When you're young, it's easy to be driven by it. But now I'm old, I'm not sad to see it go. It took up too much space.'

I leaned forward. 'What do you mean?'

'Well,' she said, 'when I think about all those years I spent pining over boys when I was young, I can't help wondering what if I had put the same energy into being a . . . an astronaut? I could have flown to the moon. I think society sells women a lie—that we need to find the right man to feel complete. They should be telling us to find our own completeness before we join to someone else. In my day especially, the find-the-man bit was it. That *was* the goal. Whereas the story sold to men about finding a wife is simply that it's a step in their bigger journey.'

I'd always thought Mum's feminism was a reaction against her traditional upbringing, but here was Nan, a feminist from her orthotic shoes to the top of her white curls. It hardly seemed possible but my affection for her grew. And I thought about what she'd said. Daniel did take up too much room in my thoughts. But the thought of desire going . . . I was not ready for that yet. I just had to find a way to master it.

Nan looked at me with her piercing gaze. 'The other lie they tell is that there is only one person who can make you feel like that. I've seen so many women fall for it. But the truth is that a man might suit you at a certain time in your life, but a different man might be better later. I saw how hard you fell for Daniel.'

I knew what Nan meant, but the thought of being with any other man but Daniel made me feel sick. 'There's no one else for me,' I said sadly; my fate had been sealed.

'The way you looked at each other . . .' said Nan.

We both smiled wistfully at the memory.

'But for the time being, you're discovering who you are on your own. I think every woman needs that too. I'm proud of you, my love.'

'Thanks, Nan.' For a moment I rested in the warmth of her praise.

Daniel and I had made no promises when he left. It had been great to work by his side over the weekend, but I couldn't leave this place. That was one thing I was sure of. I wouldn't follow him back to Melbourne and it felt strange to imagine he would come here.

CHAPTER 28

FOUR DEAD

Doc Caldicott had a small window of time at her consulting rooms on Tuesday morning and agreed to let Wozza and I fill it.

We followed her into her office and sat in the two visitor chairs.

'Hey, Doc, while we're here, I have this weird rash,' Wozza said, holding up his forearm for her inspection.

'Maybe you're allergic to pastries,' said the doc wryly.

I've never seen an arm withdraw so quickly. Then, we settled into the real reason we were there.

'Ralph at the Royal said something yesterday that got me thinking,' I opened. 'Four men from Deception Bay have died in the last . . .' I counted the months in my head.

'Since you arrived in town,' said Wozza happily, like he'd solved a puzzle.

I felt myself blush faintly. 'Thanks, Wozza. Not helping, and one of the deaths pre-dated my arrival.' Turning back to Doc Caldicott, I said, 'I'm talking about Pete McCreedy. Now Josh McCreedy is dead. Jack Barratt. Merv Evans.' Next I asked the question that had been bugging me. 'How likely is it that four men in a small town who all know each other could die in a relatively short space of time and the deaths not be connected?'

Doc Caldicott considered the question. 'Jack slipped from a cliff. Merv died after ingesting the same drug used in the drink spiking spree he himself was implicated in. Pete from anaphylaxis, and Josh from ingesting a lethal dose of medication prior to his collision. Two accidental and two due to medication.' She frowned. 'If my memory serves me correct, aren't there two men in jail for Merv's drink spiking?'

She was right. The men who'd been found not guilty of sexual assault in the spate of drink-spiking attacks last year had been found guilty of manslaughter when Merv picked up a beer that had been discarded by one of their potential victims and drank it.

I nodded, feeling a little silly. 'Maybe I'm just being paranoid.'

'Nonsense.' Doc Caldicott stood up to signal our time had run out. 'As a detective, you always have to ask these kinds of questions. What if there was a killer sneaking around out there, spiking medications, and you didn't notice? Then we'd all be in trouble.'

'Not all of us,' said Wozza, standing up and hiding the rash on his forearm with his hand, 'just men who target women.'

His comment gave me the chills.

'But Wozza,' I said in a low voice as soon as we'd cleared the consulting rooms, 'I'm serious here. What are the odds? These four men who knew each other, hell, they could have been drinking at the pub together within the last year, and now they're all dead. Different age groups, different backgrounds, but . . .'

Wozza's eyes narrowed and he took up my point. 'But they could've all been connected with the drink spiking, if Ralph's hunch is correct . . .' His voice trailed off and I could see him mulling it over.

I remembered the first reported victims of drink-spiking sexual assault had been on Australia Day the previous year. 'Pete McCreedy died in April last year, three months after the first drink spiking was reported.'

'Bloody hell,' said Wozza. 'You might be onto something.'

I continued. 'So, Pete McCreedy was the first one to go. An expired EpiPen on a camping trip in a remote location.' I thought for a moment of a case I'd had in Melbourne. 'But even if the EpiPen hadn't been faulty, he still might not have made it. I'm pretty sure paramedics follow an EpiPen by giving more adrenaline shots. Even if he'd had a single shot, his friends may not have gotten him out of there in time anyway.'

'Then Merv went after drinking the spiked beer,' said Wozza, counting the men off on his fingers. 'Then Jack went over the cliff. No drugs found in his system. And then Josh McCreedy died of an overdose of pills, and we don't know where he got them from.'

'There's a pattern there,' I said. 'Aside from Jack, there's medication involved in every death.'

'I think we're going to need to visit Filmore's Pharmacy and have a chat with Norma,' said Wozza. 'And we can kill two birds with the one stone and tell her we've finished our chocolate cake.'

'For the record, *you* finished our chocolate cake,' I corrected.

Just then, a notification pinged on my phone. I glanced at it on the lockscreen and saw the logo from the DNA company. I could see the message header too: *Your results are in!* Swiping quickly, I braced myself. If my sibling survived and had gone looking for their family, I might be seconds away from knowing. Buried deeper in my soul there was also the question of my father's identity.

I told Wozza I needed to go and left him to visit the pharmacy alone. As soon as we parted, I tapped open the message and saw two names that made absolutely no sense.

■●■

It was fitting we meet at Angie's Cafe since it was the place we had first met. When I'd called, I hadn't given him a reason for meeting and he hadn't asked.

'Hey, Antigone,' he said, waving me over as soon as I came through the door. 'I grabbed us a table.'

'Hey, Andy,' I said, sitting opposite him.

He looked at me, a question in his eyes. 'Thanks for the coffee invite.' His smile was uncertain.

'Andy, I hope you didn't mind me getting your number from Russell—'

Angie appeared at our table with her notepad in hand, cutting me off. 'The usual?' she asked me.

'Sure,' I said, and Andy ordered a Coke.

When Angie walked away, I took a deep breath and refocused. 'You took a DNA test a while back . . .' I let my voice trail off.

'Oh, I remember that.' Andy smiled. 'Must've been nine years ago now because someone gave it to me for my thirtieth birthday. When I checked the results, I didn't match with anyone or discover any bushrangers in my ancestry.' Suddenly, he looked serious. 'Has my DNA been connected to a crime?' Then he paused. 'No, wait, that doesn't make sense since I haven't committed any crimes.'

'It's not crime connected . . . well, not as far as you're concerned anyway.'

He looked uncomfortable. 'So what's this about?'

'Andy, thirty-nine years ago, my mother had a baby at the Bellanook Hospital. They told her the baby died . . . but he didn't.'

Andy's eyes widened. 'I was born at the Bellanook Hospital. My dad was a doctor there.'

I tried to find the right words. 'Recently my mum heard rumours that babies were taken from Bellanook Hospital back then and she started wondering if her baby really did die. I took a DNA test to see if that baby was out there somewhere. And you were.'

Andy leaned back and puffed out a breath. 'What?'

I gave him a minute to absorb the news.

'You know,' he said finally, 'my dad is the reason I do the work I do.'

'You protect women from violent partners, right?'

'My dad is a controlling son-of-a-bitch,' he said, flint in his voice. 'It's no coincidence that I've come back here while he's out of the country. That's the only time I want to be here. When he's not. I wanted to go through Mum's things. After she died, he was just going to dump everything at St Vinnies, so I offered to sort it all out.'

'What was your mum like?' I asked.

Andy looked distressed. 'I watched her being controlled by him for my entire childhood. As soon as I could get out, I did. I had this fantasy of making a lot of money and then rescuing her, but by the time I was able to do that, she got sick.'

It was hard to listen to him talk about his mum, knowing that this was the woman who raised my brother when it should have been my own mum doing it.

'My mother wasn't even a patient at the Bellanook Hospital. She only went there because she was on her way home from Melbourne when she suddenly went into labour. Your mum must have been shocked when your dad suddenly arrived home with a baby all those years ago.'

Andy shook his head in wonder. 'Mum wouldn't have been able to question it, either. Questions were not a thing in our family.'

I marvelled that such a strong and kind man could emerge from the toxic environment he was describing.

Andy's eyes glistened. 'So you're my sister. And here I was thinking I was an only child.'

'Same here,' I said, feeling a sudden kinship with my brand-new brother.

We made plans for him to call round to the farmhouse later. But for now, I had to get home and talk to Mum.

CHAPTER 29

YOUR RESULTS ARE DRIVING UP THE DRIVEWAY

As soon as I parked in the driveway, I could smell the barbecue. Mum must have been cooking out on the side verandah, I thought, because the smell was wafting all the way to the front door. I could get used to coming home to my family, but I knew it wouldn't last. My mum had a wanderlust that I hadn't inherited. Maybe it was because the intergenerational pendulum usually swings in the opposite direction. Nan stayed on the farm all her life, Mum couldn't wait to leave, and now I was living on the farm.

I opened the door to a very excited Waffles, who led me out the back to where Mum and Nan were enjoying the pleasures of a simple summer's evening on the verandah while dinner sizzled on the barbie.

Nan nursed a pre-dinner cup of tea while Mum sipped a rare glass of red.

'Antigone!' Nan said as soon as she saw me.

I settled in the chair next to Nan and tried to figure out the best way to broach the news about Andy. My heart was in my throat because, for the whole afternoon, I had known the identity of Mum's lost baby and she still didn't. And not only that, I had spoken to him, and Mum didn't know about that either.

Mum put the steaks on a plate and brought them over to the table. She set them next to a potato salad and a bowl of tossed lettuce and tomato sprinkled with dill and fresh basil from the garden.

'Dig in,' she said.

Looking from my mother to my grandmother, I knew that as soon as I broke the news, our little Pollard clan would have a new member and its shape would be forever changed. I wanted to savour this last dinner together as a family of three. I let them finish dinner and talk over the excitement of their day. They had visited a local National Trust house; one they'd been meaning to visit for years.

'The gardens were lovely,' said Nan. 'I managed to explore them on my walker. Your mother helped me of course.'

Mum finished eating and raised her glass. 'Here's to family,' she said.

'Hear, hear,' said Nan, lifting her teacup and tilting it towards Mum's glass.

I filled a tumbler from the water jug on the table and we clinked cups. 'Speaking of family,' I began, 'my DNA results came back today.'

Mum's eyes widened with panic. Her trademark stoicism had subsided and there was a tremor in her bottom lip. Nan reached over and took her hand. They both looked at me.

'Who is my child?' said Mum in barely more than a whisper.

'It's Andy Gilbert. You met him the other night.'

'Andy?' Mum's eyes welled with tears of wonder. 'But how . . .'

'His dad—or the man he thought was his father—is Dr George Gilbert, who worked at the Bellanook Hospital back then. We can surmise that the night you gave birth, he decided to keep your baby for himself. If other babies were taken, then he was quite possibly at the centre of those cases too.'

Mum took a deep breath, her eyes glistening. Then, without a moment's hesitation, she began making plans. 'We have to see him! Can we call him? Do you have his number?'

I went round the table and hugged her. 'Mum, I've already talked to him. He's coming around tonight.'

Mum burst into tears. Nan and I did our best to soothe her. But it's hard to calm someone when your own heart is beating faster for the exact same reason theirs is.

'Antigone, love,' said Nan. 'Might be a good idea to pop the kettle on.'

■●■

While Mum and Nan sat together on the couch, murmuring in low voices, I tidied up the dinner dishes, listening for Waffles to signal the approach of a car up the driveway. Just as I'd settled on a comfy armchair, Waffles was on his feet, hurrying to the front door. He let out a single bark. Mum stood, looking like she didn't know what to do with herself. Nan pushed herself up on the arm of the couch and stood by her daughter.

Someone knocked.

Mum and Nan stood frozen while I hurried to open the door. On the other side was Andy, looking as nervous as Mum and Nan. I leaned forward and gave him a quick hug. My brother.

'They're nervous too,' I whispered as Waffles and I moved back to let him in.

I normally walk past the portrait gallery of Pollard photos lining the long hallway without a second glance, but Andy stopped in awe. Generations of Pollards were all there. He stood in front of one sepia portrait and said, 'I look like him!'

As soon as he said it, I realised why Andy had seemed so familiar from the moment I met him. He bore a strong resemblance to several of the old black-and-white pictures of our family from generations past.

Too quickly, the hallway ended and Andy stepped into the back room, coming face to face with his mother and grandmother. I'm not sure who cried first, but it didn't take long before we all were. Except Waffles. He just leaned into my leg like he always does when he knows I need it.

Eventually, the four of us calmed enough to make tea, light the evening fire and sit for the first time in our new family grouping.

'How did you come to put your DNA in for family testing?' Mum began.

Andy shrugged. 'It's crazy but a friend gave the kit to me for my thirtieth birthday, I guess as a joke. A decade ago, people didn't do it so much to match with other people. It was more to see what proportion of your DNA was Irish or Danish or whatever. I seem to recall I had a bit of both. I think everyone wanted to discover Vikings in their heritage.' He laughed, then grew solemn. 'Never gave it another thought . . . until Antigone invited me for coffee today.'

We all turned to Mum. She needed to tell Andy her story.

I think all our hearts broke as she spoke of the night she had staggered into the hospital in labour, of the nurses and the doctor delivering the baby and taking it, while a younger version of her was sedated and lied to and left unconscious on the bed, alone. Every now and then, Andy shook his head in horror.

'And they took you and they raised you when you should have been mine,' Mum finished sadly.

Andy reached into a satchel he'd brought and pulled out a notebook and a photo album. 'I found these today, when I was going through Mum's things.' He handed the photo album to Mum. It was filled with baby pictures of Andy, who had looked extraordinarily like me at the same age. Mum and Nan turned the pages slowly, marvelling and making cooing noises like baby Andy was right in front of them. Both dabbed their eyes with tissues as they watched him grow into a sturdy little boy through the album's pages, then become a gangly teen, then a university graduate. His missing years were contained in that photo album and I could see the effect it had on my mum.

'I found this today too,' said Andy, opening the notebook. 'Mum had hidden it under a pile, no doubt to keep Dad from finding it. It's a book of her poems. One tells me that she somehow knew the baby was yours.' He flicked open the pages to the one, and read it to us:

I saw them in the street today,
The mother and the daughter—
Clinging together in their grief—
Over their missing boy.

We slowly drove past them—
And I ducked my head;
Their sorrow too profound
For mere mortals.

We passed the school, where children go
And Baby will go there—
When he is grown and happier;
After he forgets her.

In our back seat,
Tucked away—
Sleeps their hearts' desire
They can't have him so we can.

We drove past the gate
To the house where he won't live.
One loses so the other wins.
The victor thinks it's fair.

Love grows so quickly
For the baby boy
We will call him by a different name
And that will make him ours.

'It's so callous,' said Mum. 'She *knew*. She *saw* us.'

Andy looked distressed. None of this was his fault and I could see his dilemma. I could tell by the way he'd spoken about his mother earlier that he loved her, but for her to have kept him meant she had been party to what happened to my mum. To his mum.

'I don't understand any of this,' he said, 'but what I do know is that I never felt like I really belonged. And I don't want to defend my mum's choice, but if Dad had arrived home with a baby, she would have had no say. In the end, having me ended up being the only joy in her life.'

While Andy talked, I studied him. This full-grown man had replaced the lost baby in my imagination and it was hard to process. At the same time, I could see the shadows of similarity. The dimple he got when he smiled was in the same place as mine. His eyelashes were like Mum's, and so was the shape of his mouth. His existence had forced a seismic shift in my mind. Everything I knew had to be shuffled around to fit in a brother. *A brother.*

'Is my father going to be charged?' Andy said suddenly. He didn't sound worried at the thought.

Mum answered before I could. 'It wasn't just you he took,' she said. 'That's why I came to town. The story is about to break, and it looks like your—' she broke off, unwilling to say the word. 'It looks like Dr George Gilbert was at the centre of it all.'

I tapped the DNA results on my phone. 'Nearly forty years ago, he never would have envisaged how easy it would be for people to take a DNA test and uncover his crimes.'

On the long list of things we needed to talk to Andy about was the other name that had shown up as a match on my DNA test.

'Andy, there's something else,' I said.

He put a hand on his heart. 'Not sure I can take much more.'

'I matched with someone else who's connected to both of us. The other night at your birthday, there was a young woman called Dawn . . . do you know her?'

Andy looked genuinely puzzled. 'No . . .'

And then I remembered how Dawn had reacted to Andy's surname. She had obviously lodged her DNA test after his and had seen the match. 'Her name is Dawn Denholm.'

'Denholm?' Andy's eyes grew wider. 'I used to date a girl called Kelly Denholm. We broke up when I went off to uni. I was eighteen when I left town and, once I was gone, I tried not to come back too often. Are you telling me that she was . . .'

'Pregnant, by the sounds of things,' said Nan.

'And Dawn is my . . . daughter?' Andy looked mystified.

Mum's lip quivered. 'And my granddaughter?'

Then Nan. 'And my great-granddaughter?'

And then it was tissues all round. Again.

CHAPTER 30

THE NIECE

It took hours to get to sleep that night. The wonder of a new brother filled my thoughts. Mum, Nan and I had interrogated Andy about his life and his upbringing, wanting to absorb every detail of those lost years into our collective story. Andy in turn was treated to a Pollard history. Nan got out the old photo album and regaled us with stories of Pollards past. The great-grandma who liked a whisky and once made two innocent fishermen leap over the side of a local bridge when she swerved too close to them in her car. The long line of farmers. The great-uncles lost to war. Andy soaked it all up, his eyes gleaming in the firelight.

And as I tossed and turned in bed that night, our discoveries made me wonder if Maddy might not see baby Ethan again until he was a grown man taking a DNA test by chance. The thought brought more tears to my eyes before an exhausted sleep finally claimed me.

■●■

The early-morning sun had a heat to it that promised a scorcher uncharacteristic of our otherwise mild summer. Waffles and I headed off for our run as the dawn chased the shadows away. I wanted to see Maddy first thing to check how she was going. It was hard to know which was worse—my mum being told her baby had died when he was really alive, or Maddy not knowing either way.

As I pounded the dry dirt road on the way back to the farmhouse. I wondered where the media would focus their attention today.

■●■

Mum and Nan were up and making breakfast by the time Waffles and I panted in the back door. Waffles scurried over to his big water bowl and slurped happily for a long while.

'How are you both feeling?' I asked as I carried plates to the table.

'Mentally exhausted,' said Mum.

'Happy,' said Nan. 'I have a new grandson, and a new great-granddaughter who seemed lovely when we chatted the other night at the pizza restaurant.'

They'd both summed up the situation perfectly. On one side there were the complexities of rediscovering a lost connection and on the flip side was the simplicity of Andy and Dawn.

The previous night, everyone had agreed that I should be the one to speak to Dawn since I knew her better than they did. Every time I thought I'd had enough tough conversations to last a lifetime, another always landed on my to-do list.

■●■

Wheels was giving a press conference when I drove up to the police station. The usual media throng that had been there since Ethan went missing were all back. In fact, I thought their numbers might have been growing. In the media, these kinds of cases have a life of their own. I kept well out of their way and drove around the back of the police station. By the time I'd parked and come inside, the TV was on in the muster room and everyone was gathered around watching Wheels.

'We expect to find the baby any day now,' said Wheels, his chest puffed out.

'How can he say that?' Jane groaned.

'He's an idiot,' said Wozza. 'I hope Maddy isn't watching.'

On the screen, a reporter asked, 'Has the door-knock yielded any important information?'

'We have several new and promising leads,' said Wheels. 'Of course, I can't go into details.' His voice was authoritative and the reporter nodded solemnly.

'What leads?' said Randall.

'He's making it up as he goes along,' said Wozza in disgust.

I followed Woz into our office; neither of us could be bothered to stay and hear whatever else Wheels had to say.

Wozza grabbed his keys. 'We've got to head over to see Maddy,' he said. 'That press conference will need damage control.'

We were driving out just as the media throng began dissipating.

'Turn on the radio,' said Wozza, speaking with none of his usual good-natured humour. 'Three Triple P with that tosser Drew Nayle. We need to stay on top of this.'

Sure enough, Drew Nayle was in fine form, criticising the Deception Bay police, me in particular. People were phoning in with wild theories and Lincoln Steele came on, repeating Wheels's promise that the baby would soon be found.

'Jeez,' said Wozza, driving a little faster than he should to get us to Maddy's house as quickly as possible.

We beat the reporters there and Maddy swung open the door as soon as we parked in her driveway.

'Have you found him?' she cried. 'I just saw the press conference on TV.'

I hurried over to her. 'No,' I said, and watched her deflate. 'I'm so sorry he made it seem like we were close.'

Maddy burst into tears and we led her back inside before the press could show up and catch her on film.

'I hope Wheels burns in hell for this,' muttered Wozza, keeping his voice so quiet that only I could hear. The pressure was getting to all of us.

■●■

It was late afternoon before I even thought about Dawn. Wozza, Kasparas and I had spent the day following up people who'd attended the funeral to find out if they knew anything that could be helpful. There had been a couple of new leads, but mostly our efforts amounted to a big fat nothing. I needed to head to the pharmacy, but in all the crazy of the day, I realised I'd forgotten to ask Wozza about his visit there yesterday, when he'd gone to talk to Norma about our 'four dead' theories. Since it wasn't part of the current investigation, I waited till Wozza and I had a moment alone.

'How did you go yesterday with Norma?' I asked him in a low voice after following him to the station kitchen when he got up to make tea.

'She doesn't remember seeing a spate of deaths like this before,' he said. 'She looked a little worried, I reckon. Told me to keep my eyes open.'

'Why was she worried? Does she think there will be more deaths?' I could hear the shock in my voice.

Woz thought for a moment. 'She didn't say those exact words . . . but I'm a world champion at jumping to conclusions.'

■●■

By the time I got to the pharmacy, both Dawn and Crystal were already finished for the day and Norma was locking up. It gave me the chance to talk to her about our 'four dead' theories. Wozza was right. She did look concerned, and I promised her I'd stay vigilant.

When I told her I needed to speak to Dawn she suggested I pop around to her house. 'She's in the little cottage next to Holy Trinity.'

It was easier to walk around the corner than drive so I set off on foot, wondering what on earth I was going to say. We had fitted Andy into the jigsaw puzzle of our family and now it was Dawn's turn to fit the Pollards into her family. I didn't know her well enough to guess how she'd take the news, but I bet she already knew part of it, from the way she'd reacted to Andy's name at the birthday dinner.

The little cottage nestled next to the Holy Trinity church looked like something out of a picture book. Rose vines climbed across an arched arbour and fragrant jasmine perfumed the air. Someone in the family had a green thumb. I stepped up onto the neatly swept wooden verandah and knocked on the door. Footsteps sounded inside the house, then the door opened a crack. It was Dawn.

'Antigone?' she said in a low voice.

'Hey, Dawn,' I said. 'I was hoping you might have a minute to talk.'

Dawn squeezed herself through the door and closed it behind her. 'Now isn't a good time,' she said, looking pensive. 'Mum's having a bad day. I don't want to disturb her.'

'Oh, okay,' I said, stepping back on the verandah to give her some space. 'Can we talk out here?'

Dawn looked back at the closed door then at me, and suggested we take a walk. She seemed to relax after we'd put some distance between ourselves and the house. I wondered about her mother, the woman my brother had loved when he was eighteen and desperate for connection, then left without knowing she was pregnant.

'Is everything okay?' Dawn sounded nervous.

I mentally kicked myself. I'd been knocking on her door as an aunty, but of course she saw a cop. 'Dawn, I wanted to talk to you about a personal matter.'

'Yes?'

'I noticed how you reacted the other night at the restaurant when you found out Andy's surname.' I stopped, hoping that would be enough to prompt her to tell me what she knew so far.

At first, she didn't take the bait, and we kept walking in silence. Finally, though, she spoke. 'Two years ago when I first started pharmacy studies, we talked about DNA in class. I took one of those online tests, and the name Andrew Gilbert came up as a match. My mum never told me much about my father. She was really young when she had me. I asked her about him and she told me he'd left town. And then the other night when you said his name, I figured he'd come back.' Dawn looked shaken, hurt.

'Dawn, he didn't know about you,' I said, stopping.

'Have you spoken to him about me?' she said, panicked. 'You have no right!'

'Dawn.' I put a hand on her arm and felt her trembling. 'It's not what you think. Your name and his name both came up when *I* did a DNA test. I got the results yesterday.'

'What?' She stepped back from me. 'What are you trying to say?'

I looked around. This was not going the way I'd hoped. Dawn looked spooked and I didn't blame her. There was a park bench nearby, in the little community garden on the other side of Holy Trinity. 'Come over here and let's sit down.'

Once we were settled, I explained the whole story to Dawn. Her eyes widened in disbelief when I told her how my mum's baby had been taken and raised by the doctor who had delivered him, when Mum thought the baby had died.

And then I told her about how Andy had left town because that same doctor had been a father he wanted to escape from, and how he never knew Dawn's mother was pregnant.

At the end of the story, Dawn sat back on the park bench and stared at the sky for a long while. Now that I knew who she was, I could see shadows of her father and echoes of Pollards in her face.

'So your mum lost her baby. Kind of like how Maddy has lost Ethan,' Dawn said.

I stared out at the street. 'I can feel Maddy's pain because I was feeling my mum's pain at the same time. She never spoke about losing her baby, but I can see now that she's been tortured by it all these years. I mean, you met my mum and nan the other night. They're good people. They didn't deserve this.'

Dawn nodded solemnly. 'So you're my aunty?' she said finally, a smile creasing the corners of her mouth.

'Welcome to the family,' I said, giving her a hug. I was pleased when she hugged me back.

When she let me go, she told me she needed time. Unlike Andy who wanted to meet the family immediately, she didn't.

'It's going to be a shock to my mum to hear about all of this, especially Andy being back. I didn't tell her about meeting him the other night.'

'Of course,' I said, 'take as long as you need.' I meant it, but I hoped she wouldn't take too long.

I reluctantly left Dawn when she said she had to get back to her mother.

■●■

After swinging by the farm to collect Waffles, I had a maths tutoring date I had to honour. Waffles loved Crystal's farm and had also formed a weird attachment to Crystal's horse, Black Beauty. He'd run over and bark at her and she would neigh back at him, then the two would follow each other around the paddock. It was funny to watch.

After we finished maths and I was satisfied Crystal seemed to understand fractions a little better than she had when we'd started, Russell suggested a run. It was just what I needed. Running with Crystal and Russell and Waffles through the state forest just outside of town was a great way to take my mind off not finding the baby and getting a new brother. A cool change had come through and so it was the perfect evening for it. Russell had been nearly as gobsmacked as me when I told him that Andy was my long-lost brother. He hadn't really known Andy's dad but he had been really fond of Andy's 'mum'. 'She was always kind to kids,' he said. 'You know, the type who always had a jug of ice-cold cordial and freshly baked cake ready when you went round.'

I ran at an easy pace with Russell and Crystal, not speaking, just thinking. Not all cases ended well and that had nothing to do with how hard we tried. Breathing in deeply, and out . . . in and out . . . running rhythmic footsteps . . . I used the almost hypnotic motion to clear thoughts of failure with the beginnings of acceptance that the baby might be gone. That Maddy might never know what had happened to him. Australian history was full of lost children. Artists like Frederick McCubbin had painted them back in the late 1800s. I remembered looking at the pictures in the National Gallery; it was unthinkably sad that children could disappear into the bush and never be found but it happened often enough for painters to immortalise the lost ones on canvas.

Crystal called out that she wanted to hide from Waffles again. It was a good excuse for Russell and me to stop for a breather. I jogged to a halt and called Waffles over to me. I went down on one knee and ruffled the fur around his neck. He licked my face.

'Dude!' I said, wiping my cheek.

Crystal took off into the bush. Soon the sounds of footfalls and snapping twigs faded.

'How are you doing?' Russell said. 'This week can't have been easy.'

'It's been a bit of a roller-coaster,' I agreed.

He nodded.

I straightened and Waffles positioned himself against my leg. 'And as for the missing baby, we will eventually exhaust all our avenues. And if we don't find him . . .'

'It seems inconceivable that a baby could just vanish into thin air,' said Russell, wiping his forehead with the back of his hand.

Visions of Maddy and her visceral grief sprang to my mind. 'That's the thing. He didn't vanish. Either Josh hid him somewhere or someone took him.'

Noises of Crystal had faded completely.

'Find Crystal,' I said to Waffles, taking my hand off his collar. He took off like a shot, weaving in and out between trees before disappearing. Moments later, Russell and I heard delighted squeals and a couple of playful barks. Soon, Crystal and Waffles burst from the bushes, Crystal pink-cheeked and Waffles with his tongue hanging out in a pant.

'Wish he could find Maddy's baby as easily as he finds me,' said Crystal, patting Waffles on the head.

'Me too,' I said.

'It's all we talk about at work,' she said. 'And how weird was it when you saw Norma and Dawn on the CCTV right behind Josh? They were so upset about that.'

'Well, they wouldn't have realised at the time,' I said. 'They would have just had a normal lunchbreak and come back none the wiser.'

'Only Norma came back after lunch,' Crystal said, bending down to retie her shoelace.

'What?' I said, careful to keep my voice at a mixture of casual and disinterested.

'Dawn left early on Monday to take her mum to an appointment. She didn't come back.'

■●■

It took one phone call to Doc Caldicott's medical practice and a quick conversation with my friend Gail on the front desk. She confirmed that Dawn's mum, Kelly Denholm, did indeed have an afternoon appointment on the day Ethan went missing.

'Just one more question, Gail,' I said trying to sound casual. 'Does Kelly's daughter usually come with her to her appointments?'

'She has a couple of times. MS is a funny thing. Sometimes you're good and sometimes you're not good. Dawn tends to come with her when she's not good.'

'Was she there at that last appointment?'

Gail clicked the keyboard. 'I don't think I was working that day. Let me check the roster.' More clicks. 'Yep, that's right. I wasn't on that afternoon so I'm not sure.'

I wondered why Dawn hadn't mentioned leaving early. But then another thought occurred to me. Maybe she was trying to protect her mother, like she did earlier when I'd gone to her house. If Dawn did go with her mum to the medical appointment, maybe that meant she was really sick at the moment. I made a mental note to ask after Kelly. Now that we were almost family, maybe there was something I could do to help.

THERAPY JOURNAL, PRIVATE PROPERTY OF DAWN DENHOLM

Wednesday, 22 January

Sometimes you feel like Frankenstein's monster. Like the monster, you have been created piece by piece, but your creators didn't steal your body parts from cemeteries and stitch you together; they moulded you from experiences. Your heart, once open and generous, beating at a regular rate, shrinks and hardens, then pounds in your chest like a prisoner wanting to escape. Your mind, once free to think and learn, becomes obsessed with finding justice. Your immune system, once healthy, becomes infected with syphilis, which announces itself with a sore . . . down there. The sore makes it real because when they came for you, you shut down. Froze. And when it was over, your mind willed it away, willed that it never happened, and you relegated it to the stuff of nightmares.

But the sore says it did happen. The rash says it did happen. And then you are the monster under construction. And then you realise there is something else growing inside the monster.

You study and learn that the infected become infectors, which means you are tainted. You learn that women with untreated syphilis who become pregnant have a fifty per cent chance of losing the baby. And when that happens, when you do lose the baby one lonely night in the uni dorm, you are torn in equal measure by the greatest relief and the greatest sorrow. The miscarriage is blood rather than baby because you're not that far along. No one knows, only your mum who promised to be there for you regardless of what happened. The doctor who tried to fix you tells you that you'll be okay, but you know better. The damage has been done. Your construction is complete. You are infertile. Destined to be alone.

Like Frankenstein's monster, you move through the world trying to find out who you are, where you fit. Like Frankenstein's monster, you can't partner, because a monster can only partner with another monster and your creator cannot build you a mate. And so, like Frankenstein's monster, you lash out at your creator. Creators. The ones that made you who you are. They're all over town. Down the pub. In the streets. Coming into the pharmacy for their antibiotics and their EpiPen replacements . . . right after you've sat through a class on the molecular basis of peanut allergies. Peanut proteins injected into capsules, taken with food. No one will ever know where those deadly traces came from.

And then the next one. The one who escaped justice by slithering away from the net. The brother. His script for penicillin wasn't for tonsillitis. He had syphilis too. But he was able to treat his early and escape it. You could feel it. Rough-handling his baby, taking selfies before the storm, by the old grain silos where you go to think when your mum says she doesn't need you to take her to the doctor's. He was rude as usual, saying, 'Hey, Chemist Girl, got any drugs?' and looking mighty pleased when you said you did. Because you always do, just in case. Easily talked into letting you mind the baby while he chased his high, willing to swap his child for a handful of magic beans—or six capsules of pregabalin, which you tell him works better with beer. And just like that, you're complete. And it feels fair. They took a baby from you so you get to take one from them.

At least, it feels like that at first. Having a baby is like curling up in a warm cocoon. Your mum understands what you've done because she understands what they took from you. Doesn't stop her from trying to talk you out of it, but you don't budge and she backs down. Your brother is another matter, gliding around town on his skateboard, seeing Maddy's grief and reporting it right back to you. Taking the big orange dummy and tossing it off the cliffs where he heard the search was happening so people might know Ethan was okay. Telling you that taking a baby to make up for one that was taken from you was only doing to another what was done to you and that it didn't make things right; it made you just as bad. Feeding your already growing guilt.

And

Then

You

See

Your

Dad

And your world smashes around you. An alert on your phone from that DNA app tells you there's another match and it's her, the one you like but fear because if she knew what you did, you'd be a goner.

You don't understand how she could be your dad's sister. Your aunt. Her name wasn't next to his on the DNA site that night you had pizza. You checked your results again when you got home after meeting him. It was just his.

Then you see the baby's mother for yourself, coming into the pharmacy, bent with grief, and you realise something vital. You are moved by the sight. It hurts you. And this hurt fills you with wonder because you thought that part of your soul, the part that feels for other people, was dead. But it wasn't and suddenly you are flooded with feelings, overflowing with them.

And when she knocks at your door it is too close for comfort. If she'd have stepped inside, she would have found the baby she'd been looking for. You feel lucky you walked away from the house with her and she didn't come back. But between her and the door-knocks, it feels like they're all coming for you—like the spotlight shining over the whole town is swinging in your direction.

And then you know you can't keep him. And you make the call.

Shhhh . . . what's that sound? You hope those distant sirens don't wake the baby because he's just been fed and you just got him to sleep. Are they getting louder? Louder. Louder. Then you hear the screech of tyres outside. You pull on your dressing-gown and you and your brother step outside, preparing to look surprised.

CHAPTER 31

THE CHURCH

Sirens screeched and lights flashed red and blue, turning the dark pre-dawn landscape into a circus of colour. Crunching through the gravel of the car park, Wozza and I hurried around to the front of the church. The double wooden doors at the front of Holy Trinity were open, and in the centre of the tableaux of soft lighting and dancing colours reflected off the stained-glass windows was a woman holding a baby.

We rushed to her side then stopped still and looked down at the bundle wrapped in a striped blanket. I was no expert on babies, but this one looked a lot like Ethan Muir. Same peach cheeks, same blond curl on the top of his head. He was sleeping like a . . . well, it's not a saying for nothing, I realised.

'I found him here,' said the woman, pointing to a blanket-lined box at her feet. 'Someone rang me. Said they were at that phone box.' She nodded her head towards one of Deception Bay's only remaining public phones, which stood across the road. 'She said she had the baby and would leave it on the steps of the church. I rang the police and raced right over.'

'Are you Lesley Gillis?' I asked, looking over her shoulder and seeing her name and picture on a flyer pinned to the bulletin board.

The woman nodded, not looking up from the bundle in her arms.

'We keep missing each other. We wanted to talk to you about Josh McCreedy. We think this is his son. Little Ethan.'

'Yes, I imagine it is. Maddy will be very relieved to get him back. She must've been frantic.'

'She has been,' I said, watching the woman closely.

'We were at your place earlier this week, talking to your son.' Wozza held out his hands as he spoke, and she passed the baby to him.

'Such a good boy, my Christos,' she said. 'He always tried to help Josh. We all did.'

I needed to make sense of why Lesley had got the call and not the police. 'You said someone rang you about the baby and said they'd left him in the church foyer.'

'It's not the first time I've been summoned in the middle of the night. That's why we leave the outside church doors unlocked, so if people need to, they can get into the foyer to access emergency supplies.' She pointed to several laundry baskets filled with tins of food and items of clothing.

It made sense. I looked at Wozza, who rocked Ethan gently. I excused myself from them and walked out to the footpath for a bit of privacy. I had a phone call to make. Neighbours had begun to gather, most wearing pyjamas and dressing-gowns, looking startled by the lights. Among them, I noticed two familiar faces. Dawn and her brother Xavier. They hurried over.

'What's going on, Antigone?' asked Dawn in a worried voice. She pointed to her little cottage next to the church. 'We heard a commotion from our place. Is everything okay?'

'We found baby Ethan!' I couldn't contain my excitement. 'Someone left him at the church and called Lesley Gillis.'

'That's who I would call if I needed help,' said Xavier. 'She's a nice lady.'

Dawn ruffled his hair.

'If you'll excuse me, I have to ring Maddy with the news.' I had a sudden lump in my throat as I fumbled with my phone. Dawn and Xavier moved towards Wozza and the baby, and I could see Wozza handing Ethan to Dawn and reaching for his phone. He had calls to make too, but mine was the most important.

'Hello?' said a sleepy voice.

'Maddy, we found him!' I said without preamble. 'He's asleep but he looks healthy to me. We're at Holy Trinity. Come and get him!'

■●■

Ten minutes later, Maddy and her parents had replaced Dawn in the doorway of the church. With Ethan in her arms, Maddy was wrapped in the warm embrace of her mum and dad. Wozza was by my side looking up at them. I took a tissue from my pocket and handed it over to him.

He took it. 'Bug in my eye,' he said.

CHAPTER 32

WHO TOOK THE BABY?

Forensics weren't hopeful about finding uncontaminated evidence, given the crowd that turned up at the church after baby Ethan's return. Evidence preservation was always going to be secondary to reuniting the baby with his mother. And it was all moot anyway because Lesley Gillis had already picked him up from the laundry basket he'd been left in. It was one of several baskets that belonged to the church and was housed in the foyer for donations. It had probably been touched at some point by half the town, so that was no good for evidence.

The best we could do was collect everything Ethan had been wearing when he'd been found. So, after Doc Caldicott stripped him down at the doctor's surgery to examine him for injuries, I gathered all his clothes into a paper evidence bag. After the examination, Maddy lovingly dressed her baby in a crisp white jumpsuit with monkeys and giraffes on it. He flapped his arms up and down and smiled.

'No evidence of injuries at all,' declared Doc Caldicott. 'He appears fit and healthy.' She turned to Maddy. 'If it's any consolation, whoever took your baby cared for him.'

Maddy's eyes filled as she hugged her little one to her chest. 'How is it even possible to feel grateful to a kidnapper?' She kissed Ethan on the head. 'But I do.'

'Did you recognise the clothes he was in?' I asked as I sealed the evidence bag.

'No, and they weren't new,' Maddy said. 'If the kidnapper was familiar with the church, they could have got second-hand clothes from the donation baskets there.'

Baby Ethan made a cooing sound and she hugged him again.

It was time for Wozza and I to return to the station to try to pull the threads of the investigation into some kind of cohesive narrative that might point us towards the offender. Leaving Doc Caldicott's medical clinic, we ran the gauntlet of the media. This time, there were no jeers and taunts; the mood was festive. A returned baby was good for headlines and good for business. Maddy was already getting lucrative offers from TV current affairs shows to tell her story. Whether she took them was up to her. After the way they'd treated her, I wouldn't blame her if she shut the door on the whole lot of them.

Then I saw Tammy Millhouse in the crowd and she waved. I immediately felt bad for my uncharitable thoughts about the press. The few bad ones took up more space in my head than all the good ones. Tammy made her way through the throng.

'Great result, Antigone,' she said, grinning.

'Our greatest pleasure was uniting mother and baby,' I said, feeling a sudden wave of emotion. 'It's been a very rough ten days.'

Tammy did her job gently. 'Do you have any persons of interest in the case?'

'Working the investigation is still very much our focus.' And that was all I had left in me to say before returning to the office and doing just that.

■●■

Wheels was giving a press conference out the front of the station as I drove in with the evidence bag of baby clothes. Wozza must have briefed him on the details because he hadn't turned up to the church before dawn. He looked like the product of a good night's sleep, unlike the rest of us.

Inside the police station, the TV was on in the muster room and everyone had stopped to watch. I looked at Wheels and wondered how it was possible to be such a tosser and yet have no awareness of your tosserness. Maybe how others saw us was the only thing we couldn't see about ourselves.

As usual, Lincoln Steele asked the first question. He'd been absent from the throng outside the medical clinic. Not surprising that he wouldn't want to focus on the mother–baby reunion, since he and Drew Nayle had hammered Maddy all week.

He cleared his throat. 'Lincoln Steele, Three Triple P. Senior Sergeant Wheeler, do you believe your door-to-door searches were ultimately responsible for the return of baby Ethan Muir?'

'Absolutely,' said Wheels. 'Whoever took the baby saw the might of the Victoria Police bearing down on them and returned him.'

'You did express great confidence in the strategy,' said Steele, gilding the lily.

'I think any offender knows the excellent capabilities of the Victoria Police. They've clearly thrown their hands in the air and given up. We know our stuff and we get results.'

'How close are you to finding an offender?' Steele continued, cutting across another reporter who'd started to ask a question.

'Very close,' said Wheels. 'Our detectives are inside narrowing down a list of suspects as we speak.'

I couldn't watch anymore and so I went to find Wozza. I had to look twice when I walked into our office: Wozza was sitting at his desk eating chocolate cake—normal enough—but opposite him was Kasparas, also eating chocolate cake.

'You're sharing your cake!'

'Norma brought in a new one this morning to celebrate. And I'm in a hospitable mood,' said Wozza, 'now that the baby's back.'

I glanced at the empty desk next to Kasparas. 'Where's Riggs?'

Wozza giggled. 'Got sent back to Melbourne for being mean to the Chief.'

'We're celebrating with cake,' said Kasparas.

'So you're staying?'

He shrugged. 'At least until we find out who took the baby.'

'Well, I hope you like Deception Bay because you might be here a while.' I took the plate of cake Wozza offered and sat down at my desk.

'My money is on Lesley Gillis,' said Wozza, wiping cake crumbs from his tie. 'Phone records do show a call from the public phone to her mobile, but she could have called her own self.'

'And all that baby stuff at her house. Do we know if she actually *has* a grandbaby?' asked Kasparas with a mouthful of cake.

I nodded. 'I called Norma about that and she confirmed that Lesley has been minding her baby grandson. Word on the street is the baby's a screamer.'

'There's no way you'd even get a warrant to search their place,' said Kasparas.

'I hate to say it,' said Wozza, 'but do you think Wheels could be right? That our door-knocking spooked the kidnapper and that's why they ditched the baby?'

I shrugged. 'No idea.'

We discussed the world of possibilities, going round and round in circles. In the end, all we agreed on was that the person who took baby Ethan was probably local, that they might have shoplifted the missing tin of formula from Filmore's Pharmacy, and that they probably threw the dummy over the cliffs at the Devil's Corner to put us off the scent, because why else would it have been there?

'Any reports of people not showing up for work or taking unexpected leave?' said Wozza. 'Because if you take a baby, you have to look after it.'

I shook my head. Nothing came to mind. But then I thought about how Wonky George had stolen my brother. He'd still turned up to work because he'd left the baby with his wife.

Our conversation was interrupted by a commotion outside, which was followed by a round of applause.

Randall appeared at our office door, breathless. 'Maddy is here with the baby and wants to thank everyone!'

We followed him down the corridor. Maddy stood in the muster room surrounded by every uniform in the station. Everyone was admiring the baby and patting his head. Behind Maddy were her mother Tilly and, I was thrilled to see, Tamara McCreedy. Tamara might finally get to be Ethan's grandmother like she'd wanted to before Josh had discouraged contact between them. There was no sign of Keith, I noted. When Ethan smiled a big gummy smile, there was a burst of spontaneous joy, the likes of which wasn't often heard in the muster room. Jane and Randall both looked emotional. They had been there every step of the way, and a good outcome on a case like this was unexpected. Wozza and I stood back and let everyone bask in this success.

A hush fell over the gathering when Wheels entered the muster room. He made a beeline for Maddy and held out his arms to take baby Ethan. Maddy looked uncertain but passed her baby to the man who had made everything worse for her over the last ten days.

'Who's a cute little fella?' Wheels tapped Ethan's cheek.

Showing a remarkable degree of good taste, baby Ethan scrunched up his face and let out a loud wail. Maddy moved forward and scooped him back into her arms, where he immediately quietened. Wozza snickered.

Maddy cleared her throat and everyone quietened down to listen. 'I just want to express my most sincere gratitude to everyone here for bringing my baby back to me. I gotta say, there were a couple of days there where I didn't think it would happen.' Her eyes glistened and she hugged Ethan close to her. One of his little hands reached out and patted her face, and everyone laughed. Including Maddy.

'Each and every one of you bent over backwards for me and my baby. I will never forget your kindness.'

There was a round of applause. Maddy moved over our way a little while later, once the crowd of uniforms had dispersed.

'I have no words,' she said, a tear rolling down her cheek.

'Me neither,' I said, hugging her and feeling the warmth of baby Ethan between us. When the hug was over, I held up the Simba dummy that I'd grabbed from my desk. 'But I do have this. I bought it after we found the one on the beach, in the hope that I could give it to you when we found your baby.'

More tears. More hugs.

CHAPTER 33

JUST LIKE ON TV

In the early afternoon, Mum and Nan arrived at the police station to report the kidnapping of Mum's baby thirty-nine years ago. To create the appropriate degree of separation, I'd organised for Kasparas to take their statements. He told us he'd worked some historic sexual abuse cases in Melbourne which required a similar methodology of statement taking. He had found legislation relevant to the time period Mum's baby had been taken in, and was all set up in the interview room when they arrived. He took Mum's statement first, which left me to entertain Nan.

First, I took her on a tour of the police station, carefully avoiding the corridor leading to Wheels's office. '*He's* up there,' I said, wrinkling my nose.

Nan nodded and turned her walker back towards our office. Wozza made Nan a cup of tea as she vocally admired everything about our workplace.

'What a lovely desk you have, Antigone. May I take a photo on my phone?'

Mum had taken Nan shopping for a new iPhone and now Nan was obsessed. She'd even crocheted a brightly patterned pouch for it, which she'd sewn onto the front of her walker so she could film her strolls around the garden at the farm. It was the nana version of a GoPro. She hadn't quite mastered the selfie but was having the time of her life photographing everything around her. I sat behind my desk and posed for her. Wozza scrambled over to photobomb me but it just ended up being a nice photo of the two of us. Nan was pleased.

'Now one of you looking busy at your desk,' she instructed Wozza, who suddenly looked bashful. He sat ramrod straight with his hands tightly clasped together while Nan clicked away. Then she showed us the photos, which were so good that Wozza asked if she could text them to him so he could update his LinkedIn profile pic. He helped her add his number to her phone and soon the pictures pinged their way to him.

Nan started to look restless and checked her watch. 'I wonder how your mother is going with her statement,' she said.

Wozza and I both assured her it wasn't going to be a fast process and that Mum was in good hands with Kasparas.

'What's his first name?' said Nan.

'Leonard,' I said.

'Leonard. That's a nice name,' said Nan. She stood up and reached for her walker. 'I'm going to the ladies' room.'

I stood too but she waved me away.

'I remember where it is, Antigone.' Nan made her way out of our office.

'You just got burned by your nana,' said Wozza with a laugh.

'Like all Pollards, she's fiercely independent.'

'Wonder if your brother is like that too.'

While I hadn't yet seen enough of Andy to know, we had plans to catch up on the weekend. I hoped the start of the legal process to bring Wonky George to justice didn't sully the relationship that was developing. Mum's statement was one of many being collected from everyone who had come forward with allegations against him.

'It's kind of lucky his wife didn't live long enough for this. They would have arrested her too,' said Wozza pragmatically. 'Especially after Andy found her book of poems.'

I agreed. 'The one about seeing Mum and Nan in the street, knowing she had their baby, meant she was at least an accessory after the fact, even if she didn't have much of a say in it.' I looked at my watch. 'Nan's taking a while. Hope she didn't get lost.'

'Someone will point her in the right direction.' Wozza's phone pinged. 'Speak of the devil. She just sent me a text.' Wozza tapped at his screen, then frowned. 'She sent a video.'

'What?' I moved over to his desk.

A blurred image began playing, with Nan's voice whispering close to the camera: 'I'm going to do it just like they do on TV.' Then the video wobbled; it looked like Nan had put the phone into the walker pouch. The camera showed her hand reaching out and knocking on a door. A muffled 'Come in' from the other side. We watched as Nan's old hand, a little bent with arthritis, pushed open the door, and then we saw Wheels sitting at his large desk.

'Annie Pollard, as I live and breathe,' said Wheels, not unkindly.

'It's been a long while,' said Nan. 'In fact the last time I saw you was just after you took my daughter out on a date and she swore she never wanted to see you again.'

Wheels's face turned red.

Nan continued. 'I didn't like you back then and I've heard nothing over the years to make me change my mind.'

'The feeling's mutual,' said Wheels, his voice now hard.

'Just so you know, I heard Antigone and the Chief Commissioner talking about you. They know you're responsible for Amanda's crash.'

'What's she doing?' gasped Wozza, staring agape at the video.

'Shhh. Listen.' I nudged him into silence.

Wheels's expression, square in the camera lens, turned calculating. He lowered his voice, but it was still picked up perfectly by Nan's phone. 'Who's going to believe them? No witnesses.'

'But Amanda *saw* you.' Nan's voice was calm and even.

Wheels's glance darted sideways then back to Nan. 'Doesn't matter if she saw me. She's had a head injury—any lawyer would make mincemeat of her in court. Her story will never stand up.'

'Maybe,' conceded Nan. 'But then they have all that CCTV from around town that they've been gathering, which shows you heading out there just before Amanda crashed. I think you're a goner.'

'I left no evidence,' Wheels spluttered.

'You're wrong,' said Nan. 'They all talk around me and don't think I'm listening. Antigone got those accident police to photograph shoe impressions. She's typing up a warrant right now to confiscate your shoes.'

'What?' I spluttered. Nan was making this up as she went along, but she was bloody convincing.

The video ended with Wheels tugging off his shoes and then we got a sweeping view of the room as Nan slowly made her way to the door.

Wozza jumped up from his desk. 'Let's go and get us some shoes!'

I was right behind him.

CHAPTER 34

THE LAW

The defence barrister, Morris Abbott, was a puffed-up old man with unlikely hair, swept sideways in luscious waves of silver.

'That is totally a wig,' Wozza whispered in my ear as we stood in the courtroom and bowed to the magistrate.

'Ya think?' I said, trying to keep my face serious. Wig aside, I studied Abbott. *Know your enemy*, I always say. And as we were about to face off in court, he *was* my enemy. It was his job to make me look stupid. It was my job not to let him.

Wozza and I had been waiting outside the courtroom till the clerk called the proceedings to order. I wasn't allowed in until it was my turn on the witness stand. After a lot of sitting around and waiting, pacing, and the occasional game of I-Spy—*Wozza: Something beginning with B. Me: Bailiff. Wozza: Dammit!*—things swung into action, and from there, they moved quickly.

As soon as my name was called, I stopped pacing and followed the bailiff in with Wozza close behind.

I stood in the raised witness stand. 'I swear by Almighty God that the evidence I shall give will be the truth, the whole truth and nothing but the truth.' All eyes on me. I waited.

Abbott faced the magistrate, then turned to me with disdain. Took a deep breath and opened his mouth; his voice boomed in the silent courtroom as he began. 'Madam!'

I saw the magistrate flinch. The police prosecutor rolled her eyes. The use-by date for men who spoke to women like that had passed and Abbott hadn't got the memo.

'Madam! You claim that my client'—he swept his arm towards the dock, where Dimitri Christopoulos sat in a much nicer outfit than he'd worn when he stormed into Angie's Cafe—'accosted you at a bakery'—he spat the word *bakery* like it was a place peasants hung out, and made a show of shuffling papers, before looking back up with a smirk—'accosted you and *interrupted your afternoon tea*?' His voice dripped with sarcasm. 'Which, the last time I looked'—he gave a loud, condescending laugh—'isn't a crime. Indeed, Your Worship, yesterday, I was visiting my elderly grandmother in her aged care facility and I interrupted her afternoon tea when I arrived. I hope she doesn't have me charged!'—another loud, fake laugh—'And goodness! I think I touched the bailiff on the arm on the way in to court today, in the course of asking how his daughter went in her end-of-year exams. Whoops! I could get charged with assault for that one!' He chortled, then turned to me and boomed, 'Madam, how say you?'

I didn't answer. Instead, I reached into my blazer pocket and pulled out a pair of glasses. From another pocket, I pulled out a crisply ironed handkerchief, and flicked it till it unfolded. All eyes were on me. Slowly, I cleaned first one side of the glasses, then the other. Then, I put the glasses on and looked up at Abbott. His smirk was gone by then. Replaced by a sunset of red. Anger? Embarrassment? It was hard to tell.

He tried to wrest back control from my silence. 'Answer the question, madam!' he commanded.

I looked at the magistrate then back at Abbott. 'What was the question again?'

Silence. Then a faint snicker from Wozza.

The thing about power, in any situation, is this: someone takes it and holds on to it until someone else takes it away from them. You can feel when it shifts, and I felt that shift happening now. I caught Abbott's look of uncertainty: just a flicker, but it was there. Suddenly, I was unpredictable, and that is a lawyer's worst nightmare. I wouldn't flinch under his bullying examination. I wouldn't get flustered and stumble over my words. I stood a little taller. Hands by my side, feet slightly apart. Fighting stance.

Speaking directly to the magistrate, ignoring Abbott completely, I said, 'Your worship, if Mr Abbott believes that there is no difference between the way his client acted and the way he visits his nana and manhandles the bailiff, we may need to look into that.'

The corners of the magistrate's mouth twitched. 'Mr Abbott, perhaps you can rephrase your question. I forgot what it was too.'

Abbott looked completely thrown. 'Er, you say my client entered the bakery . . .'

I didn't wait for him to finish. 'Yes, he did. He stormed into the cafe in pursuit of his wife, knowing she had an AVO in place. He was asked to leave several times and created a disturbance when he refused. I arrested him, took him to the police station and charged him with breaching the AVO. During a search of his wife's car, we found a tracking device linked to his phone. It showed a history of stalking that stretched back to long before they were even separated. We've linked every time his wife reported him showing up unexpectedly to the tracking device to show these encounters were deliberate. And we found a record of purchase for the tracking device and the tracking app.'

The rest was game, set and match. The magistrate found Dimitri guilty of stalking, and Wozza and I went off in search of pastries at Angie's Cafe.

As soon as we sat down in front of our coffees—latte with chocolate on top for me and iced coffee for Wozza, as always—the penny dropped. 'Hey, you don't even wear glasses,' he said. 'What was that thing you did in court when that watermelon tried to interrogate you?'

I pulled the glasses out of my pocket and wiggled my fingers through the frames. 'These aren't glasses,' I said. 'See. No glass.'

His high-five was heartfelt.

EPILOGUE

Mum had decided to stay on the farm for a while and had just finished helping Nan move her things back in. Nothing better than full-time medical care provided by your daughter. I had my family back and I could not have been happier. And we'd just got news Amanda had been released from hospital.

I'd just spent a couple of hours with Maddy. Although she had her baby back, despite extensive enquiries and a thorough examination of the clothes Ethan had been returned in, the lab hadn't been able to find any evidence we could use. The only DNA found on the clothes had been from Wozza, Lesley and Dawn, all the people who'd held the baby on the morning he'd been returned.

Mum and Nan and I talked long into the night about all the questions that remained unanswered. Later, those questions, still swirling in my thoughts, made sleep impossible. Logic leaned us towards Lesley and Christos Gillis. I couldn't get the image of the baby clothes on their dining table out of my head. Had they kept baby Ethan out of twisted loyalty to Josh? There was no way to prove anything. Because of babysitting little Simon, Lord of Darkness, they already had baby paraphernalia like formula and nappies, which would explain the fact we'd found no sign of them buying those things in the CCTV footage.

My eyelids finally felt heavy and sleep beckoned. Snatches of words floated past me like wisps of clouds.

four dead . . .

someone's picking 'em off

medications

drugged drink

someone's picking 'em off

faulty EpiPen

exposure to peanuts

someone's picking 'em off

Hey, Chemist Girl, got any drugs?

DNA

the missing tin of baby formula

only Norma returned after lunch . . .

she was a victim of them

It all came back to the pharmacy.

I sat straight up in bed.

Dawn.

It made perfect sense. And with a dread rising from the pit of my stomach, I realised that my empathy lay with *her*. Not just because I was her newly minted aunt, but because I was a woman. These men had done shocking things to the victims we knew about. They'd knocked them out with drugs then used them like rag dolls. We'd seen the polaroids. In a recent case in France, the world's admiration had gone out to a woman who had suffered a similar fate; Gisèle Pelicot had been drugged by her husband and raped by fifty men. The world had stood with her, and I'm guessing a good part of the global population wished the worst on the rapists.

But.

My cop brain kicked in and understood that Gisèle Pelicot had participated in a legal consequence for the men, not a consequence of her own choosing. Then I experienced the haunting memory of Gemma, the victim in one of the many cases I'd investigated in Melbourne where the justice system did not work. There was no *Time* magazine cover for Gemma, no international support. Hers was just one of the many cases where the jury believed the rapist's denials over the woman's story. The phrase *he said, she said* is used to describe a situation where there are two conflicting accounts at play, and no clear evidence to prove the veracity of either. Yet those who fling the phrase about—whether in a legal context or on social media—don't use it to suggest there is equal weight in both stories. They use it to suggest that if *she* can't prove it, then *he* didn't do it. My heart hurt as I mulled this over because that was what Dawn would have been up against. I didn't blame her for not coming forward. And I didn't blame her for wanting to stop it. Stop them. Yet it was my job to uphold and have faith in the legal system, even when it failed more victims than it served.

An unexpected sob pushed up from my chest at the chaos of my thoughts. Waffles stirred, climbed off his big cushion and came over to my side of the bed. He lay his head just below mine and looked into my eyes. I reached for him and hugged him. Then I reached for my phone and selected a number. Clicked on it and listened while the ring tone repeated like a drum roll.

Then, a voice croaky with sleep: 'Pollard, this better be bloody good.'

'Sorry, Woz, did I wake you?' I could hear the worry in my voice. So could he.

A pause. 'Nah, I had to get up anyway to answer the phone.'

ACKNOWLEDGEMENTS

I began writing *The Stolen* before *The Unbelieved* hit the bookstores. I'd read an article about a baby who was taken by its father and never found, and the story idea just flowed. I have written on the subject of missing persons in my career as a true-crime author and podcaster and have seen firsthand the agony of not knowing.

A huge thanks to my brother, Andrew Burke, who is always happy to read drafts of my fiction and talk about the story as if the characters are real. Your suggestions and encouragement are invaluable, and I hope you're bracing yourself for book three. I'm also so grateful to my mum, Helen Burke, and my sister Vanessa Burke for being my first readers. Mum read *The Stolen* in a day and loved it, and there's no higher praise than praise from your mum. Ness took longer, but who's counting. Thanks to Steven Petraitis, too, for the endless cups of tea.

The Unbelieved was the first work of fiction I published after a long history of writing true crime. It moved me into a different world as an author. I got to speak on panels and was invited to literary festivals, and I also got reviewed, which isn't really a true-crime thing because true-crime reviews tend to be about the case rather than the writing. For the first time, I got to experience book bloggers and meet many of them at events. I love the way they show up to library talks and book launches with so much enthusiasm and joy for the world of books and reading. Some of you I met and some of you I know because you tagged me in your lovely reviews. To Helen and Brooke, Rina, Lily, Ash, Tash and Casey, Chrissie, Nicola, Kirra, Alyse, Michelle, Suzanne, Jess, Tel, Danni, Mary and all the other beautiful people who wrote lovely reviews of *The Unbelieved*, I am very grateful.

Being a crime writer, I have an amazing wellspring of people who I can talk writing with, including the members of my writers' group, who are all awesome: Jacqui Hawkins, Kylie Orr, Loren O'Keefe, Nicole Joseph, Madeleine Heather and Claire Halliday.

To Rory, thanks for offering you and your husband's names for my characters; I really hope Carsten likes being a villain. Thanks to the real Angie and Marina for continuing not to mind your names being used. Thank you to Maggie Baron, a forensic scientist who worked in drug and trace-evidence analysis, for offering me poisons advice at a Sisters in Crime dinner. And to pharmacist Belinda Theobald, who is always happy to answer questions about drugs; it makes things much easier when you can go straight to the source. Thank you to

Jane Varney, childhood friend and retired cop, who doesn't mind when I use some of her crazier real-life stories. And to Lesley Gillis, who won the Be Immortalised in Fiction prize at the Sisters in Crime 2023 Davitt Awards; I had great fun putting you in the story. And thanks to the real Kerrie and Marg for your many years of service to the Frankston SES. And special mention of the real Azzurro pizza restaurant in Brighton East, which has the best pizzas ever.

After thirty years of going it alone, I finally got an agent. Andrew Taylor from More Talent has made me feel at last that I have someone in my corner. And then Andrew found Jemma McDonagh in the UK, and now I have two people. Thanks to Annette Barlow, Christa Munns, Jennifer Thurgate and the team at Allen & Unwin, who assembled the troops again to get this book out. Ali Lavau, the most amazing and encouraging editor, I can't tell you what a thrill it is to open your feedback document and read such high praise. The funny thing about writing is that until others—who aren't your mum—say they like your book, you're never really sure if it's any good or not. Many thanks to copyeditor Deonie Fiford for your precision and attention to detail; and to Greer Gamble, whose proofreading was so thorough she even impressed my mum. And so grateful to Luke Causby, who designed the amazing covers for both *The Unbelieved* and *The Stolen*.

And finally to Xavier, Daisy, Deb and Anna for seeing Antigone and wanting to show her to the world.

ABOUT THE AUTHOR

Vikki Petraitis has written eighteen books, including her bestseller *The Frankston Murders*, about Frankston serial killer Paul Denyer. In 2023, she released a podcast of the same name which helped put the case on the international radar and, working as part of a dedicated team, she was in Parliament in November 2023 to witness the passing of the amendment to keep Denyer in prison for life. Vikki has written on topics from Lawyer X to police dogs. She has made several true-crime podcast series with Casefile Presents that have been downloaded eight million times. Her first novel, *The Unbelieved*, won the inaugural Allen & Unwin Crime Fiction Prize in 2022 and the 2023 Readers' Choice Davitt Award. She has just submitted her PhD in Creative Writing and is really hoping she passes.